The
Franklin
Scare

BOOKS BY JEROME CHARYN

The
Franklin
Scare

BY JEROME CHARYN

ARBOR HOUSE *New York*

Library of Congress Catalog Card Number: 77–79529

ISBN: 0–87795–167–5

Manufactured in the United States of America

Grateful acknowledgment is made to Milton Drake for permission to
quote from *Mairzy Doats*. Copyright 1943, Miller Music Corp.;
copyright renewed 1971, Drake Activities Corporation, Al Hoffman
Songs, Inc., Hallmark Music Corporation.

"My children, you are permitted in time of great danger to walk with the devil until you have crossed the bridge."

—*Franklin Delano Roosevelt, from an old Bulgarian church proverb*

Prologue: The Wizard in Bed

It was a cowtown compared to London, Paris, or Berlin, a carbuncle south of Baltimore, created by George Washington, the first American king, to house a squalid little government that was frightened of its thirteen constituent states. It was built on a swamp, around a limestone mansion for the president-king, a mansion that began to crumble and peel soon as it was put up. It was a city of mosquitoes, Washington, D.C., with a dampness that bit at you in the winter and made you feverish in the long, summer blaze. It couldn't even rule itself. Congress squatted over the city, prepared its finances, and stroked it to sleep. It had a few scattered markets and fisheries, no centers of trade, just monuments, cafeterias, alleys, and government houses. But it was the wartime capital of the world.

You found the strangest epaulettes on its shopping streets; soldiers and sailors of America's allies crowded into Washington after 1940. The District was converted into a crazy quilt of uniforms: men of the Belgian Corps de Marine *in civilian raincoats, peaked caps, and ragged shoes; Chinese admirals in old American Navy jackets; British seamen with horizontal pleats running up their trousers; glum-faced Polish brigadiers with daggers hanging from their belts; officers of a Free French battalion in "walking-out" clothes, with the Cross of Lorraine stitched into the cloth over their right breasts. There were pom-*

pons, scarlet piping on a shirt, and more military daggers. The kings and princes of occupied countries went into department stores wearing generals' uniforms. No one blinked at them. The District had gotten used to kings.

It was no accident that this many foreign armies and navies had arrived. Washington was the command post of the Free World. And these admirals, generals, princes, and kings had come for their twenty minutes with the American Commander-in-Chief. It was easier to get near FDR than to beg an audience with Churchill and his general staff. The British were always putting you off. Churchill didn't have time for every Polish brigadier. He would give you over to an undersecretary of his, who might scowl at you or not. But the White House was much more receptive to stranded brigadiers and kings without a throne. FDR took you into his bedroom and sat you down with an interpreter from his Navy and a bowl of nuts. The most powerful man on earth met you in a lumpy gray robe. He didn't surround himself with footmen, generals, and bodyguards. Officers didn't march in to salute the Commander-in-Chief; only a butler with a glass of orange juice.

He wasn't pompous with a brigadier. He shook your hand and wouldn't let you curtsy and say "Mr. Roosevelt." You had to call him "Brother Franklin," in the Polish way, or he would begin to pout. It troubled you at first, because you hadn't expected such informalities in a chief of state, though you'd heard often enough that the Americans were an odd tribe; rambunctious and familiar, they liked to grab your clothes whenever they had a point to make, talk to you with their fists in your chest.

But FDR didn't handle your clothes. He had a dog under the bed, an overstuffed Scottie named Fala, the best known animal in the world, who wheezed through his nose and wouldn't be quiet until FDR rubbed his scalp. So you uttered a tiny joke about the animal through the Navy interpreter, and Franklin Roosevelt laughed. It wasn't an ordinary chuckle, *meant to be polite. This President of all the Allies threw back his forehead and roared. FDR's famous pince-nez nearly dropped off his nose. The bed rattled under his weight. The gray lumpy thing he wore popped open for a minute and you could see a President's bosom; he had a large, deep chest that squeezed out a mighty shiver in the middle of his roar. The noise drove Fala into a basket next to the interpreter's chair. The animal whimpered and dug under his blankets as far as he could go.*

Then the roaring stopped; the pince-nez was pushed back up the bridge of his nose, as FDR recovered himself. You nodded to the interpreter and thanked the President for welcoming a brigadier of the third Polish dragoons when he had to command a global army and oversee the fighting on many, many fronts. So you begged Pan Franklin's *pardon, but you were worried about the integrity of Poland after the war. It wasn't Hitler's dying soldiers that alarmed the brigadier. It was the Red Army. Russians were about to cross the Oder. Would they roost on Polish soil and create their own puppet government? Or could the President guarantee an independent Poland?*

FDR didn't shrug off the brigadier. The President was also alarmed about Stalin's ambiguity toward Poland. He would meet with the Russians in another month. And he promised to resolve the Polish question with "Uncle Joe."

The brigadier was pleased. He couldn't help curtsying to FDR. There were no men alive more just than these Americans. He got up to leave. But the President kept him with a story. Now the brigadier strained to listen. The story had something to do with a Bulgarian priest, the devil, an old margrave, and children on a bridge. The interpreter must have lost the President's nuances. The words made little sense. Was FDR piecing an allegory together for the brigadier? Were the children on the bridge meant to be the Poles? Who was the devil? Stalin? Hitler? Churchill? Or Roosevelt himself?

It was lucky for the brigadier that a young sailor popped

into the room, or he might have eaten his mind away on the President's riddle. This was a curious sailor, with a head full of eyebrows, white pants in December, and a rumpled neckerchief. He could be surly with FDR. "Time's up, Boss. You got two kings in the hall." Fala nipped at the sailor's heels. "Dog," he said, "I don't want no trouble from you."

The brigadier found it hard to believe that such insolence could exist that close to FDR. The sailor didn't even have to knock. He was free to move in and out like the quartermaster of "Brother Franklin's" bedroom. FDR wouldn't punish the sailor. He leaned into his pillows, tugged on his robe, and said, "That child keeps his Poppa in a straitjacket. Gosh, he won't let you breathe . . ."

And you left with the interpreter, noting two straggly kings parked outside the bedroom in simple camp chairs. Your trip to the White House began to take on the auras of an uncomfortable dream. The ceilings over you were cracked, the chandeliers were filthy, the rugs had bold wounds in them, as if tigers prowled the floor. But not one soldier on the stairs to guard "Brother Frank" from insurrection. Any lunatic could visit the President of the United States. All you had to do was get past the sailor with the eyebrows. Were those really kings in the hall? They looked unsavory to the brigadier. What could he write to his people? He'd been to "Brother Franklin's" home. The White House appeared to be under a murky spell. He wondered if the rest of America was one monstrous hallucination conceived by FDR to dupe Polish brigadiers? Franklin Roosevelt was like a seedy wizard in his bed. He shook hands with you, laughed, offered you peanuts, told you a riddle, fondled his dog, but what could you say about him? The smile, the pince-nez, the cigarette holder, the young sailor, the lumpy robe, they were all conundrums. The brigadier nodded to the cannon on the lawn. He got out of Roosevelt's city with the sense of having been spooked by a sailor, a dog, and a President who wore a magical robe to bed.

The
Coming
of Oliver

He was a common sailor, a boy in summer clothes, Seaman Oliver Beebe. He hadn't come off any ship. He was only a barber, a barber who stayed on land. He mingled with obscure admirals at the old Navy Building on Constitution Avenue. He went from office to office, clipping hair. The admirals trusted him. He was quiet, discreet, and he had small, lovely hands that could massage a bald spot or powder the runnels behind a Navy man's ear. Seaman Oliver Beebe.

He came through the north gate with a card signed by the Chief of Naval Operations. A soldier inspected his barbering tools. A Secret Service man accompanied him to the usher's office. It was routine business. One of the admirals had recommended Seaman Beebe. The President's other barber was sick. An usher escorted him up to the second floor. He was gone in half an hour.

No one expected to see him a second time. It was the end of May. He wore the same summer "whites." The weather in the mansion was intolerable, but the sailor didn't seem to sweat. He had the President's signature on his pass. He was given full authority to come and go. The Boss snatched him from the admirals. He had nothing to do with the Navy now. He was assigned to Headquarters, the Commander-in-Chief.

The Secret Service didn't appreciate the kidnapping of Oliver Beebe. It hadn't been warned of the President's move. Kirkland Horn, chief of the White House detail, had to step around the President. Agents scuttled through Washington, investigating the boy. He was twenty-three years old. He came from New Jersey. His mother and father were dead. He lived in a room off "H" Street, in Chinatown. He had only one relative, a sister of twenty-seven. He was neither a Republican nor a Democrat (the boy had never registered to vote). His schooling was sparse. Two years of high school in Wee-hawken. He had nearly failed the Navy's intelligence test. He didn't have a criminal record.

Horn couldn't fathom Oliver's duties at the White House. The boy was with the President every day. He was given his own bedroom in the attic. Who was this Oliver? Did he clip the President's neck morning and night? There was an odd nimbus surrounding Oliver Beebe. He was more than a barber, but not quite an aide. He walked the President's dog. He wheeled the President around the second floor. He delivered letters to the President's wife. He played with the President's grand-children inside the jungle gym on the south lawn. His function was no more definite than that. He seemed utterly replaceable, in Kirkland's head. The Boss liked a young sailor around him, that's all, a boy who wouldn't chatter very much. He didn't take Oliver to Hyde Park. The sailor was strictly for the White House.

Problems arose from the natural secretiveness of the boy. The press corps seized hold of Oliver. The newsmen in the lobby couldn't ignore the whereabouts of the President's sailor. They examined the markings on his sleeve, all his insignias, and didn't come up with a clue. He wore no specialty badge. A barber? Why not a cook? Was he a communications expert, a boy who decoded messages for the President? None of them ever saw Oliver enter the Map Room. So they cashed in on whatever they could. The boy was photogenic. They exploited his uniform and his face. They photographed him tugging at the leash of the President's little black Scottie. They had him pose on the jungle gym. But they couldn't loosen his tongue. "I help the Boss," he said. The barber wouldn't give them any other news.

TWO

Oliver was in the attic. It was midnight, and the house was dead. Mrs. Roosevelt had left for her cottage at Hyde Park; most of her entourage went with her: secretaries, companions, a Yugoslavian princess, newspaper friends, a stray soldier she'd met at Washington Circle. Apart from the Negro butlers and maids, who didn't interfere with Oliver, there was only one other person in the attic. This was Zena of Bulgaria, an ex-empress, and a grand lady of fifty-five. Zena had lost her husband, Emperor Charles, her children, her jewels, and her crown. A pauper in America, she was a permanent guest of the Roosevelts.

Zena wouldn't go to Hyde Park. She was frightened of trains and soldiers with bayonets. She kept to her attic home, wandering through the corridors with her hands on the wall. She couldn't use the sun porch; there was a machine-gun nest stationed on the roof. So she had to hunt for a breeze in the corridors if she didn't want to be roasted alive.

The machine gunners were having a party. They walked over Oliver's head. There were two of them up there, specialists from Fort Meyer, drinking watered rum. Oliver knocked on his low ceiling with a shoe. "I'm reading. Cut it out."

One of the specialists tumbled off the roof. He landed on the balcony outside Oliver's window. He came into the room, his leggings untied, the chin straps of his helmet tight against his nose. "Ollie, come on up."

Oliver grabbed the specialist by his Army pants, took him out on the balcony, and hoisted him up to the roof. He closed his French window and got into bed with a movie magazine. The sailor was a fanatic about Alan Ladd. This month's *Silver Screen* pushed Sonny Tufts, Turhan Bey, and Willard Parker, the Golden Boy of 1944. Oliver grew hungry reading about Turhan Bey's childhood in Istanbul.

The attic had its own kitchen. Oliver could have gone there for graham crackers and a bottle of milk. He could have woken the valet and gotten him to scramble three eggs. The valet would plague him with stories about Mrs. Roosevelt and her miraculous chafing dish: no one could scramble eggs like the First Lady.

Oliver climbed into his Navy pants and combed his hair. Zena of Bulgaria grazed his overshirt in the hall. Her bathrobe hung loose against her sovereign belly. The ex-empress had paper-white skin. She accepted Oliver's invitation to a glass of milk.

He brought Zena to her room and went downstairs. He didn't have to face Kirkland Horn, who watched over the main galleries whenever Roosevelt was around. Horn was in Hawaii with the President. He'd left a skeleton crew of Secret Service men to guard an empty White House. Oliver didn't use the front door. Newsmen were always sleeping in the lobby, and they'd think Oliver was running over to the Navy Department for a midnight chat with a few key admirals.

The back porch was free of newsmen. The sentry had to come out of his hut to open the south gate, which was kept closed since the beginning of the war. Oliver could have gone to Chinatown and drank bourbon out of a teapot. The proprietors of "H" Street were familiar with Oliver Beebe. He could have fondled a waitress in an obscure corner of the Old Shanghai. But he wasn't in the mood to tamper with garter belts. He hiked to Sailors' Row.

Oliver hadn't always been a barber. He was once a sailor of the line. He'd scraped rust and handled pelican hooks on a light destroyer out of Guantanamo Bay, Apprentice Seaman Beebe. But his captain took a liking to Oliver and got him off the deck. The boy was turned into a steward's mate. He uncorked wine at the captain's table. He learned to cut an officer's hair. The captain went to Washington and brought Oliver along. Nobody gave the boy a steward's badge. A few months of shore work, they said. He shuffled among admirals for two years until the President took him away.

He smelled of hair tonic. He had notches in his thumb from the scissors he used. He carried flea powders for the President's dog. He lived in an attic among cooks, maids, and an empress who would have starved without Mrs. Roosevelt.

There were shacks in the alleys of Sailors' Row. Oliver was in the Filipino colony. Women in their sixties, with dark stockings covering their veins, and enough rouge to smother a cat, began to pester him. They were whores from the Penguin. Oliver tried the Ship's Cafe.

Swabbies, seamen recruits, and petty officers slept on their feet at the Ship's Cafe, their only nourishment a sailor's beer with flies swimming in the glass. Oliver stood at the bar with a gang of petty officers. The petty officers were attacking Mrs. Roosevelt. "She's the ugliest bitch in America. She bends down to niggers while we get our asses shot off."

"She doesn't bend so much," Oliver said. He wasn't fond of Mrs. Roosevelt. She made him nervous with her loose chatter, her knitting needles, and her chafing dish. If she didn't scramble eggs for you, she talked you to death. But he couldn't let these petty officers insult the Boss' wife.

They glared at Oliver. "What's that?"

"I said the lady doesn't bend."

It wasn't much of a brawl. Five petty officers were on top of Oliver. They could have broken his neck. They wanted to humiliate him, to slap his tiny butt. They started to take down his pants. A string of blood ran from Oliver's nose to his ear. They had his pants around his ankles when the Shore Patrol arrived.

The two SP's arrested Oliver, after getting him into his pants. He was reviled by the rest of the cafe. Sailors spit beer at Oliver. They thought he was a spy from the Penguin, come here to make trouble. The SP's threw him into the back of their DeSoto. The boy couldn't scream. His mouth was stuck against the window. "I work for Mr. Roosevelt," he managed to cry.

The SP's shone their flashlight into Oliver's face. They went through his pockets. They pulled out a card authorizing Oliver to enter the White House. Holy shit. They had a sailor in their car who belonged to the Commander-in-Chief. Roosevelt's pet. They could lose their armbands messing with Oliver. The thought of sea duty made them sick. A man could drown at sea. They gobbled potato chips and planned their next move. They could take this Oliver to the Navy Yard and process him there; they could drop him at the Penguin; they could telephone their captain and explain themselves to him.

They did nothing for half an hour. Then they drove to the White House. They grabbed Oliver's arms and legs, brushed him off, and gave him to the sentry at the north gate. "He lives here," they said. "Oliver Beebe."

A Secret Service man came down from the White House. He accepted Oliver and thanked the SP's. Oliver wandered into a bush and scratched his eye. The Secret Service man brought him up to his room.

THREE

Oliver woke with pieces of blond hair in his mouth. He saw another head on his pillow. Ethel Rosenquist, assistant chief of the White House switchboard, was under the covers with him. Ethel had a craziness for Oliver. When her need was very great she would come into bed with him around five a.m., cuddle, and sneak back to her post. She must have overslept. The sun was high on Oliver's window. He could sniff coffee in the hall. The maids were up.

Oliver nudged her out of bed. He dressed her in panties, skirt, and bra. He was still out of sorts from his scuffle at the Ship's Cafe. Checking the corridors he guided Ethel to the stairs. Then he searched his closet for old movie magazines. His phone began to ring. He knew it would be Ethel. It rang nineteen times.

"Darling, will you take me to the movies tonight?"

"No."

"Why did you come home with a purple cheek? Oliver darling, did you go to the Navy Yard again?"

He was silent with her. She liked to parlay these early morning naps into a permanent thing. She was a graduate of riding academies and a tough finishing school, a third-generation Wisconsin girl, one of the

Sheboygan Rosenquists, come to Washington for war duty at the White House. But she was in love with a sailor in the attic, an obscure boy who didn't even have the grace to treat her to a movie.

He got her off the phone, not with silky promises. Oliver didn't have the gift of tongues. He said goodbye and hung up. She buzzed him a second time. A thin despair entered his heart. He was condemned to living under a machine-gun nest, saying no to Ethel Rosenquist with a telephone in his hand.

"Oliver darling. . . ."

"What?"

"FD is on the line. He's calling from a battleship, I think. He wants to talk to you."

Oliver didn't hear any static, just that familiar frog-like voice, as if the President were downstairs, in his oval office.

"Ollie, Fala misses you. He's in wretched shape. The sailors on board have been scalping the Pup. I guess they wanted some souvenirs."

Oliver was glad the Boss hadn't stuck Fala on him. The Pup would have moved into the attic, and Oliver would be feeding him, walking him, brushing his hair, while the dog moaned for FDR. He was jealous of the Pup. Roosevelt took his dog to the Pacific and left Oliver behind.

"Boss, you should put a sign on the Pup, saying 'Touch At Your Own Risk.' Don't you worry. I'll shampoo him when he gets back. Boss, who's been cutting your hair?"

"Butcher boys," the President said. "Ollie, they've been burning my neck with their Navy clippers. . . . Well, child, Poppa has to go."

Oliver forgot to ask the President about his sinus attacks and his cough. Did the President need any more of his stamp albums? Oliver could have dropped them into the pouch that left the White House every morning. FDR was the number one stamp collector in the Free World. He sketched ideas for stamps, bartered with dealers, fought with the Postmaster General over the print order of a stamp he happened to admire. Oliver was forever running over to the Bureau of Printing and Engraving to collect the die proofs of a new stamp, so that the Boss could pick the one he liked best.

The attic was driving him crazy. Machine gunners clumped on the roof. Ex-Empress Zena was in the corridors, scratching wood. The maids were in the laundry room. The smell of shirts being cooked on ironing boards clung to the sailor's bed. Oliver shaved in the tiny bathroom he had to share with the President's valet. He put on a laundered overshirt and left the attic. He wasn't going to skulk out of the mansion today. The newsmen caught him in the lobby. They sensed a story in Oliver's discolored face. "Ollie, did you bang yourself in the dark? Did you run into a fist, a wall, or a juniper tree?"

He walked out the front gate, squinting at the cannon on the lawn, the bronze shells, all the accoutrements of an antiaircraft battery that couldn't have shot down a kite. The cannoneers would flirt with secretaries from the West Wing. They were arrogant boys in metal hats who talked about balloons, bombers, and cannon bores. The meanest sailor was superior to them.

Oliver had a room off Mount Vernon Square. Whenever he was disgruntled with the White House, he would visit his room. Out of the President's grip, he could distance himself from butlers, aides, and the Secret

Service. The room cost him seven dollars a week. Washington had become a crazy house after 1940. With the influx of servicemen, secretaries, lonely kings and queens, apartments were impossible to find. And Oliver was a sailor with two homes.

His landlady scowled at him. "Your missus is upstairs," she said. "You never told me you had a wife. That'll be six dollars extra for the month. And tell your missus she has to get rid of her friend. This isn't a hotel, Mr. Beebe."

Oliver couldn't explain the appearance of his "missus." He would have remembered if he had a wife.

His sister was in the room with a strange man. She sat on his bed with her stockings off. She had black hair, like Oliver, and a beautiful neck. She smiled at him. The man wore a baggy suit that might have been the rage of 1930. It seemed ridiculous in 1944. Oliver got his sense of clothes from the President, who never threw out a shirt, a tie, or a pair of pants.

"Ollie, I told Vivian you wouldn't mind if we stayed in your room. The hotels are packed. We couldn't get in. Vivian's a journalist. Vivian de Vries."

Oliver shook hands with Vivian de Vries, the scarecrow who came with Anita. Vivian had a hollow face, with small eyes, a small mouth, and small gray ears. Oliver couldn't tell where Anita had picked him up. She was supposed to be in Milwaukee with a commercial artist who was hiding from the draft. Anita had a special sympathy for draft dodgers. She'd been with the guy over four years. They'd had a child, but Anita wouldn't marry her commercial artist. The child took its mother's name. Michael Beebe was two and a half. Oliver saw him only once. His nephew had bright red skin.

"Vivian's doing articles," Anita said. "For an independent magazine. He writes about all kinds of governments. That's Vivian's field. He wants to interview you."

Oliver squeezed his eyes. "Interview me? What for?"

"You live with the Roosevelts, don't you?"

Oliver had spent half his childhood fighting with Anita. They both had faint claw marks under their lips to remind them of these fights. He couldn't get along with her. She liked to bully him, force him to do her will.

"I don't live with anybody," he said, truculent, staring at Anita and her journalist, a man with a woman's name. "I'm Mr. and Mrs. Roosevelt's page. I carry her messages. I cut his hair. They have a dog. I feed it. That's what I know about the government."

This de Vries bothered Oliver. He looked forty, forty-five. What was he doing with a twenty-seven-year-old girl? And where was Michael Beebe? Oliver didn't have aunts or uncles who could house Anita's child. Did she fob Michael off on the nuns of Milwaukee? Anita was relentless, shrewd. She could convince any stranger to lend her money, hold Michael, buy her a meal.

"I'll fix it with Mrs. Saunderson," he said. Saunderson was his landlady. It was no good coming here. He wouldn't have much peace with Anita in the room. But he didn't get away so fast. She touched his Navy collar before he was out in the hall.

"Aren't you going to kiss me, Oliver?"

Her tongue leapt at him with a mottled cry. Even as quarrelsome children they wouldn't give each other cold pecks on the cheek. Anita demanded a passionate allegiance from whoever crept close to her skin. Brother or mailman, she didn't care. Oliver kissed her on the lips and said goodbye.

He pacified Mrs. Saunderson. Mistake, he said.

Anita was his sister, not his wife. She was married to a man who wrote for the magazines. Told government stories. Interviewed people. Mr. and Mrs. de Vries. The landlady softened to Oliver. "A married couple? Your sister and a writing man?" She wouldn't bleed money from a nice couple. They could have the place at Oliver's usual rent.

He sat inside the Old Shanghai with bourbon in his teapot. A visit from Anita always upset him. It obliged him to recall the shards and bric-a-brac of his family. Raised in Weehawken, with a father and mother who were drunks, Oliver and Anita had to occupy themselves. They were orphans within their father's house, playing little sinister games, pretending they were dead. Anita moved out at sixteen and a half, abandoning Oliver, who was twelve. She had a succession of admirers, always solemn men, older than Anita, with suffering looks: they couldn't take their eyes off his sister. She lived with them, one after the other, threw them over, while Oliver walked through a house full of whiskey bottles, with a mother who couldn't creep out of bed and a father who neglected to come home from the dockers' bars of Wee-hawken.

Oliver showed up at the north gate with bourbon in his ears. The sentry called the White House. An usher got Oliver inside, without using the front porch. The secretaries would have frowned at a wobbly sailor. The newsmen would have picked at his clothes. It was barely noon. Only Oliver would think of getting drunk at such an ungodly hour. He was shunted through the basement and brought up to the attic in Mr. Roosevelt's elevator car. An ordinary page would have been dismissed. But no one could touch the President's "child."

Eleanor

Oliver heard the thump of bare feet in the attic: the First Lady had come home from her cottage at Hyde Park. She was visiting with Zena before breakfast. She loved to clatter up the stairs in her morning robe, rush through the halls, give instructions to her personal maid, sit on Zena's bed for a short while, squeeze the ex-empress' hand, console her for the loss of her three sons. The First Lady had a high voice. Oliver shut his door. Mrs. Roosevelt was liable to come in, inquire about the puffs on his face, and send Oliver to the dispensary.

An usher pounded on Oliver's door five minutes after Mrs. Roosevelt left the attic. He was a Southern boy, dressed in a black suit that was beginning to crumple in the heat. "Ollie, you'd better climb into your duds."

"How come?"

"Mrs. Franklin's inviting you to breakfast."

Oliver tied his neckerchief and went down one floor. Mrs. Roosevelt was scrambling eggs for her coterie in the West Sitting Hall. She didn't say a word about the peculiar coloring on the sailor's cheek. She smiled. He couldn't understand her bashfulness. She usually chirped at him with her arm over the chafing dish.

He ate his eggs near the window. "Thank you,

ma'am." Even her secretaries smiled at him. None of them liked Oliver. He was Franklin's property. The White House was split into enemy camps. Franklin's people collected in the West Wing; they scorned the other part of the house. Eleanor's people were twice as ferocious. She had actresses, poets, college boys, Negro educators, and newspaper women in her camp. They were full of contempt for the generals and politicians who surrounded Mr. Roosevelt. The ushers and Secret Service men sided with the President. The cooks, butlers, and maids were partial to Eleanor.

Oliver had nothing to do with politics and the West Wing. He was a boy who came down from the attic to perform small favors for Mr. and Mrs. Roosevelt. But Eleanor's people could never welcome a sailor who cut the President's hair. So Oliver was disturbed by the smiles, the gentle swish of teacups, the signs of goodwill.

He saw one of Mrs. Roosevelt's girls clutching last night's edition of the *Washington Star.* The girl, an actress Oliver couldn't remember, winked at him. Oliver was much too uncomfortable to wink back. He couldn't understand why she would flirt with him in front of a dozen ladies. The actress rose out of her chair to kiss Oliver's damaged cheek. No one reprimanded her. "Oliver, you were wonderful," she said.

Oliver succumbed to scrambled eggs and a stinking kiss. They were taking liberties with him. He wasn't any lummox of theirs. He should be the one to say who could kiss him and who could not.

"Why am I so wonderful?" he asked.

His sullen looks amused them. Except for Eleanor, all of them laughed. The First Lady continued to scramble eggs. The actress wiggled in her chair with delight.

"Don't you know?" She thrust the newspaper at Oliver. "Doris Fleeson spent a quarter of her column on you."

Oliver didn't read the *Washington Star.* He couldn't abide newspaper print. The stripes down a page confused him. But the maids in the attic talked of Doris Fleeson. She was some kind of tattletale.

"What does Fleeson want with me?"

The ladies wouldn't stop laughing at him. "Oliver, behave."

"Look," the actress said, pointing to Doris Fleeson's column. "You're our hero. . . ."

The barber was still amazed.

"Didn't you fight nine sailors at a bar for making fun of Mrs. Roosevelt?"

"Less than nine," Oliver said, and he wouldn't mumble anything more. The ladies took his silence as an act of extreme modesty. Then the conversation switched. Oliver had fallen into a breakfast conference on Negroes in the Army and Navy. Eleanor's people wanted statistics from him. He was questioned by a female poet. "Oliver, did you ever serve under a Negro officer?"

"No, ma'am."

"Did you ever *see* one?"

"No, ma'am."

"Were there Negroes aboard your last ship?"

"Yes, ma'am."

"What kind of work did they do?"

"They were mess boys . . . and barbers, like me."

The breakfast table was consumed with noise. The ladies were shouting at each other. Oliver wasn't surprised. The head usher had warned him about Eleanor's people. Bolsheviks, he called them. Oliver couldn't tell what a Bolshevik was. But it had to be something noisy.

He watched them with a bitterness in his heart. He wasn't going to throw dirt on the Navy for a tribe of Bolsheviks.

Mrs. Roosevelt must have sensed his embarrassment. The First Lady pulled on the collars of her morning robe and the quarreling ceased. She shoveled eggs for Oliver. She was always kind to him. He would have liked her better if she didn't go around in bare feet.

Oliver stayed his twenty minutes. He could excuse himself now. He had to fulfill the duties of a page. He would bring Eleanor's mail up to her little study after the Secret Service screened packages and thick envelopes for a possible bomb. Then he had to collect the Roosevelt grandchildren from different floors of the White House and lead them in exercises on the front lawn. The poet tried to keep him longer, but Eleanor let him go. "Good morning," Oliver said, nodding to everybody, and he went for the mail.

FIVE

I t was a rainy July. Admirals and servicemen stood under the oak trees along Pennsylvania Avenue muttering to themselves. The wax on the leaves was so thick and powerful, it reminded you of a tropical city. The admirals had nowhere to go. Like the servicemen, they were stuck in Washington seven days a week. Responding to this universal restlessness, newspapers began to drum up stories of sabotage. A fever struck the District. Rumors were coming right out of the Navy Department: a midget submarine was caught plowing the bottom of the Potomac. Washingtonians waited for the Japs to appear in Rock Creek Park. The Army put more bayonets on every bridge. Navy men walked the marshlands of the Potomac with clubs swinging from their belts. Soldiers, sailors, and marines crawled through the Ellipse in back of the White House. A saboteur who got close to East Executive Avenue would have been kicked to death.

The Secret Service wouldn't leave Eleanor alone. Agents attempted to shadow her. It's a scary time, they said. Mrs. Roosevelt would have none of them. The agents didn't dare shout at her. It was hard to call down the First Lady. And they couldn't squeal to Kirkland Horn. The chief of the White House detail was in Singapore, or Hawaii, playing cards with the President.

Mrs. Roosevelt took pity on them. She mentioned Oliver's name to the Secret Service. The agents stared at her huge teeth. "Don't you worry. My husband's barber will protect me."

They telegraphed Kirkland Horn, expecting a million noes from their chief. They were bewildered when Kirkland approved. They talked of outfitting Oliver with a wooden gun. Then their excitement paled. They withdrew from the task of guarding Mrs. Roosevelt.

Oliver didn't have the constitution of a bodyguard. His stamina was poor. He couldn't growl at people, or appear menacing to strangers. He blamed Mr. Roosevelt. The Boss shouldn't have left him in the attic for the whole July. Oliver climbed stairs in a state of gloom. The ushers would catch him in the hall and feed Oliver disgusting news. They told him it could be wicked business riding with the First Lady. Eleanor wouldn't use a White House limousine. She had her own little Chevrolet. "Mrs. Franklin's a terrible driver. The worst." She'd lost her front teeth in one of her little cars. She would go through the District bumping fenders, sidewalks, and trees.

Oliver wasn't dreaming of Chevrolets. He had a man called Vivian on his mind. His sister was living with a scarecrow in Oliver's room. She'd come to Washington without her little boy to stay with this Vivian de Vries. His gloominess began to multiply in Mrs. Roosevelt's car. Driving, she had busy hands and feet. There were three more ladies with her, squashed up in the back, their shoulders touching like flattened knives. Oliver had the chosen seat, next to Mrs. Roosevelt. The three ladies chattered without end. Their topics eluded the boy. They could jump from politics to facial creams in the middle of a sentence.

Eleanor was mostly quiet. From time to time she would ask favors from the boy.

"Golly, it's hot. Oliver dear, would you open your window, please?"

The three ladies got off at Dupont Circle, and Oliver had Mrs. Roosevelt to himself. They chewed biscuits, talked about the interiors of the White House. Woodwork made the best barometers, she said. If the wainscoting in the Blue Room swelled an eighth of an inch over the course of July, the White House would be a swamp in August. The First Lady had beans in her head. But Oliver wasn't harsh with her. She could turn the Blue Room into a weather station, if that's what she liked. He was growing fond of her in her little car. He didn't begrudge her tennis shoes and her severe white socks. But he thought a woman her age should have to wear a girdle.

The traffic cops along Rhode Island Avenue recognized the Chevrolet. They ignored the fenders she bumped and waved her on to the next red light. A whole fleet of heads popped out of car windows to gape at her. "There's Eleanor." Oliver thanked God she didn't hit any trees.

They arrived at a school for the deaf on Florida Avenue. Oliver saw acres and acres of grass and woods. This was Kendall's Green. The First Lady couldn't go anywhere unnoticed. Teachers and children paraded in front of her car. Oliver had never been so close to deaf mutes. The noise they could make with their curled mouths put goose bumps on his neck. Eleanor didn't seem to mind these steady wails.

Oliver wanted to sit in the car with his knees in his face. Mrs. Roosevelt wouldn't allow it. He had to leave her Chevrolet. Children grabbed his hand. He was the sailor who came with Mrs. Roosevelt. He could swear the children were trying to squawk his name. Oliver was amazed. The school for the deaf was so good, even the mutes could speak.

They were brought into a building for lunch. Oliver had cooked pears, lettuce, and cottage cheese. Deafness didn't interrupt the children's appetite. They could spoon a pear better than Oliver. And they didn't get cottage cheese in their laps.

The First Lady talked to them after lunch. She didn't have to gesture with her fist. These were smart children. They could all read her lips. Oliver became demoralized. The children followed her words as fast as any sailor could.

Mrs. Roosevelt wore him out. She played volleyball with the school champs. She sat in a huge dollhouse that the deaf girls themselves had built, and helped them dress and undress their dolls. She conducted a sewing class. She visited the sick and the lame in the school's infirmary. She was never cross with a child. She would lean over a sick boy, hug him with her long arms. Oliver left her in the middle of her rounds.

He intended to smoke near the edge of the grass, but he saw a man curled up on the running board of Mrs. Roosevelt's Chevrolet. The man's hungry face couldn't fool Oliver. It was his sister's grubby sweetheart, Vivian de Vries. Oliver woke him up. "Did you follow me here?"

Vivian took the boy's fingers off his throat.

"Are you deaf and dumb?" Oliver said. "It's a crime to follow the President's wife?"

Vivian laughed. His eyes were still raw from his nap on the running board. "Can't you tell when you're being used? Half the country could manipulate you, and you wouldn't know the difference."

Oliver frowned at him. "Who's manipulating me?"

"Eleanor the Queen. You're her decoration, the good sailor. She brought you around to advertise her cause, to prove what a decent little democrat she could be. Oliver, it's a put-on, a show to impress the natives."

"That's baloney," Oliver said. "I saw her sweat. She stabbed her thumb on a sewing needle. She banged her head in the dollhouse."

"The old clumsy routine. Don't leave the place without a wound. A drop of the queen's blood is a fantastic souvenir. Get smart. She came down from the White House to smile at her subjects, to make the prisoners happy."

Oliver's frown got very deep. "It's not a prison, it's a school."

"Yeah, a school for the lily white. Rich people can throw their retarded babies behind the wall. It's a way out for them. This school cares for the babies, and nobody has to know. If you're poor and deaf, they send you to Maryland, to the nigger school."

"Who says?"

"How many Negro boys or girls did you meet on the premises?"

"I can't remember," Oliver lied. "This is Washington. Coloreds don't play with whites."

Oliver was sick of Vivian de Vries. "Go away," he said.

Vivian wouldn't move. Oliver would have had a shoving war with him on the grass if Mrs. Roosevelt hadn't come towards him with a party of teachers and

children. The children were walking her to the Chevrolet. She smiled at Vivian. "How do you do? I'm Mrs.
Franklin Roosevelt."

Vivian took her hand, pumped it once, and let it go.
"I'm a friend of Ollie's sister. I write for *Contempo.* It's
a little magazine."

"Would you like a lift?"

The scarecrow backed off. He was afraid to sit with
Mrs. Roosevelt. The children opened the door of the
Chevrolet. Mrs. Roosevelt drove off with Oliver. The
children waved to her. She said, "Goodbye, goodbye,
goodbye."

The Wild Man
of Tangier

It didn't stop with a school for the deaf on Kendall's Green. Eleanor took him everywhere, to old-age homes, hospitals, civil defense stations. She wasn't choosy about her visits. She went into all the colored wards, without skipping a bed. She would go from patient to patient in her tennis shoes, touching hands, scribbling notes, helping nurses change the sheets. No one mocked her. No one threatened her life. She could survive with a bodyguard as docile as Oliver Beebe.

Patients liked to find a sailor in the ward. And Mrs. Roosevelt had a companion during her drives. With Oliver around, she couldn't fall asleep at the wheel. He began to appear in her newspaper column. "One of my husband's aides, Seaman Oliver Beebe, has been visiting Washington area hospitals with me. He is a forthright, excellent young man. Doctors and patients adore him. Nurses want to know if the handsome sailor has a bride waiting for him somewhere. I won't disappoint them. Oliver is single. But he is dedicated to the United States."

Oliver became a celebrity in the attic. Even the ex-empress of Bulgaria, who did nothing but bump into walls, read about Oliver in *My Day*. The maids tittered at him. Ushers brought up huge packets of mail. In one week Oliver got eighteen marriage proposals. The furor of so many words depressed Oliver. He couldn't get through his mail.

Something else bothered him. It was impossible to shake Vivian de Vries. The scarecrow would spring up suddenly on the steps of a hospital with that tight, sneering face. He badgered Oliver with a crazy story. Several oystermen had discovered a Japanese sailor on Tangier Island, in Chesapeake Bay. The Jap was hiding in a tree. The oystermen bound him hand and foot and delivered him to the mayor of Tangier. A dispute arose on the question of who owned the Jap. He was claimed by the Army, the Navy, the Congress of the United States, Maryland, and the mayor of Tangier. The Jap was acting funny. He screamed in a language that didn't sound much like Japanese. The Coast Guard whisked him off the island. He was brought to a federal institution, St. Elizabeth's, and put in a cage. Vivian swore that the wild man of Tangier was a demented Negro and not a Jap.

"Then why does he look like a Jap? Who gave him the yellow skin?"

"Roosevelt," Vivian said. "It's a war scare. The Navy painted him yellow so King Franklin could have his fourth term. You manufacture a Jap, parade him around, create enough hysteria, and people say you can't switch presidents in the middle of a war."

Oliver didn't believe the Navy had invented the wild man of Tangier. But why wouldn't Mrs. Roosevelt bring her car to St. Elizabeth's and examine the wild man? If he's a nigger, she could tell. Oliver didn't have to brood very long. Eleanor mentioned the wild man in her column. "Are there really Japs on Tangier Island, or has the Navy incarcerated an innocent man? Only scientific tests can tell. The prisoner must be scrutinized openly by a panel of experts. The public has the right to know the true history of the wild man of Tangier."

A great clamor broke out in the city. Certain hysterics would have liked the wild man to lose his head. A few of the "aborigines," the older natives of Washington, wanted to pull out his eyes. Military men spoke of restoring the calm: they expected the Army or the Navy to have him tried and shot to death. The wild man had some partisans too. The children of Georgetown collected pennies to throw in his cage. Government girls made pudding for him on their hot plates and sent it on to the wild man at St. Elizabeth's. A clergyman from Virginia Avenue promised his congregation that he would storm St. Elizabeth's with an army of righteous gentlemen and set the wild man free. His church was closed for a few days. Who had stifled him? The Navy or the FBI? No one was willing to say.

News of the wild man must have reached the President. But no word came from him in the pouch that arrived at the White House every morning. It was an election year, the newspaper boys reminded everyone. A wise President wouldn't intervene. They hadn't counted on Eleanor. The First Lady marshaled all her wits in behalf of the wild man. She formed a committee with Doris Fleeson of the *Washington Star.* She descended on St. Elizabeth's with geologists from the Smithsonian Institute, churchmen, Doris Fleeson, Oliver, and the rest of her loyal band. Fleeson stood with Oliver. The boy had the jitters around her. He was afraid she would talk of his ordeal with the petty officers. Fleeson didn't say a thing. She smiled and called him Mr. Beebe.

The warden came out of St. Elizabeth's to greet Mrs. Roosevelt. He wasn't surly with her. He recognized the authenticity of her people. But he wouldn't grant her permission to interrogate the wild man. They were standing on federal property. The lunatics inside St. Elizabeth's belonged to the United States. Mrs. Roosevelt didn't lay claim to the prerogatives of a President's wife. "We're as much of the United States," she said, "as the stones and bars of this institution."

The warden made a phone call. A team of Navy geologists arrived. The warden was beneficent now. He let Mrs. Roosevelt's people into the lunatic asylum. Everybody went down to inspect the cage. The wild man was guarded by two marines. He had long brown fingernails edged with little teeth. His beard covered most of his face. His complexion was invariably yellow. Oliver looked for signs of paint behind the wild man's ears. If the Navy had brushed the wild man into being, slapped an old mad Negro into a sailor and a spy, Oliver couldn't spot any giveaways. The wild man's freckles were real. His eyes were slanted enough. He didn't have a nigger's mouth. He couldn't be anything but a Jap.

The warden led him out of the cage. He didn't jump. He didn't attack the two marines. A noise came out of him, a peculiar howl, like the deaf and dumb children of Kendall's Green. "The poor man's hungry," Mrs. Roosevelt said. She took a bar of chocolate from her bag and fed it to him. The warden didn't object. The wild man made gentle sucks at Mrs. Roosevelt's thumb.

The geologists were eager to get at him. The men from the Smithsonian didn't want clothes on the wild man. They would only examine him in his natural state. The Navy men had to agree, or the investigation would never have begun. The two marines grabbed the wild man's shoulders and plucked off his hospital gown. His coloring didn't change. His buttocks were as yellow as his ears. The women in Mrs. Roosevelt's party tried not to peek at his genitals. But they couldn't help themselves.

The geologists asked for a barber. Oliver had to deliver the wild man from his beard. He used some rough scissors that the warden supplied. It wasn't easy. He had to cut into that fierce growth with all his might. The wild man was left with stubble on his cheeks. The skin under his beard didn't reveal very much. It was a sickly yellow. Mrs. Roosevelt's geologists walked around the wild man. They measured his skull with a set of wooden clamps. They tapped on the walls of his chest. They all laid their heads on the wild man's bosom and listened to his heart. They felt his scrotum with a rubber glove that passed from hand to hand. Their minds were made up. They gathered near Mrs. Roosevelt in complete accord. "Ma'am," their spokesman said. "He's definitely a Jap."

You could feel the disappointment spread through Mrs. Roosevelt's party. There was great bitterness and chagrin. Her people seemed ready to fall upon their own geologists. Then one of the Navy men approached the Jap. He rubbed the wild man's face with a wet rag. He was persistent, this Navy man. The Jap's howls couldn't stop the Navy man's rag. Soon the yellow began to peel off, one spot at a time. "That's mud from the Chesapeake," the Navy man said. "Yellow mud."

They were staring at nigger eyes, nigger ears, and a broad nigger nose. The warden was appalled. You couldn't house a nigger at St. Elizabeth's in 1944. A movie starlet fainted at the spectacle of a semi-yellow man. Oliver revived her, fanning the starlet's lips with his sailor hat.

SEVEN

No one claimed the nigger of Tangier. There was some talk of enlisting him in the Navy, but nothing could be done about his vocabulary of howls and grunts. Psychologists primed him for a week, but he failed to pass even a simplified version of the Navy's intelligence test. The Army backed off after the Navy rejected him. A movement rose up among enlightened people to restore the nigger to his original habitat. Those oystermen shouldn't have snatched him from his tree. The mayor of Tangier balked at this proposal. He had no use for niggers on Tangier, tame or wild.

The nigger was thrown at the mercy of the government. A federal judge scolded the adoption agencies of the District for their unwillingness to help the former wild man. He had to lease the nigger to Mrs. Roosevelt until a permanent home could be found for him. This kind judge gave the nigger three dollars and suit of clothes, and called him Jonathan, because that had been the name of his own dead son. Washingtonians held Mrs. Roosevelt in disrepute for bringing Jonathan to the White House. Civilized niggers were bad enough, they said. A wild nigger would hang from the chandeliers.

All the calumny in the world couldn't injure Mrs.

Roosevelt. She followed the instructions of the judge. She didn't allow Jonathan to become a showpiece. He wasn't trundled out at breakfast time to amuse a guest. Members of her party were cautioned not to feed him any tidbits. Ushers and Secret Service men were told not to bump him on the stairs. Reporters couldn't get near him for an interview. He was given over to Oliver.

The machine gunners on the roof were delighted by the goings-on in the attic. "Lord," they said, "there's an ape living right under us." Oliver was less amused now that he had Jonathan for a brother. The nigger's grooming was left to him. He had to be sure that Jonathan's sleeves didn't stick out of his summer coat. He shaved the nigger, buffed his shoes, taught him the refineries of a toilet seat. He was the only tutor Jonathan ever had.

Oliver couldn't romp in the attic, with an ex-empress clogging the halls. The nigger had to have his exercise. So Oliver ran him on the south lawn, in front of policemen and gardeners, and shoved him through the open tunnels in the jungle gym. But he didn't want to cloister Jonathan inside a garden. The nigger's education was far too narrow to satisfy a landlocked sailor such as Oliver. He meant to give Jonathan a touch of the city. He took him across the road, to Lafayette Park. They sat opposite the Episcopalian church, a good quarter of a mile from the admirals and generals who came out of the Map Room in the White House with their salt shakers and a box lunch.

Oliver had no luck. He could avoid nosy admirals, but not his sister's man. Vivian de Vries had an instinct for creeping up on Oliver. He was only a bench away. He stared at Jonathan with pebbly eyes.

"Don't talk," Oliver said. "I'm not interested."

He would have liked to run. But the Admirals might have seen him clutch Jonathan and push him out of Vivian's way. You couldn't gallop with a nigger in Lafayette Park and remain undiscovered for very long.

"You ought to visit Anita," Vivian said, without taking his eyes off Jonathan. "She doesn't have your options, son."

"I'm not your son," Oliver said.

Vivian ignored the surliness of the boy. "She can't come over and knock on your door. You live on Pennsylvania Avenue with all the kings."

Oliver developed a murderous streak talking to Vivian. But Lafayette Park wasn't the place to claw a scarecrow. He would invite him to Sailors' Row, feed him to the whores and the bar rats at the Ship's Cafe. Vivian's journalism would fail him with pieces of glass in his mouth. "Anita don't need visits from me," Oliver said, "when she's got a fox like you in her hair."

Oliver waited for him to call the nigger one of Franklin Roosevelt's election freaks. But Vivian was quiet. Then he said, "That's quite a lady, adopting a wild man, making him a cousin to you."

"Shut your mouth," Oliver said, no longer cautious of the admirals. They were lords of the Map Room, but they couldn't push their little war pins in Lafayette Park. He raced with Jonathan across the green. The nigger enjoyed himself. He moved with his tongue deep in his mouth. He seemed to have affection for Oliver.

The nigger's presence in the attic irritated Ethel Rosenquist. She would come upstairs at three in the morning and find Jonathan in Oliver's bed. "What's *he* doing here? Doesn't he have his own room?"

"Ethel, he isn't used to ceilings and walls. He likes to stay with me."

Days and nights with Jonathan left Oliver a sorry man. The nigger's howling was like a hatchet in Oliver's brain. He couldn't think. He couldn't perform his chores. He couldn't pilfer through his movie magazines. He let the maids borrow Jonathan for a single afternoon. Jonathan could sit with them in the laundry room and watch his shirts being ironed, and the maids could have the pleasure of accompanying him to the toilet. Oliver drank a potful of bourbon in Chinatown. He fondled a waitress behind the kitchen of the Old Shanghai. With cooks going in and out of the kitchen, they couldn't take off their clothes. It was grueling for Oliver. He had to copulate with bourbon sitting in his belly. He scrounged on the floor in white pants. Then he buttoned up his fly and walked to Mount Vernon Square to see his sister.

Anita sneered at him. She wasn't blind to the sawdust on his pants. "Did you have a nice party?" she asked.

The bitch had gone into his wardrobe. She'd ransacked his civilian clothes. She was wearing one of his old shirts. Anita scorned Oliver's buttons. She twisted up the ends of the shirt into a knot over her tits.

"Tell Vivian to leave me alone," Oliver said. "I'll tear off his lip, he follows me again. Let him do his journalism on somebody else."

"He can't. He's writing about the Roosevelts."

"What kind of name is Vivian? It don't fit on a man. And where the hell is baby Michael?"

"That's not your worry. Michael belongs to me."

"Close your shirt," Oliver said.

She tied a stiffer knot, leaving her stomach exposed. She had stretch marks that went under and over her navel. Oliver was rude. He stared at the stretch marks until Anita turned her belly away. The sailor couldn't relax in his old room. He'd fucked a waitress and come to Anita with wet pants. The waitress wasn't Chinese. She was a blonde from Philadelphia who had a softness for Oliver's looks. The owners of the restaurant hadn't discouraged her from meeting Oliver behind the kitchen. They would never have allowed a Chinese girl to get that close to Ollie. They hired blondes from Philadelphia to bring tea and smile at the soldiers and sailors who flooded the District in 1944. Oliver didn't have to damage the blonde, bruise her tits. He liked the girl, valued her generosities at the luncheon table. But he had to make himself savage for Anita. He was afraid of the bitch.

So he sparred with Anita, took her bite for bite, or she would have swallowed him whole. He'd been her prey for the first twelve years of his life. She'd sit in the bathtub and beg him to scrub her back. She could reduce Oliver to a pitiful boy with the different parts of her body. He'd have been glad to cut out his tongue for a peek at Anita's ass, legs, and shoulder blades. She loved having Oliver spy on her. When she moaned on the couch with an admirer of hers, she was moaning for Oliver. It excited her to copulate with her brother's eyes on her. He remembered the shudders in her back, her pinched waist against a pillow, her admirer's big ears.

She must have seen the terror lines in his face, the tightened grip of his ears, the harshness of Oliver's jaw. "Ollie," she said. "Michael isn't lost. Jesus, would I abandon my own child? I left him with a friend. You can't go traveling with a baby in these times. Food's hard to get. You never know if bugs are going to be in the water."

"Where's that other guy of yours? Philip, the draft dodger. Did you leave the baby with him?"

"Don't be such a goddamn boss. I'm with Vivian now."

"Vivian's a feather. Can he look after a child?"

Anita puffed out her nose. "Ollie, stop. . . ."

"He is. A feather. You could blow him off the street. And he's crazy. He sees niggers in the bushes and he likes to call Mrs. Roosevelt the queen."

Anita put her hands on Oliver's blouse. "Take off your sailor suit," she said. "It's a mess." She deprived him of his neckerchief. She'd gotten into his clothes. Oliver couldn't believe it. She started to nuzzle him. Her head was in his lap. He could smell the roots of her hair. His shorts were still on, thank God, his prick housed in white cotton. He couldn't control her nuzzling head. The boy was petrified. He didn't have the energy to scream or grab portions of her face. One of his knees jerked out. He tumbled off the bed. He ran out of the room clutching his shoes and pants.

EIGHT

T he wild man's ordeal wasn't over. Phonologists
from the old Navy hospital came into the White House
with bundles of sound equipment. They tied earphones
onto Jonathan's skull. They clamped pieces of metal into
his mouth. They dug out bacteria from under his tongue.
They fondled his organs of speech. They announced to
Mrs. Roosevelt that Jonathan was a mute. His howls
meant nothing to them. His wild man's grunts bore no
resemblance to the mellifluous noise of human beings.
He must have training at a school for the deaf. They
couldn't get him into Kendell's Green. He would have
to go to the colored school, in Maryland.

Jonathan didn't want to leave his attic home. He
held on to Oliver when the phonologists tried to carry
him down the stairs. Oliver kept thinking, that son-of-a-
bitch Vivian didn't tell a lie. The nigs go to Maryland. If
the wild man had been a little more white, he could have
had the sunshine at Kendall's Green. The phonologists
tugged at Jonathan's legs. Oliver was glad he hadn't
trimmed the wild man's nails, or Jonathan's grip
wouldn't have been snug at all. There were deep grooves
in Oliver's shirt. Blood trickled down his sleeves, but he
prayed that Jonathan wouldn't have to go. "I'll get you

out of the nigger school," he promised in the wild man's ear. It was futile work. Jonathan couldn't understand Weehawken English. His nails broke off. The phonologists pried him loose.

Oliver hadn't realized how fond he was of the wild man, until Jonathan was pulled away. He cursed the wickedness of governments, their absolute ability to transport human beings from one place to the next. In this world you could get to the White House from a tree on Tangier, and then find yourself in Maryland.

For two whole days Oliver wouldn't look at Mrs. Roosevelt. Eleanor belonged to the government, didn't she? Who else was the First Lady of America and mistress of the White House? He began to forgive her by the third day. She would have saved Jonathan, if she had been able to do so. He went down to her breakfast parties. He chewed her scrambled eggs. He listened to her people plan a huge campaign to knit socks for unwed mothers. There was much talk of adopting Chinese babies. Oliver seethed in his chair. His eggs grew cold. No one but Mrs. Roosevelt understood the boy's grief. "Ollie, we had to give up Jonathan. We couldn't deprive him of his schooling. Don't worry. He'll have a splendid home."

One of Mrs. Roosevelt's knitting companions cut in. "Heck, Eleanor, you couldn't keep him here forever, you know. Jonathan would have made a nuisance of himself."

Oliver left the breakfast table with lumps of egg and bile around his heart. Where's the Boss? Did everybody forget that this was also the President's house? Mrs. Roosevelt's people took over all the better rooms. You couldn't climb the stairs without stepping on an actress or an educator. The President's people were ensconced in the West Wing. They weren't invited to breakfast, lunch, or tea. Oliver was going crazy. He had a sister who tried to eat his underpants, and a President who was loitering in the Pacific with his admirals of the fleet. Oliver had only gotten one communiqué from Mr. Franklin in a month: it was a doll that arrived in the mail pouch, an Hawaiian doll with a deep purple face and eyelashes that must have been plucked from the head of an animal. With the doll was a note: "Dear Ollie, This is a tribal piece. It will act as your conscience, I've been told. If you do any evil, the doll is supposed to sting. Fala misses you. Stay well. Franklin D. Roosevelt."

Oliver didn't admire the doll. Its purple mug provoked him, made him want to tear the stuffing out of its neck. But he wouldn't abuse a gift from the President. The doll sat on Oliver's bureau, neglected, unloved, in a cramped position that allowed its belly to hide most of the purple. He felt hounded in his room. The doll was persecuting him. His anger for Anita had started to boil. She hadn't kissed his underpants out of any deep passion. The bitch wanted something from him. Oliver returned to the boardinghouse.

This time she wasn't in a shirt of his. She wore a dress. Her figure startled Oliver. She had the body of a fourteen-year-old if you forgot the stretch marks around her navel. She was the girl who entertained her admirers on the couch, while Mr. and Mrs. Beebe drank themselves into a stupor in the next room.

"Where's Vivian? Is he out canvassing for the Republican Party?"

Anita wouldn't answer him. She was dusting the walls with an old, smelly rag. Her domestic rituals were strange to Oliver, who had never seen his sister wash a dish.

"What's going on? Is Vivian trying to make an idiot out of me? Why'd you bother to take off my pants?"

He took her rag away. Anita didn't object. He grabbed her wrists, squeezed. Her body only softened. They stumbled onto the bed. He could smell her skin. The musk was so familiar, it frightened Oliver. The bitch had crept into his blood. He should never have shunned the Boss' doll. All that purple might have scrubbed Anita out of him. He had his sister's arms over her head. Her shoulders curved out at Ollie. She had the sheen of an animal. Without thinking he licked her hair. The boy wasn't confused. He was on a mattress pocked with cigarette burns. Most of them were from Lucky Strikes. Oliver had a habit of dozing with a cigarette in his mouth. The smoke would stir him soon enough. He'd wake with a cough and slap bits of fire away from the bed.

What should you do with a sister's teeth? They kissed with a rumbling in their mouths. They undressed. He had his prick inside Anita. It amazed him that she was wet. "Love you," he mumbled, the words sticking to his tongue. It wasn't curious for him to move in her. It was as if the two of them had one rhythm to share and one flesh.

Oliver lingered in his old room. He watched her for any signs of regret. They drank apple juice from a big can. Anita didn't put on her clothes. She was a girl of twenty-seven, a woman almost, with a child in Milwaukee. Oliver adored her stretch marks. He touched her pubic hair while she finished the can. He would have given up the White House for another afternoon with her. He was sick of the attic and a President who

wouldn't come home. He'd gotten to like Mrs. Roosevelt, but he could live without her good deeds. Anita
pouted at him, her lips full of apple juice. "Oliver, you'd
better go. Vivian's gonna be here in a minute."

That scarecrow couldn't bother him. Why should he
worry if Vivian saw his prick? But Anita's eyes went gray.
She wouldn't look at his body any more. Oliver left. He
didn't say when he was coming back. The barber had his
scruples. He wasn't going to make appointments to fuck
his own sister. He stopped in Chinatown for dumplings
and black tea. Blonde waitresses couldn't get a nod from
Oliver. A man called to him from the next table. "Say,
aren't you Oliver Beebe?" Oliver didn't smile or blink
hellos. He swallowed a dumpling and paid his bill.

Anita de Vries

NINE

She was a Weehawken girl who lived in a house on Jupiter Street. The boys followed her home from school. She was the beauty of her class. Voluptuous at twelve, she had Packards driving up to her father's door, Packards with stove-pipe exhausts and mirrors that made you look pink. There was a brother in the house, baby Oliver, who went along on the rides. Anita wasn't watching over her baby brother. She brought Oliver to terrorize him, make him whimper for his life. He was eight years old, in short pants, with a smelly rabbit's foot in his pocket. The boy never talked. He wouldn't eat unless Anita stuffed his mouth with food. She mashed a banana for him. The banana would end up on Oliver's cheek.

Anita dangled her admirers, kept them for a month, and then wouldn't go into their cars. This month's Packard belonged to a shoe salesman from South Jersey. Murray was what he called himself. He had a wife in Hackensack, a bunch of kids, and broken shoetrees in his trunk. He was mooneyed about Anita. Murray had no sense of caution. He lived in a soda shop, among twelve-year-old girls, eating chocolate sundaes and banana splits. He abandoned his route to buy dresses for Anita. He taxied her to junior high school. He supplied her family with shoes.

And he couldn't escape the boy. Oliver's head would rise over the shoe samples in the back, pucker up, like a greedy eye, and the salesman would lose his erection in the car. Anita didn't object. She would puncture his condoms with a bobby pin, wiggle a finger into one of his socks. They would kiss for hours, Anita winking at Ollie from the salesman's lap. He had nothing to do but stare at his sister. That month he smelled of leather from all the shoes. No matter where the salesman crept, Anita wouldn't close her eyes. Oliver was quiet. He learned to sit on a shoebox without swaying his behind.

The salesman didn't last. His wife showed up on Jupiter Street with a brood of little Murrays. The brats cried in front of Mr. Beebe's house. Mr. and Mrs. Beebe were much too drunk to care about the noise. But the neighbors listened. They heard a wife lament over the future of her little boys. It was getting dark. The wife disappeared to Hackensack. Her brood left a deep impression. When the salesman brought Anita and Oliver home, the husbands of Jupiter Street pulled him out of the car. They had their way with Murray. They punched him up and down the block and stole his supply of shoes. The husbands scowled at Anita while they inspected her clothes. They carried her into her father's house with their hands clapped in their thighs. The husbands felt more of her than the salesman ever did.

Oliver was left on the sidewalk. The husbands marched out with their jawlines split from grinning so hard. They patted Oliver on the head. They pitied him for having been born into a family of Beebes. Oliver got away from them. He found Anita upstairs in the john. The husbands had cinched her to the toilet seat with the shreds of her skirt. It took him an hour to unravel Anita.

It wasn't the ferocity of the bindings. Oliver worked with his face in the wall. He didn't want to peek into the area of his sister's legs.

There were no more Packards on Jupiter Street. They were afraid to come. Anita was landlocked for a while. Her suitors had to meet her in the park, or take her indoors. She had four years of petting on her father's couch. Then she grew tired. She wrote a letter to Murray. She needed a small vacation, she said. Away from Weehawken. Murray obliged. He threw over children and wife for his former darling. Her appearance was a shock. The girl had aged in four years. Skinnier at sixteen, she'd lost the edge of her loveliness. The salesman was just as mooneyed about her. They went to live in New York. He took a flat on Irving Place for his Anita. He bought her two vanity tables and a bed. But he couldn't hold a job. The vanity tables were sent back to the furniture store. Anita got gifts from other men. She wasn't a venal girl. She wouldn't accept anything from a man unless he made himself vulnerable to her.

Murray returned to Hackensack on his knees. His wife jabbed him with a broom. His children ate his cuffs in a long choleric fit. But they took him in.

Anita's boyfriends began to overlap. Her suitors were coming in strings that tightened around Anita. She became a terminus for all her men. They would crawl into her body, grab whatever delight they could, and cling to her until she found a way to shove them out. She got through her teens with a small patch of gray in her hair. She fell into her twenties without a permanent suitor. She was starving now. Anita didn't have a capacity to work, and she wouldn't lie down with a man who didn't please her. She met Philip in 1941, an unemployed cartoonist. He had as few strategies for survival as Anita did. Philip sold shoelaces in the street.

He was a fugitive, hiding from the peacetime draft. They could kill him, he said, throw him in the penitentiary and pull out his teeth, before he would put on a uniform. He stopped selling shoelaces because he was timid about going into the street. Roosevelt had his agents everywhere. Anita wallowed in Philip's hysteria. But they had nothing to eat. They moved to Terre Haute, near the college of St. Mary-of-the-Woods. Philip did odd jobs for the nuns at the college, who were terrified of Roosevelt and the Democratic Party. He felt comfortable around the nuns until they asked why a healthy boy like him hadn't received an induction notice. They fled St. Mary-of-the-Woods and landed in Milwaukee, where he found work with a greeting card company that did too much volume to worry about the civilian life of its employees.

He begged Anita to have a child with him. "I'm not right to be a mother," she said. "There was too much neglect in my house. The only time I saw my father was when he had to puke. My mother would have strangled me if she had stayed sober. That's how jealous she was. Anyway, I had one child. I raised my brother Ollie. Both of us are jumpy. We could never sit still."

Plagued with morning sickness, she vomited for seven months. Weird brown spots developed on her nipples. Her belly turned dark. Her navel was wider than a thumb. She had enough pubic hair to put fleece inside a glove. The veins on her legs crawled like worms. She tramped through the Milwaukee winter without a coat, her skin on fire. Her labor was horrendous. The contractions nearly split her eyes. On the way to the hospital her water bag broke. She sat in her own fluids for three quarters of an hour. The doctors tore a baby out of her. Michael was born with a purplish head.

It was 1942, and Philip was frightened to announce his paternity in the middle of a war. The infant took Anita's surname. He was Michael Beebe.

Philip was good to baby Michael, so good that he crept between mother and child. Anita didn't mind being scorned. She was grateful for Philip's devotion to the brat. Coming from a disjointed family, she had no idea how a young mother should behave. She was awkward around Michael Beebe. Michael arrived at the age of two without interference from his mother. Anita didn't stray from the house. She knit socks for the baby that never got done.

A salesman happened to knock on the door while Philip and Michael were in the park. He was trying to push a magazine stuffed with politics and art. She couldn't unscramble a paragraph, or connect two lines of verse. The salesman's hat was oily, and his cuffs were beginning to shred. She had mercy on him for peddling such rotten wares. He didn't get coy with her. He wouldn't come in until he told her who he was. Vivian de Vries, the sole editor of *Contempo.* He had a grayness that petrified Anita. She couldn't tell what he wanted of her. They necked on her couch while the coffee boiled. It was like kissing a cool piece of stone. Vivian had a salesman's tricks. He wouldn't take off his hat. "My boyfriend's in the park," she said. "You'd better leave my panties on just in case."

He hadn't touched her clothes. She struggled to undress herself. She needed that stone body of his. He entered her like a claw. She thought she was giving birth

all over again. The salesman had a miraculous way of
loving her. Nothing jumped except his groin. She
couldn't reconcile that delicious pain inside her with the
stillness of his hat, limbs, and chest. She bit him on the
shoulder to find out if the salesman was alive. His salty
blood only served to confuse her. He came without shuddering once, with the clipped snarl of a dog. Then he was
out of her. She hadn't even noticed the color of his
underpants.

She clucked to Vivian, hoping to delay him with the
resonance of her voice. She mentioned Oliver, Weehawken, Hitler, Terre Haute, the things that came into
her head. Vivian acquired a sudden taste for Anita's
coffee. He unbundled his magazines and steered her
back to Oliver.

"He lives at the White House," she said. "But he
keeps a room in Chinatown in case Roosevelt gets too
smart. He's short, my brother. Five foot six. His scalp's
so black, he looks like a crow. He used to be a sailor.
Now he gives shampoos."

The salesman had a weakness: he was crazy to hear
about Oliver. She'd tell him anything to hold his curios-
ity. "Ollie loves me. He always has. Vivian, where's your
next stop?"

"Washington, D.C."

Anita was packed before the salesman could grab his
magazines. She didn't take her scarves or her bran-new
spikes. Just the necessities. Walking shoes, blouses and
skirts, a stack of underwear. She hadn't planned to run
off with the editor of *Contempo* magazine. Milwaukee was
no trouble to her. She could have continued with Michael and Philip, an unnecessary mother around Lake
Michigan. But when Vivian said Washington, she had to
go.

She could barely get into Vivian's car. The old Plymouth was stuffed with magazines. Anita had to sit on a pile of *Contempos,* or not go at all. The engine spit a vile green blood. A fender would fall off every three miles.

He was some kind of scoundrel, Anita assumed, but he had a magician's way with cars. He could nurse a dead machine. He recited poetry with his cheek in the steering wheel, lines about bean rows, crickets, and honey that enthralled a Weehawken girl. He was purring to the car. That man had sweettalked the Plymouth into getting them to Washington.

He dropped her at a small hotel on New Jersey Avenue, and disappeared for eight days. She had to live on a handful of dimes, the last of Vivian's money. She saw black faces outside her window. She was stranded in niggertown because of him. She would have dialed the President's house and begged to speak to her brother, but Vivian had told her not to call. "Don't want Ollie boy to know we're in Washington, sis. We'll surprise him when the time comes. He's a celebrity, your baby brother. He sticks his fingers in Roosevelt's hair."

She'd go downstairs every afternoon to buy cupcakes at the colored grocery store. That was her only trip abroad. She sat in her room pecking holes in the cupcakes and licking out the cream. Vivian returned with a scratchy face. He'd gotten shabbier since he disappeared. He devoured all her cupcakes, smashing them into his mouth. Anita thought he'd swallow his thumbs. "Pack up," he said.

"Where we going, hon?"

"To hide in Oliver's room."

They got into the boardinghouse by letting Anita pose as Oliver's wife. Vivian shook hands with the boarders and introduced himself as Oliver's Navy friend. The cans of soup in Oliver's cupboard kept them alive. "Hon, we might eat a little better if you sold some of your magazines."

Vivian twisted the collar of her blouse. His knuckles bore into her throat. "Shut up about that magazine."

Oliver arrived before her throat could heal from the knuckling it got. He looked pretty in his sailor pants. Anita would have leapt on him, ruffled his clean white jersey, but her man didn't like displays of affection between brother and sister. The talk was somber in the room. She could feel the pulse in Oliver's eyes. She shouldn't have left Milwaukee.

She grew listless after Oliver was gone. Vivian wouldn't let her out of the room. He disappeared on her again. Then he stumbled into the boardinghouse with a sheath of fifties in his pocket and whiskey on his tongue. He wanted to dance. He hugged Anita and trotted around the floor with her, grinding out music with his throat. The boardinghouse creaked. Vivian had this idiotic refrain that he mumbled in Anita's ear. The whiskey gave his words a sour pull.

> *Ollie and the President*
> *Ollie and the President*
> *Who's the pauper, who's the king*
> *Who's the barber, who's the fool*
> *Who's the clippers, who's the purse*
> *Ollie and the President*
> *Ollie and the President*

It was like the poetry in Vivian's magazine. A pack of stupid words, good for making fun of people. But those fifty-dollar bills did get her out of the room. Vivian was on a spending fit. He picked out a cocktail dress for her at Garfinckel's department store. She walked in front of mirrors with a fluffy bodice and crepe around her heels. The editor of *Contempo* was an aristocrat. He'd grown up with the rich ladies of Charleston, if she could believe his stories. And he took her into a store with cherrywood on the walls. All the Senators' wives shopped at Garfinckel's, Vivian said.

She didn't go dancing in her cocktail dress. They sat in an obscure diner that belonged to another nigger-town, near Dupont Circle. The people in the diner stared at the crepe between her tits. Vivian had dressed her up like a miserable crepe dummy, to sit with ketchup bottles and niggers in straw hats. A man came in. He went straight to Vivian. Jesus, they hugged in front of all the niggers. "Sis, meet my buddy, Orlando Frayard."

He had powerful manners, this Orlando Frayard. He gave Anita a wet kiss on the hand. A Spaniard who had grown up in the American South, he was tall and blond and thirty-nine, Vivian's age. They'd gone to school together at The Citadel in Charleston.

He bumped her under the table with his knee. It might have been a mistake. The Spaniard had an advantage over her. He was tall enough to peek through her bodice. He didn't stay very long. They could stick her in mummy's clothes, but they couldn't fool a Weehawken girl. Anita had spent her childhood in a dark house, with her mug in the banisters. She had an infallible eye. You didn't meet friends in a nigger cafe without a good reason. That tall Spaniard had come to check her out.

"Why's Orlando so blond?" she said.

"What the hell do you mean?"

"Did you inherit your money off of him?"

"Sis, you'd better shut up."

She didn't have to sneak into the boardinghouse with the cool smell of crepe on her bodice. Vivian booked a room at the Willard. It was a fortress on "F" Street, a stone hotel with little balconies, a melange of roofs, and a dirty white face. A plaque on the wall claimed Charles Dickens had slept at the Willard in 1867. "Who's that Dickens?" she asked.

"An Englishman," Vivian said, hiding his scorn. "He wrote *Oliver Twist.*"

Anita wasn't crazy about Vivian's hotel. Its lobbies were overrun with government girls who polished their nails and read a book, rather than sit in a rooming house. Older, more adventurous girls invaded the cocktail lounge, scratching for men. The Willard was lousy with women. It made Anita unsure of herself. The girls in the lobby eyed her with envy and distrust, because she'd come in with a man. She was registered as Mrs. Vivian de Vries.

Vivian hadn't disappointed her. Their room was at the top of the Willard. She was going to live inside a roof, just like Oliver. She stuck her cocktail dress in the closet and took possession of the room. She was softening to the Willard. You could see the White House from her window.

That son of a bitch returned her to the boarding-house after breakfast. Vivian kept the room for himself.

Now she had that dreamy interval, waiting to seduce Oliver for *Contempo* magazine. She'd been curious to sleep with Oliver for years and years, and Vivian gave her the excuse. It was bravura on her part, a bravura nursed in Weehawken, where she'd had enough suitors to choke off Roosevelt's Army and Navy. "I know Oliver," she said. "He'll do whatever I ask."

So she waited for Ollie, slept with him in that stinking room, a room for widowers with phlegm in their throats and sailors without a ship. You couldn't take a bath, standing or sitting in Oliver's room. It had nothing but a sink. The boardinghouse was fickle about its water, which came out of the pipes a scummy brown. Anita boiled some of it on her brother's hot plate. She smelled of Oliver. His sperm dripped between her legs. She crouched over the little sink and washed herself, rubbing her body with an old towel. Oliver wouldn't come off. He was an attic sailor. He never went into the sun. She could picture his white knees. The pale, hairy bumps nauseated her. She shouldn't have settled close to Oliver. Washington was an evil city.

One of the lodgers screamed something through her door. She crept into the hall wearing Oliver's robe. She despised the graceless, baggy lines she had inside her brother's clothes. Vivian barked obscenities at her on the phone. Anita interrupted him.

"Oliver was here," she said. She had to whisper with so many lodgers around.

"Congratulations, sis."

"Aren't you going to ask what we did?"

"Why? That dimwit's a sucker for you."

"He's smart enough to work for a President."

"That's because Roosevelt can only tolerate dummies nowadays. Everybody else talks back to him. He's got a whole line of Olivers shuffling through the White House. He steals them from the generals if he has to. He's got a knack for it. That man's a thief."

"Then why's it so important to get Oliver for your magazine?"

"Because I'm not on speaking terms with every single dummy in the White House. Oliver's the one that's related to you. Now come on over, sis."

She got to the Willard, but she couldn't watch the sun sink under the roofs. Vivian hogged the window. He crouched with his binoculars and expected her to please herself.

"Vivian, can I have some champagne? I'm easier to be with when I drink champagne."

"Order a piece of cake," he said, without turning his back. "Chocolate cake."

Room service was unpredictable at the Willard. A boy arrived with apple cobbler in a special humidor. It was a curious pie. It had no crust on the bottom. She didn't know how to eat a cobbler. The smell of pie got Vivian away from his binoculars. He brought the cobbler to the window. The crust on top looked like pieces of rubble to Anita. Vivian broke under this rubble to pick at the fruit. Anita glowered at him. There's a Southern gentleman. Eating pie with his hands.

She'd hustled her own brother for that man at the window, and he stole her pie. He'd come to the Willard for an open view of the White House. That's the only reason Vivian lived in a roof. He romanced a pair of binoculars and stuck her in a boardinghouse. She would have peeked at his notes, which were on the windowsill, but she couldn't come to grips with Vivian's sketches or his scrawl. He was fond of drawing curtains and flagpoles, it seemed to her. She'd never been with a writer before. His words were like the pincers a grocer used to knock down packages of toilet paper from a high shelf. Vivian could pull your underpants off with the sentences he wrote.

Someone slapped on the door. She hoped it wasn't room service with more apple cobbler. Vivian's face wasn't deep enough to support another pie. "Open it," he said. It was the blond Spaniard, Orlando Frayard. He ducked into the room with a bottle of Old Kentucky under his summer coat. Frayard ignored her after kissing her hand. He went to the window with his Old Kentuck. Bourbon's a gentleman's drink, she understood. The bottle passed between them. They pulled on it with their mouths like good Christian boys. They traded stories about Washington numbskulls, the niggers, actresses, and idiotic generals who stayed at the White House to suck leather off Roosevelt's shoes.

Vivian left his binoculars on the window. "Sis, I'm going down for cigarettes."

His gestures were too pronounced, patting his wallet, reaching for his shoelaces and tugging on the bows. "Bye," he said, and she was stuck with Orlando Frayard. People were going berserk to grab a pint of whiskey, and Frayard had his own supply. He called her over to the bed. Anita could have resisted his Old Kentucky mouth. She wasn't a lump of chocolate pudding for blond Spaniards to stick their fingers in.

Frayard had the Spanish touch. He liked to kiss her with his hands in her brassiere. It didn't hurt. She could think of Oliver while Frayard blew passionately on her neck. Her brother's pale, sunless body felt like a reptile on her skin. His dark eyes were unhealthy. His hair was coarse and dusty, like coal. Frayard clung to Anita. She was grateful for blond shoulders and a blond chest. The Spaniard made love to her in Oliver's wake. His eyes glistened over her in smooth, natural colors. At least his hair wasn't dusty.

Summer Storm

The barber was summoned from the attic. He went down to the West Wing with his tools. The Secret Service men were lonely without the President and Kirkland Horn. They had nothing to do. They couldn't order Oliver Beebe to trim the wild hair on their necks. Even the admirals in the Map Room had lost that privilege. He was only obliged to cut the President's hair. The Secretary of State could grow potatoes in his ears and Oliver could ignore it. But the Secret Service men knew what a good boy he was. He didn't complain. He devoted a half hour to each of them, cutting perfect halos around the edges of their scalps.

He nibbled on a Baby Ruth between haircuts. That was Oliver's lunch. He couldn't go back to his movie magazines. The First Lady wanted him in her sitting room. She was surrounded by her usual retinue of tough ladies and college boys. Eleanor's people were giving a lawn party. They screeched and hurled pencils across the room as they prepared an invitation list. The list would shrink and grow with the smack of pencils against the wall. They scratched off names and scribbled them in again. They couldn't agree on who *not* to invite.

Oliver almost lost an eye ducking pencils in the

sitting room. The raucous energy of her comrades embarrassed Mrs. Roosevelt. She invited Oliver to the party
with a dull smile. Both of them stooped to pick pencils
off the rug. "Ollie dear, bring your sister, will you
please?"

Oliver shuddered inside his clothes. "She's busy,
ma'am. She knits socks for the USO."

"Fine," Mrs. Roosevelt said. "She can knit with me
at the party."

Oliver left the room with "Anita Beebe" scratched
on a little gold card. He didn't tell Anita about the invitation. He was too scared. Eleanor's people would catch a
brother and sister holding hands on the White House
lawn. They'd wiggle their pinkies and go "Shame,
shame," and Oliver would be out of a job.

Guilt began to gnaw at him, to thin his eyebrows and
pull in his nose, but he couldn't keep away from Anita.
He brought her flowers from Mrs. Roosevelt's garden,
summer tulips that could sweat in the dark, roses with
enough pink in them to kill, irises that could have swallowed a fingernail. Anita thought she was with one of her
crazy suitors again. The flowers breathed a thick perfume
in the boardinghouse. The irises left crumpled blue bells
on the floor that stuck to Anita's toes. The tulips exhausted themselves, their petals tucking under like the
curled knobs on an old man's back. The roses refused to
die. The morbid sweetness in Oliver's room stuffed
Anita's nostrils with a special kind of glue. She sneezed
most of the time. She lay with Oliver in the presence of
flowers that pinkened the air. It wasn't romance. It was
the colors of a funeral parlor.

Only Oliver didn't come to her in mourning clothes.
He had laundry privileges at the mansion. The maids

starched his uniforms and did his neckerchiefs by hand. He visited Anita in proud summer whites. His old anger was gone. He could admit his blind love for her. In Weehawken Oliver didn't have his own toys. He played with Anita's dolls whenever she wasn't in the house. He combed them, rubbed their skirts, took the dolls into his bed. He wasn't a womanish boy. He had no interest in dolls that didn't belong to her. Anita was too bitchy in person. He could only display his affection to her dolls.

They didn't fight any more. He could stroke her without the threat of being bitten on the hand. "Love you, 'Nita." He was at rest in his sister's body, her hips rocking like the burnished sides of a boat that could ride him out to sea. She was Oliver's Navy. He could forget barbering and jungle gyms, the mishaps of a sailor in the attic. The scratching wars he'd had with Anita began to make sense. They were a perverse, upside-down love-making, preparations for this. He would have shucked the White House and taken his chances with Anita, but she always made him put on his pants at the end of an afternoon. And Oliver would sneak home to Pennsylvania Avenue.

He got incautious once while stepping into his pants. The little gold card fell out of his pocket. Anita saw her name in blue ink. "Lawn party," he said. "I told the President's missus about you. She invited us together."

Oliver was miserable. He kept to the attic on the eve of the party. But he couldn't escape the smell of asparagus from the big kitchen down below. Workmen were setting up tables in the south garden. The slap of wood on wood rumbled through Oliver's walls. The workmen's shouts stuck to the sun porch outside his window. He heard varieties of curses and nagging refrains. The workmen lashed Eleanor, Fala, and FDR without mercy. The rat-tat-tat of hammers drove him under the pillows. The barber was going mad.

Eleanor's people clucked through the mansion enlisting all the bodies they could find. The machine gunners on the roof had to leave their station to lug crates of strawberries. They climbed up to the roof mumbling to themselves, their shirts stained a grizzly red. The bitches got hold of Oliver. He had to run across the road to Blair House, which, in 1944, was an unofficial annex of the President's mansion. It became a hotel for minor royalty, the uprooted princes, queens, and dukes of the smaller European states, men, women, and children who had arrived in America with the ambiguous status of pure-blooded refugees.

Blair House was shy of princes the first week of August. Most of them were deep in Maryland, on their summer holiday. Oliver couldn't bring back any recruits. Those tough ladies would have sent him across the District to sniff for royal blood if Oliver hadn't been smart enough to hide from them. He sat in the basement, locked inside one of the dressing rooms that belonged to the President's swimming pool, smoking a solitary Camel he'd swiped from the machine gunners and eating his Baby Ruths.

But Oliver had to emerge for the party. He met his sister at the gate. Anita had ruffles on her tits and a naked back. She'd come to the mansion in her cocktail dress. She didn't have another thing to wear for this occasion. The sentries rubbed their eyes and goggled at her, tilting their sun-bleached hats. It was still morning to the sentries, whose strict belief in etiquette had turned them into snobs. Girls didn't wear gowns at high noon. The sun blazed on the lawn. The umbrellas covering the tables began to cook. Blisters formed in the webbing. You could burn your fingers touching an umbrella pole. The rest of the ladies wore trim summer articles that cooled their legs, linen skirts, a light cotton dress, something in seersucker. They drank tomato juice and wouldn't stray from their escorts.

There were different clots of people, each with its own special sanctity. Words cracked on fire around Anita, who had never heard such gabbing in all her life. She didn't intrude. She stood on the periphery, outside endless strings of talk. Oliver had abandoned her. He went upstairs to fetch ex-Empress Zena, the only piece of royalty in town. Eleanor didn't want Zena to be disturbed, but her own bitches had overruled her. If they couldn't have a prince from Blair House to grace their party, a broken-down empress would do. The bitches instructed Oliver. "Tell her not to be morbid. She can mention all the kings she wants, but not the dead babies she carried in her arms."

Zena arrived in one of Mrs. Roosevelt's morning gowns. She curtsied to strangers like a bear on a leash. No one called her *majesty,* or pressed her knuckles in the royal way. She would have been forgotten without Oliver Beebe, who put her and Anita together with Mrs. Roosevelt. They were a foursome now, Eleanor, Zena, the barber, and his sister, standing under Andrew Jackson's magnolia tree.

Anita was prepared to growl at the First Lady. Vivian had stuffed her head with mean reports on the Roosevelts: ghoulish aristocrats, he said, eager to suck out your blood if it would help them get the vote. That was the nature of politics. The White House was overrun with gruesome animals, men turned into swine by the Roosevelts; those swine-men would bleed to death groveling for Franklin and Eleanor. All Anita could find were Negro butlers in bright red coats, carrying tidbits from the White House to the party. Anita ate mushrooms on a cracker and minted melon balls. The butlers did sweat like pigs, but that was because of the sun and not the horrendous quality of their labors.

She was getting to like Mrs. Roosevelt's puckered face. Vivian had called her ugly. It wasn't so. A mousy chin and big teeth couldn't hurt her. There was an excitement in the wrinkles, a flow that animated every bump and line. The discordant parts met in a luminous shiver that held Anita and was beautiful to her. She couldn't take her eyes off the President's wife.

Several important ladies from the Agricultural Department began to pester Anita. "Are you one of the Philadelphia Beebes?" they asked, edging up to the magnolia tree.

Anita smiled noncommittally and kept looking at Mrs. Roosevelt. The ladies edged closer.

"The Boston Beebes? Colonel Edgar's daughter?"

Anita scratched her nose.

"The Beebes of Dupont Circle? Chevy Chase?"

The ladies were staring at the crepe and tulle on Anita. "Jupiter Street," she said. "My father was a plumber in Weehawken. When he worked."

The ladies said, "Sorry, so sorry," and edged away from the Jackson tree.

The girl from the switchboard, Ethel Rosenquist, left her telephone plugs to be with Oliver under a tree. She grew despondent in the shade. A glimpse of Anita was enough to put terror in her eyes. "My sister," Oliver said. "Anita Beebe." Ethel could tell that there was more than sibling rivalry between her Oliver and this Anita Beebe. They had the same burnished skin that exuded the arrogance and complacency of lovers. This was Oliver's darling. A black-haired creature in silly clothes. Who else would come to the President's lawn wearing artillery on her chest? Ethel cried into a pink napkin. She couldn't conceal her jealousy and her scorn. She shook Mrs. Roosevelt's hand and trudged across the grass, vanishing into the shrubbery near the West Wing.

Mrs. Roosevelt watched over Zena, fending her from upstarts and the talkative wives of bureaucrats, but the ex-empress couldn't tolerate people, sun, and magnolia trees. She gazed at the caterpillars dropping from the Jackson magnolia, and tore off the bosom of her gown. Many of the wives were shocked to see the pale white breasts of an ex-empress. Eleanor's bitches pumped their arms in desperation and started to shriek. They blamed Oliver for Zena's filthy exhibitionism. He should have kept her hands out of her bosom. Eleanor was much calmer than the bitches on her staff. She didn't give up her smile, or her pity, as she spoke into Oliver's ear.

The sailor covered Zena's breasts with his own Navy jumper. He walked around in his undershirt, leading the ex-empress into the house. Guests tried to catch him by the elbow, and ask what was wrong. They saw a haggard lady in military sleeves. Oliver shoved them gently out of the way. He never gritted his teeth. Zena lost her sense of direction. She jabbered about hunting parties and her winter home. She mentioned streets in Sofia and the fortress city of Ruse that Oliver couldn't have understood, and the shame of the Bulgars, who were fighting on Hitler's side. With Zena in a daze, mumbling on her feet, Oliver didn't trust the stairs. He rode with her up to the attic in the Boss' elevator car.

He put her to bed, made her drink a glass of hot water with half a lemon inside, and sat with her while she talked to the pillows. It was too early for an empress to sleep. Oliver was still in his undershirt. He wouldn't take his jumper off Zena's breasts.

Without the barber to cover her flank, the First Lady was obliged to drift from the Jackson tree and say hello to the admirals and generals who had come out of the Map Room for hors d'oeuvres. Anita was left alone again. Eleanor's bitches swooped up behind her and began to prattle about the guests on their list. They were cunning girls. A legion of Eleanor's friends would have made a dull party. They invited a few enemies of the White House, a fascist, a neutralist, a senator who was skeptical about the war, so they could have a supply of people to jeer at, a quota of straw dogs.

They developed a delicious sway in their backs at the sight of a little man in the naval dress of a foreign power. Their favorite bugbear was at the party. The marqués de Estrella had a withered arm, and a tiny black glove jutted out of his sleeve where his left hand should have been. Anita wasn't used to a man without fingers. The glove frightened her. It curled up at the marqués' side. "That scum is the most important Nazi in the United States," the bitches told Anita.

The little marqués had burn marks on his throat, a mottled splash of purple that looked like dead bark. Anita decided that the marqués was lucky to bring his Navy jacket. A military collar could hide the greater portion of his throat. It was the prettiest uniform she had ever seen. He had white lace under his mottled throat, on his pockets, cuffs, and shoulder boards, and blue embroidery on the skirt of his jacket. His sword came in a gold scabbard that clung to his leg. With him was another man, in civilian clothes, with his back to Anita. Much taller than the marqués, he had to bend his knees to hold the marqués' attention and converse with him. The man's blondness soon became apparent to Anita. It was the Spaniard, Orlando Frayard.

Eleanor's bitches didn't seem terribly interested in Frayard. Most of their vituperation went to the little marqués. Anita couldn't understand why a tall, blond Spaniard failed to arouse deeper feelings in the bitches. Orlando turned far enough to recognize Anita. He gave her nothing but a single twist of his lips that could have been a smile, a frown, or both. He made no effort to move towards her. This was Washington, where a man could undress you in a hotel, taste your body, and then snub you on the south lawn.

The sky cracked over Anita's head without the slightest warning. It didn't get dark. A twitch of lightning nearly struck the magnolia tree. A wind blew on the lawn. Anita's cocktail dress shivered crepe and tulle. Guests ran towards the White House with sun in their eyes. In an instant the weather was foul. Rain beat down from a sky that was more than half blue. The bitches screamed at the fates that could wreck a party. The Secret Service was prepared to meet storms, fires, bombings, and acts of God. They herded men and women through the South Portico, while other agents collapsed in front of the Map Room with their bodies in the shape of a pudgy screen. Battles were being fought in that room, with colored pins on a wall. Admirals could spend a day on one pin. They wore pistols in the Map Room. The pistols weren't for show. An admiral had to defend his war charts from nosy senators, saboteurs, foreigners, and Eleanor's guests.

Anita was reluctant to scramble into the White House with the rest of the party. The mansion seemed enormous to her, with windows, porches, and columns that could swallow up a girl, make her feel puny in a President's house. She would have loved to see Oliver's room if she could have gone upstairs with him alone. But she would have been too anxious to lie down with Ollie in the attic. Mrs. Roosevelt lived there. Kings and ministers probably sat on the porch. The President signed bills and ate his dinners and lunch. She wouldn't fuck a soul in the White House.

Anita stayed under the Jackson tree. It couldn't protect her from the storm. Branches slapped against the wind and shook wet leaves in her hair. Cold tulle bit through her underpants and left an imprint on her ass. Her cocktail dress was in ruins. The crepe balled up under her armpits. She wanted to die.

Some mysterious force that could uproot a girl had seized her by the arm and was pulling her away from the tree. She would have choked on a mouthful of rain trying to protest. Anita was right to have believed in Vivian. The Roosevelts *were* devils. They could create a storm out of sunshine and spook a whole lot of grass. She blinked into the storm. Frayard, with blond hair in his face, had swept her up and dragged her over the lawn.

She was sitting in a huge sedan with rugs on her feet, surrounded by men. She could smell their cologne, wet shirts and frail beards. Something cold, bitter cold, caressed her ankle. It was the scabbard of a long sword. She had her bearings again. She was stuck between Frayard and the little marqués with his mottled throat.

They took her to an apartment building on Dupont Circle. It wasn't a suspicious place. It had a doorman, a plugboard in the wall, old ladies in the lobby who smiled to the marqués and watched the storm with cookies in their mouths. Then she was in a suite of rooms on a high floor. She was too disheartened to look at furniture. She would scream and kick if the marqués tried to fondle her with his tiny glove. She didn't belong to Frayard. Vivian was the only one who could tell her what to do.

A maid had come for Anita, an enormous woman with pleats in her hair and a complexion that seemed ambiguous. She was a criolla from Panama, neither black nor white. Frayard called her mamá Salomé. Was the woman going to tie her down and push her legs apart so the marqués could have his way with her? Mamá Salomé led Anita into another room, stripped off the cocktail dress, and scrubbed her with a bathing mitt.

Anita was returned to Frayard and the marqués bundled in velvet that revealed nothing beyond her shins. They fed her coffee with the texture of thick black mud that you were supposed to drink with the help of your tongue. She swallowed cognac and little brandied cakes that could only poison her and make her more accessible to the marqués. How much longer did she have to wait for them to clutch at her under the velvet?

Mamá Salomé had her cocktail dress. All the crepe had been restored. She went into a closet to change her clothes. She got out in a hurry. The marqués stirred his pear-shaped glass of cognac in goodbye. Then they whisked her out of the apartment.

The doorman didn't stare. He jumped for his umbrella and walked her to the marqués' sedan. She got in with Orlando Frayard. There were blinds on the window that Anita hadn't seen before. Frayard tightened the blinds and gave instructions to the chauffeur who sat on the other side of a glass wall. She felt pillows under her ass. The back of the car had been turned into a bedroom while Anita was upstairs. She didn't mind. The marqués had rescued her from the storm, given her coffee to drink, and ironed her cocktail dress. She crawled into the pillows with Frayard. He was careful about the tulle. The sound of rain drumming on the roof was pleasant to Anita, as long as her legs were dry. Frayard snuggled against her like a boy. The storm didn't have to end. Anita was satisfied to live with Orlando in the back of a nobleman's car.

ELEVEN

A wind blew over the capital seven days and nights. It was the worst storm to touch the White House since 1839, when the old roof fell in and porch rails landed in the grass. The porches held in 1944, but every window split on the east side of the house, which had to bear the full brunt of the storm.

The wind dismantled machine guns and knocked the different pieces over the walls. Clumps of iron dropped like shrapnel. The admirals in the Map Room were convinced that the war had come to Washington. They reshuffled their pins on the big chart. The machine gunners collected in Oliver's room and grieved for their lost materiel. The wind hit them by surprise. They would have been torn from the roof if they had stayed up there with the guns. Oliver made hot toddies for them with lemons from the kitchen and a bottle of potato whiskey. But he had to get out of drinking toasts with the ex-machine gunners, or he might have fallen into a ruinous sleep. The attic was his sovereignty. A drunken man couldn't have watched for leaks, or tested the durability of an inner wall.

The ceiling swayed in the little laundry. Oliver stood on two washtubs holding the ceiling up with a broom, but he couldn't spend himself in one place. The attic would have crumbled without him. He propped chairs into walls. He chalked a yellow x over sunken areas in the floor. He sat with Zena. He comforted the maids during the loudest winds. He had to keep the ex-machine gunners from climbing back up to the roof. The toddies had warmed their heads with patriotic notions. Bereft of their machine guns, they wanted to save the flag, which was shredding in the storm. They could hear the flagpole twist and shake over the South Portico. They were going to form a chain of hands that would take them out to the sun porch and onto the roof. The lead hand would grasp the flag and haul it in. They were halfway to the sun porch when Oliver interrupted them. He gave the ex-machine gunners a scolding that was positively fierce.

"Nix," he said. "Don't you dare. That flag represents the President. It flies rain or shine."

Oliver felt a responsibility to other parts of the house. He went down to the second floor, where Mrs. Roosevelt lived, to see what he could do for her. He knocked on the door of her sitting room. None of her bitches were inside. She lay on her narrow bed in a rumpled morning gown. Her fingers weren't occupied. They seemed shrunken and raw without the grasp of pencils and her knitting needles. The shocks of gray hair on her forehead were rough as steelwool. Her eyes sat deep in their sockets, vacant, watery, and blue. She'd been dreaming of her warrior sons. The oldest boy, James, was in the Marines. John, her youngest, was in the Navy with Franklin, Jr. Elliott was in the Army Air Corps. The storm had filled her with vague terrors about the harm that could come to her boys. She hated giving in to the vicissitudes of weather. Imprisoned in the mansion, she had succumbed to a growing morbidity. She couldn't exercise, knit, or write her daily column. She wouldn't take bread and butter with her staff. But she welcomed Oliver. He wasn't demanding. She could wait out a storm with him.

"Ma'am," he said, "would you like some crackers and milk?"

"Not now, Ollie dear . . . thank you."

His smile encouraged Mrs. Roosevelt to start her column. She didn't ask for her secretaries. She had a gentle sailor to sharpen pencils during the rain. She would dictate to Oliver.

"People have been calling our storm 'Franklin's Hurricane.' They think my husband is preparing the nation for the November elections. Let me tell you, he isn't so powerful as that. No one knows exactly where the President is. He travels in secret, as any wartime President must. But you have my word, as a mother and a President's wife. Franklin is much too busy to play with wind and rain. The storm came out of the best Washington sky. No meteorologist had predicted it. The magnolias are bending outside my window. Inside, the chandeliers rock. Plumbers, carpenters, and a few marines are in our basement dealing with the flood. I cannot say why this storm has visited us, or when it will leave. But I can promise you it isn't 'another Roosevelt plot,' as Franklin's enemies are so fond of announcing on the radio and in the news."

Oliver took down each of the words. However thin his education was, he didn't make spelling errors. He'd learned the art of dictation in 1943 from admirals at the old War and Navy Building. He would scribble notes for them after cutting their hair.

Working on her column had cured Mrs. Roosevelt

of her listlessness. She wouldn't let herself be responsible to a hurricane. She gave Oliver a set of instructions for her bitches, who were camping in the Green Room. The sailor went down another flight to deliver these instructions. On his way to the Green Room he met an old man in the hall. This old man was skulking through the mansion in a foul-weather coat. Oliver remembered the old man's walk, stiff knees on top of powerful, resilient shoes. Only Secret Service agents were allowed to wear rubber soles in the middle of World War II. It was Kirkland Horn, head of the White House detail, who had no love for Oliver. Kirkland saw him as an intruder, a pest, a dumb boy with a strange hold on the President. The old man's red mustache had never turned gray. In October he would be sixty-five. He'd been guarding Presidents since 1901, when the first detail of Secret Service men was assigned to the White House.

Kirkland said, "Beebe, your shoelaces are untied."

The old man didn't sound hellos. He looked in your face, riffled his mustache, and told you what was in his mind. Oliver hunkered low to work on his laces. "Thank you, Mr. Horn."

Kirkland stood over him for a second, as if he were contemplating some negligible act, a little bit of violence maybe, a knock on the barber's head that would carry him out a window and into the rain. Nothing happened. The old man continued on his rounds. Oliver got off his heels. He knew one thing. Kirkland hadn't come home to measure the flood under the South Portico. That red mustache was a sign that Mr. Roosevelt would soon be in the house.

The Boss

TWELVE

It was Roosevelt weather.

A rainbow appeared, a perfect arc, with streams of color that held on to their radiance for an hour and a half. Then the arc broke into smaller pieces, and the radiance was absorbed in a brown sky. The colors washed, but they wouldn't go away. If you were an ex-machine gunner standing with Oliver on the porch, you would have been convinced that insanity was upon you. The colors brightened again, as if a fucking rainbow could revive itself. The barber had more of a scientific head. He pointed out that a second rainbow was appearing within the dead image of the first. The arc wasn't so perfect. Its radiance was spent before Oliver could find his telescope (a gift from FDR) and study the new rainbow.

Water receded from the basement without the help of White House marines. Windows were fixed. Painters and restorers lugged cans of putty through the house. Machine-gun parts were picked off the grass. Carpenters stood on enormous stanchions to contemplate the roof. The sun shone on all their work. It was Roosevelt weather.

Three raps on a buzzer brought Oliver out of a wretched, dream-plagued sleep. The noise had traveled up from the usher's closet on the ground floor. Its tremors were unmistakable. The Boss was in the house. Kirkland must have sneaked him through the gates last night. The chief usher was alerting everybody that Mr. Roosevelt had left his bedroom for the oval office in the West Wing.

Oliver was morose. He'd slept through the Boss' homecoming. He needed an usher's alarm to tell him where the President was. The laundry girls had more information than Oliver did. From their chatter he heard that "Mr. Franklin's dog" hadn't arrived. The Pup was in quarantine. The surgeon general of the Navy declared that Fala had to be isolated for a month to make sure he hadn't picked up a disease in the tropics.

Oliver didn't expect to be summoned early in the day. A barber couldn't have top priority on a President's appointment list. The Boss had to worry about the railroads, bombs for his aviators, butter for his men in the field. But he thought Mr. Roosevelt would ring him on the phone, tell him a story about the Pacific Ocean, and how he missed having the Pup. Oliver waited in the attic. The Boss never phoned.

After three days Oliver went for a walk. A horn blared at him on Constitution Avenue. The scarecrow shouted to Ollie from the window of his car. "I'm going to the movies," Vivian said. "Come on." They didn't drive to any of the movie palaces at "F" and Fourteenth. The scarecrow stopped at a yellow house on Dupont Circle, known as the Floridian. The doorman parked his car. That's a dumb-looking theatre, Oliver muttered to himself, hoping it would be a movie with Alan Ladd. The Floridian had flower pots in the hall. The scarecrow took him up an elevator and into a lousy apartment. Oliver was chagrined. He wouldn't get much Alan Ladd out of this place.

He sat in a sunken living room with a few other guys: one of them was a petty officer named Daniel Matisse, who worked at the Army and Navy man's club on Pennsylvania Avenue. "Hey, what's the movie about?"

"Roosevelt," said Daniel Matisse.

Matisse had a pack of Camels tucked in his petty officer's pants. He wasn't greedy about the cigarettes. Whenever Ollie had a Camel, he would snip it in half and make two "runts" that could keep him for an afternoon. A Baby Ruth and half a Camel was all Oliver could want. Even the President was short of Camels. Matisse gave Oliver a fistful of cigarettes. "Puff on them," Daniel said, "float them in the crapper, crumble them up for the birds in Lafayette Park. I don't care. Ollie, there's plenty more. I run the concessions at the sailor boy's club. I can get you all the Camels you need."

Behind Matisse a tall, blond man was fiddling with a movie projector. It was Orlando Frayard. A fat nigger maid arrived from the pantry with cucumber sandwiches and glasses of red wine. Mamá Salomé fed all the moviegoers in the sunken living room. Oliver said "No thanks" to mamá. He didn't trust the sandwiches or the wine. He sucked on a Camel until the room went black. The projector rattled and shot pictures on the wall. The titles came in three giant blobs.

THE EMPEROR
IN
THE WHITE HOUSE

A battleship blinked in and out of that swollen light on the wall. Then cannons, a crying girl, coal miners with humps on their backs, a nigger hanging from a tree, rotting corn in a field, and then the Roosevelts. The First Lady with the miners, the First Lady at tea. Then she was in jodhpurs, riding her horse at Rock Creek Park. Then the Roosevelt boys. Elliott in a night club with his actress wife, Jimmy on the links. John and Franklin, Jr., at a swimming pool. Then the Boss with his Pup. FDR walking with metal braces and a cane. FDR in his wheelchair. FDR with dark bags under his eyes. And a narrator's voice jumps into the living room, sneers at all the Roosevelts, calls Mrs. R. a rich lady crow with brats for children, spoiled brats, the Boss a crippled squire who expects to run the world, a corrupt old man who had heart attacks and apoplectic fits that he's hiding from the American people.

Then the lights went on, and Oliver was in a rage. What kind of movie would make fun of a President's dog? And shame a man for wearing braces on his legs? The movie was touched up. The Boss had bags under his eyes, but they weren't black. And nothing was wrong with his heart.

Talk about cripples! A little guy with splotchy skin comes into the room with his arm dangling and everybody bends to him like he's the Count of Monte Cristo. He introduced himself to Oliver with a long rumble of names. José Something Something María, the marquis of Something Else. Oliver could never get a title straight, even though he lived next to kings, and ran errands for the minor dukes at Blair House. This marquis was the lord of the living room. You had to discuss the movie with him, or sink into your chair. His blood was too fine to have him shout. He could cut at you with a gentle shake of his tongue. He cursed the Roosevelts in such smooth tones, Oliver had to juggle his head to pick up any meaning at all. The little guy had to be the veteran of another war. Nobody but a ruined sailor would wear a glove on his hand in Washington during the month of August.

The discussion took an evil twist. Matisse reported some news he'd heard at his canteen. "People are willing to swear the President died in Honolulu. They buried him at sea with his dog. His double is sitting in the White House. The Navy rigged it up. The admirals found an old gimp who looks like Roosevelt. They painted his nose and glued him to a wheelchair. The admirals own the country. They dictate orders to the stooge and he carries them out. They're in the clear unless he forgets to give the Roosevelt smile."

The blood beat over Oliver's eyes, and his forehead rippled and swelled up like bangs of red clay. "Nobody's dead," he muttered. "The Pup's in quarantine." He hurled his unsmoked Camels at Daniel Matisse and blustered out of the room, with no regard for Vivian, the blond man, the marquis, or mamá Salomé. His swagger was gone by the time he landed in the street. Could he say for sure the Pup was alive? And where was FDR? The Boss wouldn't have neglected Oliver for three whole days.

He arrived at the White House in a wretched state. A government that snatched the wild man Jonathan away could also plant the Boss' double in the West Wing. Ollie was too disheartened to read about Dick Powell and Veronica Lake. He crawled into bed at five in the afternoon and lay with the covers pulled over his mouth. He could no longer tell who Oliver was. A barber in the attic, a boy who fucks his sister and once worked for FDR? Six blasts on the telephone couldn't get the covers off his face. The fools rang again. "Nobody's deaf," he spoke into the covers. The switchboard was signaling Ollie that the President wanted him in the oval office with his barbering tools.

It was a funny time for cutting hair. The Boss made him come down in the middle of a cabinet meeting. Oliver had to put his clippers and his comb between the Secretary of State and the Secretary of War. There wasn't any room on the President's desk for Oliver's wide-tooth comb. It was crowded with figurines of bears and pigs, donkey emblems of the Democratic Party, match boxes, a Navy barometer, a magnifying glass, cigarette holders in a tray, a ship's clock, stamp catalogues, a mangled pack of Lucky Strikes, a water carafe, ink bottles, a conglomerate of telephones with different-colored buttons, pencils, lamps, and playing cards. These weren't dead things, the junk yard of an old President. The Boss could create a frenzy on his desk with one push of his sleeve. He would stroke a pig at the end of a story, clutch his magnifying glass and peer at you if he disliked an answer you gave, or throw cards on his knees in a game of solitaire. The cigarette holders weren't for display; all of them had the President's teeth marks on their ivory grips.

You couldn't have tricked Oliver Beebe. He would have known in an instant if the man behind the desk was the Boss' double. He didn't have to sneak around a President's shoulder to witness how his pants lay under the desk. This was FDR. And Ollie was hurt. After five weeks of not seeing Oliver, the Boss didn't halt his conversation once to say hello.

Ollie wrapped his barbering sheet around the Boss' collar. The President had always been playful during a trim. He'd banter with Ollie, hum a tune, talk about the lunch he'd had with Linda Darnell. But they were alone then, with the President in his study or in the bathtub, astride his special board that allowed him to bathe without being stranded at the bottom of the tub. And Ollie would think, that's the toughest, kindest President in the world. The Boss can't even get to the Map Room on his own legs, but Hitler and Mussolini have a fit when somebody mentions Roosevelt to them. Ollie wasn't smug about his position or his tools. It used to make him happy to cut the Boss' hair.

They were in a cabinet meeting now, and Ollie had to avoid snagging the Secretary of War with his clippers. The President told a story while Oliver clipped his neck. It was about his boyhood at Hyde Park. Oliver had to concentrate on little pesky hairs, and he couldn't grasp all the turns in the story. It had something to do with an outhouse spilling over in a blizzard, and an Irish lady caught with her bloomers spread around her toes. The Secretary of State chortled close to Oliver. Splits appeared in the Secretary of the Treasury's owlish face. The Secretary of Commerce sniggered behind his red fist. The laughter he was causing must have infected the President. He threw his head back, his eyes crinkled up, and he bellowed in a way that would have been impossible for any man to duplicate. No one laughed like FDR. His body rumbled until the pigs and bears and cigarette holders on his desk shivered so hard, Ollie had to pray that the pigs wouldn't land on the Secretary of War.

The haircut was soon over. Ollie brushed the President's back. In the bathtub, hovering over that board,

Ollie would have had more work to do, but he couldn't massage the Boss' scalp in front of the cabinet. The President finally spoke to him, called him by his pet name, while Oliver put the clippers down. "Child, I have a present for you."

It came in a small bundle that Oliver unwrapped. A bosun's pipe fell out. The Boss was a fanatic about his Navy. It was natural for him to assume that any sailor would prize an article off a battleship. Oliver thanked him for the bosun's pipe. It was a dangerous gift. If he took it up three flights to blow on it in his room, Ollie would have destroyed the ears of every maid in the attic, the whistle had such a high pitch.

Oliver was pleased, even though he couldn't use the whistle. It showed the President hadn't forgotten him. Ollie shouldn't have squashed the Camels in Matisse's face. He could have had a gift for FDR, who loved to bite on his cigarette holder with a Camel between his eyes.

THIRTEEN

Ollie had nothing but a silver pipe that couldn't
be blown indoors. The President had gone to Hyde Park
with his missus and a retinue of aides and Secret Service
men. Oliver could only scratch himself. He was reduced
to a perfunctory barber who didn't merit a goodbye. He
would tootle on his bosun's pipe, smash windows, ear-
drums, and presidential china with the high-pitched
noise. His craving for violence didn't last. He packed the
whistle under his pajamas and looked at splinters in the
wall through the far end of his telescope. The machine
gunners were back on the roof, talking politics. They
would guard the Boss' life, but they wouldn't vote for
him. Dewey was their man.

Oliver went out on the sun porch to scream at them.
"Only a jackass would vote for Governor Dewey."

The machine gunners crawled to the edge of the
roof and looked down on Oliver with a hot face. "Fourth
term, fourth term," they jeered. "We got an emperor in
the White House."

Oliver balled out his fist. "No emperors."

The machine gunners didn't jump on Ollie and
knock him to the ground. They were kind to the President's sailor from their perch on the roof, explaining to

him that the Boss didn't go to Hawaii on a fisherman's holiday. He went to bully MacArthur and behave like a Commander-in-Chief. He was stumping for the elections.

Oliver said, "Wrong. Didn't you notice his tan? He fished."

"You won't catch much flounder off the side of a battleship."

The machine gunners withdrew their heads and abandoned Oliver to his own contemplations on the porch. The barber was in a muddle. There'd been too much talk of emperors. What did Oliver care about a fourth term? He was twelve when the Boss came to Washington in 1933. For almost thirteen years Roosevelt had been the only President in his life. America would have made no sense to Ollie without FDR.

He could use the comforts of a sister now. But he ran in vain to the boardinghouse. 'Nita wasn't there. Her absence infuriated him until he saw how spoiled he'd become. He *expected* Anita to be in his old room. Yet he hadn't visited her in twelve days. It wasn't entirely his fault. The storm had intervened and kept him in the attic, and then the Boss came home.

Oliver didn't want to poke about on the landlady's steps. He'd have to chat with her lodgers. So he waited for Anita in the park at Mount Vernon Square. He should have phoned her during the storm, asked her if she had enough cans of soup. Shut off in his attic with a telescope and movie magazines, he'd been too preoccupied to take an interest in his sister's affairs. What did she do between Ollie's visits? How much money did she have? Was she living off a scarecrow's bounty?

"Ollie boy."

You couldn't escape that stringy son-of-a-bitch. Vivian stood behind Oliver's bench with those inhuman gray ears.

"Ollie, come with me."

"I'll sit a while," Oliver said. "One movie with you is enough."

"I wasn't talking about the movies. We can go to a meeting of the Liberty Club."

"Does that club have a petty officer named Matisse and a little guy with a loose arm?"

"Maybe."

"I like this bench. The birds are pretty over here. You can take in that meeting by yourself."

Vivian moved away from Oliver. "Go 'head. Sleep your brain off in the White House." He took another few steps.

Oliver watched the scarecrow's back. "Wait," he said. "I'm going."

He was already sick of the park. The birds made twitchy music in Mount Vernon Square. The Boss had pulled his entourage out of the mansion for a long weekend at Hyde Park. A barber would only have been extra baggage. Oliver could commune with machine gunners and the ex-empress of Bulgaria, or hunch like a toad in his attic room. A meeting wouldn't hurt him. He'd explain the Boss' generosities to members of the Liberty Club. No other President would have taken his mind off world affairs to give his barber a telescope, a doll, and a bosun's pipe. "Emperor?" Ollie would say. "Dictator? *Yeah.* A dictator who runs out of Camels."

Vivian

FOURTEEN

The scarecrow, Thomas Vivian de Vries, grew up on Beaufain Street, at the edge of Charleston's gentle class. The de Vrieses had established themselves as Charleston stablers and dealers in manure prior to the Revolution. They had their money and a big house and the taint of horseshit on their Sunday clothes. They couldn't climb far enough over the manure to mix with better people. They got rid of the stables, but their fortunes declined. The house on Beaufain Street fell into disrepair. There were rats in the cellar and lice on the walls. They had to sell their furniture, their bedding, and their silks, to stay alive.

This self-looting of the family stock had been going on for almost a hundred years when Vivian was born. His father was a sometime music teacher. Vivian never saw a pupil in the house. In his childhood he was known as Thomas, or Baby Tom. His middle name, *Vivian,* was seldom used. It had been thrust upon him at birth to commemorate a maiden aunt who lived to a hundred and five. He had few friends on Beaufain Street. He existed on a diet of books. Baby Tom devoured Dickens, Swift, and Edgar Poe before he was ten. The de Vrieses cannibalized themselves, giving away half their garden and the old slave quarters in back of the house, to educate Tom. They sent him to The Citadel, Charleston's military college, hoping that an officer's hat would make a gentleman out of him. But Baby Tom followed the aesthetics of his hero, Edgar Poe, who had himself thrown out of West Point. Tom signed all his documents "Vivian de Vries." He wore an earring in the barracks, like an old Charleston pirate. He would arrive on the parade ground with only half his clothes. But he couldn't get dismissed. Whatever was lacking in the name de Vries, it had been around for two hundred years. That was ancient enough to keep Vivian inside The Citadel.

He happened to meet a fat blond cadet, Orlando Frayard, the son of a Spanish merchant living in Atlanta. Orlando was as rottenly placed at Capers Hall as Vivian was. They despised drills and laboratory work and the obsequious bending that a "skinhead" had to do in the company of senior cadets. They chewed tobacco and swilled cheap bootlegger's wine. They read Baudelaire after curfew, and knew the history of Rimbaud by heart. Vomiting in the chapel after a five-day drunk, they went beyond the limits of a good family name and had to be expelled.

Orlando was put to work in his father's importing house, and Vivian began to drift. He took odd jobs to prepare himself for the rigors of an artist-priest. Grooves appeared in his fingernails. His mouth turned slightly black. The poet began to age. He was thirty in 1935. He fell out of love with Baudelaire and returned to Charleston to seek a fresh vocation and some of his old roots. The house on Beaufain Street had been dismantled, the garden torn up to make way for a school. Vivian had traveled too long. His mother was dead, his father had remarried, and his last surviving cousin was in a nursing home.

Vivian became a guide for the Charleston historical society. He took busloads of up-country people through the quainter parts of town: the Battery, the Confederate Home on Broad Street, the Charleston Orphan House, Cabbage Row, the masked piazzas of Bull Street, the old Cotton Exchange, the old Slave Market, the home of Gullah Jack (the dreaded Negro conjurer and insurrectionist), the pirate house at the corner of Church Street, where Blackbeard and Stede Bonnet made their headquarters, and the old Powder Exchange.

Dressed in an official red touring coat, he would embellish the stories of pirates and nigger insurrectionists and calamities of nature, so that Stede Bonnet, who ravaged the Carolina coast in his ship, the *Royal James,* was now the savior of Charleston; the earthquake of 1886 became a landslide that lowered the roofs of Charleston and toppled the seawall; and Gullah Jack, who led the Negro insurrection of 1822 and was hanged in the jail yard on Judith Street with twenty-one of his followers, became the Charleston Cagliostro, a nigger with enough pizazz in his fingers to wreck a plantation wall and blister a white man's throat.

It wasn't any romanticism that compelled Vivian to falsify the sad history of Gullah Jack, turn pirates into cavaliers, earthquakes into avalanches. He was trying to delight his customers, the up-country people. He knew that a corrupt port existed alongside the picture-book streets. Charleston still had its pirates, and they weren't as proud as Stede Bonnet, who only disturbed gentlemen at sea. The pirates of 1936 were lesser men. You could lose your wallet and your vest in many a Tradd Street cafe. Vivian steered his customers to the safer spots.

He lived in Charleston without ambition, without politics, without Baudelaire. He ate lunch out of a box with the up-country people, indifferent to Roosevelt, Mussolini, the Spanish Civil War. He continued to read. By accident, in a stall on Savage Street, he discovered certain pamphlets and books by a little Jew with a goatee, Lev Davidovitch Bronstein. This Bronstein had an arrogance that appealed to Vivian. The little Jew liked to call himself Leon Trotsky on the covers of his books. He was no shut-in philosopher, picking words out of soapstone in a dingy room. He'd had the Red Army under his control. He could harangue a soldier better than any man alive. It was this combination of idealism and ferocious talk that helped make a convert of Vivian. He saw a place for himself in Trotsky's regime. Trotsky welcomed poets, even hard-luck ones who had to eat sandwiches near the Charleston seawall, tell and retell stories about earthquakes and nigger rebellions.

The little Jew was in Coyoacán, a suburb of Mexico City, where, Vivian had heard, he was surrounded by an armed camp of admirers who shot at strange people. Vivian wrote Trotsky an impassioned letter about coming to Coyoacán and serving at the master's feet. He got no reply.

He became a drifter again, a drifter with ideals. He started a magazine with the money he'd saved as a Charleston guide. Out of touch with other writers and editors, Vivian was the only one who contributed pieces to *Contempo*. It was a confusing magazine. Printed wherever Vivian happened to be, on whatever paper he could find, it stood for a mingling of politics and art that he figured Trotsky could approve, if only Lev Davidovitch were still alive (the Stalinists had come to Coyoacán and murdered him with an axe).

He washed dishes all over the country to support his magazine. Most of his enthusiasm was gone by 1943. He had trouble feeding himself. He lived in the same red coat that he'd put on for the Charleston historical society. The lining had begun to shred years ago into a patch of loose ribbons. He was desperate in Milwaukee, in 1944. He went from house to house trying to sell his magazine. People stood in their windows glaring at him when he rang the bell. He couldn't get in with his pile of *Contempo*s. After a week of fruitless work, Trotsky faded from his eyes. He was left without any visions of a pure politics and art. He vowed to rob *and* kill the first man or woman who opened their door to him.

It was Anita. Wandering near the lakefront, he happened to pick her door. She was an appalling girl, so beautiful and dumb, that Vivian forgot to menace her and grab her around the throat. He didn't even get to steal her pants. She put his *Contempo*s away, nibbled his tongue, and stepped out of her clothes with Vivian on the couch, stuck in his red Charleston sleeves. The little bitch liked to peel in front of a man who had on his hat and coat. He'd come to rob and do worse, not cuddle with strangers on a couch.

But the smoothness of her belly undermined Vivian de Vries. She made love with the absolute frenzy of a child. She'd clutched him out of nowhere, squeezed him with her thighs, howled into the brim of his hat. He could still rob her, break her windpipe, if he wanted to. He decided to run. Who could tell what proposals the bitch would make next? She babbled to him about a brother in the White House, Oliver Beebe, Roosevelt's only barber. Vivian frowned. He said he was going to Washington. Goodbye. His old buddy, Orlando Frayard, had something to do with the Spanish ambassador in D.C. Vivian could sponge off him for a while, sell *Contempos* at the ambassador's house if he needed pocket money. The bitch was packed before Vivian could get out the door. The glint in her eye told him he couldn't shake her so fast. He'd come to the wrong town. The bitch meant to climb on his back like a hot little monkey and scoop the blood out of his ears.

He had an inspiration in the car. Once they got to Washington, he'd park her in a cheap hotel and hide out with Orlando. But Orlando wouldn't have him. Frayard wasn't the fat blond cadet of 1924 who always joined Vivian's pranks. He was tall, skinny, and mean. They sat in the little chancellery behind the ambassador's house, Frayard in a hundred-dollar suit with thin gray stripes. He didn't seem very eager to shake hands with his old buddy. He crisscrossed his fingers with an irritated look and said, "What can I do for you, cousin Viv?"

Vivian had expected stronger allegiances, memories of Baudelaire and bootlegger's wine, and Frayard wouldn't give him anything more than ten locked fingers on a diplomat's desk. Vivian would have to play shrewd, or get out.

" 'Lando, I didn't come here for a chat. I have information to sell . . . stuff the Nazis could use."

He told Orlando about his "contact" in the White House. "Ol' Mr. Franklin has a barber named Beebe. I own that boy. He can walk into any room, spy on generals, if you get what I'm saying to you."

Frayard opened his humped fingers and tittered into them. "If anybody told you we ran a clearing house for

Germany, cousin Viv, they told you wrong. Haven't you heard? Hitler took to losing the war. We can't go around embarrassing Mr. Franklin Roosevelt with stories his barber is giving out. We have to be kind to that old man. Vivian, come with me."

He swiped his hat off a peg in the wall and left the chancellery without bothering to notify the clerks. He whistled with his hands in his pockets. His shoes were wine-red. His shirt and tie had the feel of a major department store. Vivian had two nickels in his pants. A block from the chancellery Frayard's expression began to change. He sneered at Vivian and gave him a hiding in the street.

"This isn't peach leather country, you Charleston ass. We don't suck apricot pits inside an embassy, and come knocking on the door like a grubby spy. Birdhead, you know how many J. Edgar Hoovers they got watching us? The boy who comes to shine our shoes is a goddamn double agent. So don't you holler shit about the Nazis. Nobody's waltzing with Germany in 1944. Now tell me about the barber, and don't you lie."

Vivian had to confess. "Crazy Anita . . . Milwaukee . . . Oliver . . . I didn't meet him yet."

The sneer went away. Frayard grew companionable, and Vivian could recognize a fat cadet under the trim suit of clothes. "That's better, cousin Viv. We'll sell him to my boss."

"The ambassador?" Vivian said.

"No, you idiot. Spain doesn't swap ambassadors with the United States. I work for don Valentin, the naval attaché. He's cuckoo about Hitler, and rich enough to buy your story."

Frayard couldn't make an appointment with don Valentin until the day after tomorrow. Vivian dreaded going back to Anita. " 'Lando, can I stay with you?"

Frayard stuck a dollar into Vivian's fist. "You can eat in the cafeterias and sleep in your car."

He lived on his own for two days, like a country wolf, scrounging in the District of Columbia. He saw generals in the cafeterias, men who arrived in limousines to crack eggs on a table. He rinsed his mouth in government buildings. He refused to sleep in his car. D.C. was having a tropical July, and he couldn't get much of a breeze to pass through his windows. He camped on the Mall, behind a government shack. Most of the grass had been usurped by the United States. Little houses were springing up on the Mall to make room for a growing army of agencies, secretaries, and clerks. Vivian had no peace. Tanks rolled on the Mall at four a.m. Holy Christ, were they looking for the Japanese Navy to ride up the Potomac in long canoes? They lumbered close to the shacks, making an incredible din. The impact could rattle a man's cheeks.

Frayard didn't take him back to the chancellery. They called on Spain's naval attaché, don Valentin José María Mistral, the marqués de Estrella, at an apartment house. The marqués had a fat cook, mamá Salomé. She fixed a paella for the three of them with chicken, shrimp, and saffroned rice that couldn't have been torn out of any ration book. Vivian lost his Charleston manners in the diplomat's house. He had bits of saffron on his nose throughout the meal.

Don Valentin had purple blotches under his ears, and only one good arm. He ate, drank, and blew his nose with the same clutching fist. Vivian said very little. Frayard spoke for him, in a jibber of Spanish and English.

Vivian didn't hear a word about Oliver Beebe or himself. Mamá Salomé poured Vivian's wine and filled his plate as if she were feeding a neighbor's dog.

Vivian left don Valentin's flat with a bellyache. "When do I get paid?" he said.

"Don Valentin fed you, cousin. Don't be impolite."

"How come he wouldn't look at me while he ate?"

"Cousin, you were chewing food with a marqués. He don't like to stare."

Vivian was still a beggar who had to camp behind a government shack. He gathered an old shirt around his head and survived the nightly squeal of tanks on their phantom run over the Mall. He would never make money on Oliver Beebe. He wanted to get out of a city where generals outnumbered clerks, tanks passed near enough to loosen your teeth, and paella came in apartment houses with a fat mama and a runty naval attaché, but he didn't have anyplace to go. Frayard kept him on a leash with his dole of dollar bills.

There were no more visits to don Valentin. No trips to the chancellery. No paella. Nothing but rendezvous with Orlando in a nigger restaurant. Then, after a week of sleeping on the grass, like an animal with popped-out eyes, he nursed his own despair, and blubbered in the restaurant over cups of milky tea.

"Stop it," Orlando said. He slapped Vivian's wrist with a small bundle. It had the familiar, crusty smell of paper money. Vivian revived. A bundle of fifties was sitting in his hand. "You get that crazy bitch of yours to make it with her brother, and we'll all be sitting high."

" 'Lando, she's not that crazy. How can I ask her to strip off Oliver's clothes? She'll never do it."

"Ask her and see what she says."

He went back to the hotel where he'd dumped the girl, figuring she'd want to scratch out his eyes, but all she did was coo. He mentioned this article he was intending to write on the Roosevelts, and how it couldn't be done without Oliver's help, and son-of-a-bitch, she just about offers to go down on her brother, so he'll be sure to come into Vivian's closet. "Ollie loves me," she says. They moved into Oliver's boardinghouse. But Vivian didn't live in that dinky room. Orlando gave him a pair of binoculars and a key to the Willard Hotel. All he had to do was make little drawings of the White House for don Valentin.

And then the barber showed up at the boarding-house. You could go crazy looking at him. The boy was as beautiful and dumb as his sister. Dark, with big eyes, they were like longhaired and shorthaired replicas of one face. Vivian couldn't understand what this boy was doing at the White House. Roosevelt couldn't have rubbed off on him. The barber didn't have a twist of politics in his handsome babyish skull. Vivian told Frayard the news.

" 'Lando, he's so dumb, it's a miracle he can hold on to his scissors without cutting a finger off."

"Don't care. I want you to dog that boy. He can't take a stroll without you. The minute he steps out of the White House, you sit on his head."

Vivian growled at the prospect of becoming the barber's full-time shadow. He didn't relish chasing a boy without brains. What else could an unsalaried poet do? He'd starve without Orlando's packages of money. So he dogged the boy. While he clung to Oliver Beebe, Orlando had Anita's bloomers in mind. The fuck moves like a whirlwind. Vivian can't go near the girl any more.

All he's got now is Oliver Beebe. And the Liberty

Club of don Valentin. The stupidest society Vivian ever saw. A Nazi marqués in love with Washington's colored people. The Liberty Club didn't carry guns or knives. It went into every niggertown, from Bloodfield to Goat Alley, with bags of oranges to feed pickaninnies and their grandmothers. That's all right. He took Oliver on most of the tours. "This is Roosevelt country, cousin Oliver. There aint enough nutrition in this part of town to keep a rat alive. And I'll bet Queen Eleanor throws turkey sandwiches to the squirrels in her garden."

The boy would stare into Goat Alley and turn morose. "The Boss' wife doesn't have turkey to give away. The cooks are always out of ration stamps."

Let him babble. He'd steer that barber off the king and queen. Vivian hated FDR. Didn't he read in a pamphlet somewhere that Roosevelt's State Department kept Trotsky out of the United States? Stalin would have screamed if the little Jew had landed in New York. Roosevelt was to blame for the axe that murdered Trotsky. King Franklin didn't have to leave his wheelchair to swing that axe. He sentenced Trotsky to die in Mexico. And now he kisses Stalin on the mustache, calls him comrade, and they'll split the world between them. Vivian didn't care. He'd bow to a Nazi marqués, take orders from Orlando, deliver bags of oranges, if that could help pluck some feathers off King Franklin's back.

Baseball 1944

Oliver didn't have trouble with the princes and kings who slept at the White House. None of them wandered above the Roosevelt floor. But the attic wasn't immune to unrest. The Secret Service could interrupt a sailor's dreams. Horn's agents got him out of bed in the middle of a hot September night. Oliver's pajamas were soaked. He'd been chasing his sister through the Washington alleys in his dream. Anita kept escaping from Oliver. She would turn into a cat or a nigger lady before Oliver could grab hold of her ankle. It was this constant lunging and disappearing of Anita that had made Ollie perspire. The Secret Service wouldn't let him shower or comb his hair. He had to dress in front of these agents.

Oliver was worried about the Boss. "What's wrong? Did the President hurt himself?"

The agents wouldn't answer Ollie. They marched him out of the attic. Neither of them stopped on the Roosevelt floor. So Ollie knew the Boss was safe in bed. All the correspondents were assembled at the bottom of the stairs. They crushed into Ollie. Their shouts came like a smack on the head to a boy who was only half awake. "Ollie, Ollie, is the Tuskegee Ox gonna surrender to you?"

The boy's shoulders slumped under his Navy collar. "Who's the Tuskegee Ox?"

The agents pushed him through the White House correspondents and brought him to the south gate. The sentries waved to Oliver from their huts on the lawn. "Sailor, tell Otto that we love him over here."

Why were so many people encouraging him? He didn't have any idea what he was supposed to do. The boy was shoved into a Secret Service car outside the gate. He sat between the agents in a funk. A police escort arrived, four ancient sedans. Oliver noticed a scattering of rifles with telescopic sights as the little fleet of cars scurried to Pennsylvania Avenue.

The agents couldn't believe the President's barber was so dumb. The whole District had gotten into a fever over the Alabama Ox. Otto Tutmiller was the thirty-nine-year-old rookie wonder of the Washington Senators. He'd come up from obscurity in June to play first base and hit doubles and triples for the boys of Griffith Park. The Ox was batting .389. But he'd gone amuck tonight. He'd taken over a bar on "E" Street, the Anacostia, in Pawnbroker's Lane. He'd smashed windows, mirrors, benches, and chandeliers in a drunken fit and was holding the patrons of the bar in captivity. Nobody could get in or out. The Tuskegee Ox was six-foot-six. He meant to break every bone inside the Anacostia if the police interfered with his drinking. The cops had marksmen in their ranks. They could have shot out the eyes of Otto Tutmiller. But they adored the Ox. How could you kill the town's first baseman?

A man in a white suit showed up. He was short, with dark eyebrows and a deep sun tan, Edgar Hoover of the FBI. Police chiefs rushed out of his way. He patted his

jowls with a handkerchief, climbed under the police barriers, and went into the Anacostia. The chiefs looked at
their watches. Hoover spent nine minutes with the Ox.
He returned to the chiefs without a mark on his face. He
had a wonderful smile. "Gentlemen, don't be afraid.
Otto swears he would never think of taking a human life.
But you'd better hurry. He'll give himself up to no man
but the President's barber, Oliver Beebe." Then an FBI
chauffeur took Edgar home, and Beebe was summoned
from the White House.

The chiefs barked their instructions to him. Tutmiller. Beer and wine. Don't blink at the Ox. Oliver
nodded to the chiefs. He was under the barriers before
they could feed more details into his head. The Anacostia
didn't have a door. Otto had ripped it out of the bar's
front wall. The boy had it easy. He stepped through a
hole in the wall and was gone from the chiefs. He walked
on piles of rubble inside the bar. The Anacostia's fixtures
had been dropped to the ground. There wasn't a stool or
a light bulb in place. The counter leaned on its spine, at
the end of the room, with balding wood where the zinc
used to be. Oliver tripped over men and women, who
were lying in the rubble, making their bodies flat as
possible, so they would provide a minimal target when
the Ox began throwing mirrors again.

Otto stood near the broken counter in his baseball
knickers and a pair of street shoes. He'd come from
Griffith Park without fully changing his clothes. The Ox
had spectacular powers. He could produce sobs with a
rumbling of his back. Oliver had never seen such a big
man cry.

The Ox was grieving over the death of baseball. The
war had made a travesty of the game he loved. He'd been

a minor leaguer all his life. The Tuskegee Ox, who could hit a straightaway ball out of any park, but couldn't touch a curve. He'd been on the Tigers' roster for three days in 1935. Then he'd voluntarily retired from baseball, an old man of thirty. He couldn't hit with Greenberg, he couldn't hit with Gehrig, he couldn't hit with Foxx, or with lesser people like Zeke Bonura and young Hal Trosky of the Indians, who slapped thirty-five home runs before he was twenty-two. Otto returned to his plows. He farmed the blue earth near Montgomery. He followed the careers of the newer stars, DiMaggio, Williams, Johnny Mize. The Ox wasn't unhappy. He'd worn the uniform of Detroit for three days.

The moguls recalled him in 1944, the granddads who ran the game. They needed "colorful" players and they remembered the Tuskegee Ox. They were frightened that attendance would lag if the war didn't end by 1946. Their stars were in the Army, Navy, and Marines. They had to put a club together with whatever dregs they could find. Why not the Tuskegee Ox? You couldn't see his gray hairs from the bleachers. The Ox was way over six feet. He would look terrific with a blond bat in his hands.

So Otto came to Washington in June. He was in his farmer pants with a bib on top. He had dirt under his nails and a hump on his neck from being a plowman nine years. The Ox expected a week of limbering exercises. He was installed into the line-up on his second day. The old swing was gone. Otto had bursitis. He had to chop at the ball. He delivered two doubles that first game. The Senators didn't win. But the fans forgot to notice. They were staring at the Tuskegee Ox. They had something better than DiMaggio at Griffith Park. A giant who could drill doubles and triples with a frozen right wing. It didn't matter that Washington was in the cellar. Their ace, Dutch Leonard, was thirty-five. Johnny Niggeling was forty. Their best catcher was thirty-eight. But the fans wouldn't deny an eighth-place team if it had one or two Tutmillers.

The Ox was miserable. Where were the curve balls of 1935? Why should a farmer like Otto be the terror of the American League? The game had become a circus. The moguls were buying up freaks. The Brownies had already groomed a one-armed outfielder for 1945, a guy named Peter Gray. Otto himself was the big freak of 1944.

He began searching for bars in every city. He broke mirrors in Cleveland and St. Louis with his own first baseman's mitt. The management paid all his bills. But the Ox went too far at the Anacostia. He hadn't kept hostages before. He'd smacked three triples that afternoon. He cleaned the bases, drove in five runs. The fans sang, "Ox, Ox, Ox." Otto raged in the clubhouse. He wouldn't take his knickers off.

He stumbled from bar to bar, getting to the Anacostia long after dinner time. His anger settled into the hump on his neck. The Ox couldn't shake it off. He began to pull at things. He left nothing upright except a picture of Roosevelt on the wall. Otto wouldn't put filth on the President's image. He warned the patrons not to go. He wasn't the kind of man who liked to drink alone.

Then the white suit comes in, grabs Otto's paw and shakes it. "I'm Hoover of the FBI." Otto grimaced. His shoulder was stiff as hell. He didn't mind having the little man around. It took a pair of balls to visit the Tuskegee Ox. The Anacostia was in heavy shadow and Hoover had to pucker up his eyebrows to recognize the portrait of FDR; the gray lamps of "E" Street provided tiny stings of light. "Tutmiller, what would happen if the police moved in?"

"I'd have to slap their peckers off. I don't like cops."

"What do you like?"

"Roosevelt. Eleanor. Beebe the sailor man."

Otto had read about the good sailor in Mrs. Roosevelt's column. And there were pictures of Beebe in the *Star.* Beebe's sad face could comfort the Ox. The sailor must have known what it was to hit tainted doubles and triples. Otto looked under his shoulder for the little man. Hoover was gone. So Otto grieved by himself. He promised the Lord never to wear knickers again. He'd rather chew the earth of Alabama than belong to a baseball circus. He could feel the tremors of a body sucking air. Otto looked down. He noticed two eyes in the dark. Mustard-colored eyes. And a sailor hat. Another little man was under his wing. Oliver Beebe. "Mornin'," Otto said. "I'm glad to see you." The Ox had too many gnarls in his shoulders to walk without help. He leaned on the good sailor. Oliver had to carry most of Otto's weight. The cops met them near the threshold of the ripped-out door. They pushed Oliver aside and fell on Otto with their clubs. The clubbing was very soft. They wanted to stun the Ox to sleep.

"Fuck," Oliver said. "Lemme have Otto. He can stay in the attic with me." Oliver must have embarrassed the Secret Service. He was whisked into their car and driven back to the President's gate like a man under house arrest.

The Pup

SIXTEEN

Ollie began to follow the Senators' box scores after that. He would sit in his room with the *Washington Star* folded on his knees, but he couldn't find Otto's name in the batting order. There was Kuhel, Myatt, Sullivan, Torres, Powell, Spence, Case, Farrell, and Johnny Niggeling, but no Tuskegee Ox. The sailor had two disappearances in one week: Otto and Anita. The Secret Service couldn't tell him anything about the Ox. Horn's agents leered at him. "Tutmiller? He must have gone back to his plow." Oliver would sit across the road from the White House, in Lafayette Park, dreaming of box scores and Anita with a Baby Ruth in his mouth.

Vivian would appear at Oliver's bench, and they'd go off together to the Liberty Club, no matter where it happened to convene. Vivian was as mournful as Oliver. Both of them seemed deprived.

"Where's Anita?"

"Can't say, Ollie boy. Maybe she's out scattering seeds. She's *your* sister, not mine."

And they'd lose themselves in the Liberty Club. The barber was growing fond of the little marqués. Old glove-on-his-hand took them into the meanest places, a diner on New Jersey Avenue where a white man was lucky not to drink up poison in his soup; nigger cribs and cathouses belonging to Odessa Brown, a lady with scars under and over her eye, who demanded money for all intrusions of the Liberty Club, even though she didn't offer any of her girls; a gym on "N" Street where young black boxers of thirteen and fourteen would stand around in satin shorts waiting to beat each other's brains out for the customer who'd give them half a dollar.

The little marqués didn't come to gape. He proselytized wherever he could. He was the first to taste the soup, the first to wink back at Odessa Brown when she manipulated the scars on her eye into a hideous knot to scare off the Liberty Club, the first to sway the colored boxers from wearing satin trunks and skulling themselves for money. He was generous, irascible, and argumentative, but he would smile when he prodded you this way or that. For the countermen at the Jersey diner he had felicitations, advice, and remedies for chapped lips and a cold. He had presents for the boys at the gym: less gaudy boxing trunks. And he would argue dialectics with Odessa Brown. Oliver had never heard such words thrown back and forth between a whore lady and a marquis. He called her a greedy exploiter, an entrepreneur who ate the blood of her people, and she called him a shrunken aristocrat, a foreigner who tried to poke into her affairs. The dialectics would end with a great Odessa laugh and a bottle of calvados smuggled in from France especially for her.

The girls in Odessa's cribs went gaga over Oliver Beebe. They hadn't known a sailor with good manners and lovely hands, a boy without a drop of lechery in his face. They were used to rascals with a wife and family at home in Michigan, or Tennessee, philanderers who would crawl into your loins and then vomit on Missus Brown's best carpet. These girls were making proposals to Oliver behind Odessa's back. They offered to take him into their cribs free of charge.

They were beautiful girls, eighteen, nineteen, and twenty, who didn't wear lipstick or mascara to work, girls with brave hip sockets and long thighs and only the tiniest of bellies, but the boy was in love with his sister, and he had to refuse. The whores didn't get surly. They figured Oliver was engaged, and wouldn't lie down with other women.

Oliver liked these excursions into the bowels of D.C. He was sick of the monuments, museums, and trim grassy rows that stuck to his window like some flattened pie. This was Oliver's view from the attic. It could disturb a boy looking for a human face among all the monuments. Washington's needle was only a dumb parcel of stone in the grass. The Liberty Club took him to a city hidden between the central avenues, an area of hovels and burnt paths, niggertowns behind an important hotel, whore cribs three minutes from the White House. He no longer blinked when the marquis would say Washington was two countries, independent and blind to each other, running on different energies and different clocks. There was the country of Franklin Delano Roosevelt and the country of Odessa Brown.

As long as the marquis didn't curse the Boss, Oliver was glad to listen. He began to think more and more that he belonged to the country of Missus Brown. His obligations were split. He was barber to the President with a home in the attic, and a member of the Liberty Club, who shuffled from one time zone to the next, who had tea with Mrs. Roosevelt and calvados with Odessa Brown, who met admirals on the stairs, coming from the Map Room in starched white pants, and young boxers from the Washington alleys in cotton shorts that were donated by the marquis of Something and the Liberty Club.

Oliver would disappear into the alleys like a sailor sliding off the face of the earth, and then come home to sleep in the White House. While he slept, a marine arrived at the northwest gate holding an animal carrier with tiny windows at the top. An usher was summoned to the gate with a Secret Service man, who signed the marine's papers and stared at a hump of black fur in the tiny windows. He brought the carrier into the White House and opened the latch. A fat dog tumbled out, no bigger than a Secret Service man's shoe. It was Mr. Roosevelt's Scottish terrier, Murray, the Outlaw of Fala Hill. He wasn't a dog who could run very fast. Fala waddled near the ground. He went between the Secret Service man's legs and climbed the Boss' stairs, mostly with his belly.

Ushers and maids didn't interfere with Fala's route. He entered the Boss' bedroom with a bark that landed in the woodwork. That's how soft it was. It couldn't have gotten the mice in the walls to move. But it was perfect for warning a President that his Pup was out of quarantine. Only the Boss wasn't in his bed. The bark became a miserable whine. Fala hunted in the bathroom. The tub was dry. The Pup could reason as well as any two-legged man. A dry tub and an empty bed had to mean his master wasn't in the house.

The Pup climbed one more flight. He wasn't out to amuse himself, to pick up dust on his belly. He was looking for Oliver. The sailor slept behind a closed door, and the Pup had to scratch on wood. That relentless scratching under the doorknob broke into the vague territory of Oliver's dreams. His head drifted off the pillow. He yawned. "Holy shit. The Pup is here." Oliver opened the door. Fala wandered in, his tail beating against the wall. The Pup liked Oliver best, after FDR. He wouldn't go on the leash with an ordinary Secret Service man. Ollie had to accompany him to the rose garden, or walk the Pup on Pennsylvania Avenue.

He dressed in front of the Pup. They went into the kitchen. Ollie had to fry strips of bacon for him, because the Pup wouldn't eat bread soaked in milk. They had their coffee together, Fala drinking out of a bowl. The maids spied on them from the laundry room. They were happy for the boy. Oliver was always in a better mood with the Pup around. You could hold conversations with that dog. The Pup wasn't stupid. He'd been trained by FDR and the White House staff. He could grunt, bark, growl, and grit his teeth with terrible persuasion. The Pup didn't waste a sound.

Ollie got his leash from the usher's office. He couldn't evade the newsmen in the lobby. They petted the Outlaw of Fala Hill, saying "Nice dog, nice dog," and hounded Oliver.

"Ollie, is it true the Pup was lost in the Pacific for thirty days? Did they have to send a company of marines to find him? How'd the Pup come home? On the President's plane? Will it cost the taxpayers a fortune to keep one dog in the White House?"

"Quarantine," Oliver said with his usual pithiness. "The Pup wasn't lost. The Navy put him in a cage. A dog can pick up diseases in Honolulu, just like a man. They had to test."

Oliver waded through these reporters with Fala on

the leash. He didn't stick to the rose garden. He took the Pup off the President's grounds. He went up New York Avenue towards Mount Vernon Square. Ollie might have been invisible walking alone, because of the number of sailors in the street, but the Pup couldn't go anywhere incognito. He was as famous as Betty Grable or Bob Hope. Letters arrived for him from dog lovers throughout the Free World. All you had to do was scribble the word Fala on an envelope. Postmen knew about him in Peoria, Moscow, and Istanbul. He had more fan mail than Mrs. R. Letters to Fala had to be screened with everything else that came into the White House. The Secret Service couldn't disregard a dog's mail: there might have been a threat to the President in any one of those letters.

Government girls tried to swoon in the presence of Ollie and the dog. The sailor was obliged to write something for them in their steno pads. "For Marsha. From the Outlaw and Oliver Beebe." He had to give the Pup's signature away fifty times before he got to the boarding-house. He didn't expect to find Anita. He'd come on a whim, hoping the Outlaw might bring him some luck. The dog wouldn't fail him. Anita was home. She'd arrived ten minutes earlier than her brother, after spending the night in Georgetown, with Orlando Frayard.

Anita crossed her arms and yelped with pleasure as the Pup wiggled into the room. "Is that Roosevelt's dog?"

"It's him," Oliver said. "The Outlaw."

The twitters in Anita's face touched Oliver to the bone. His sister took her delight with a ferociousness that troubled the boy. She could scar herself with a smile that made her cheeks turn crooked and put dark, rumbling lines in them. The sailor was in love.

" 'Nita, where you been?"

How could she explain Orlando's methods of court-ship to a brother who liked to take off her pants? Hadn't she grown up with him? She wasn't dumb to the misery in his voice. "I went shopping," she said.

"What did you buy?"

"Jesus, are you going to pester me for leaving your room? Am I supposed to sit here every morning until you can sneak out of the White House? Give me your god-damn schedule, or don't complain."

Anita frightened him with her arguments, and he became a petulant sailor. "Waited for you, 'Nita. Five days. In Mount Vernon park."

"Did I ask you to wait? I'm not the Washington shuttle. You come here at your own convenience, with the President's mutt, and you want apologies from me."

Fala nuzzled into Oliver's leg, unused to a shouting girl. The Pup felt menaced by her pointy heels. She was taller than Ollie, standing in her pumps. They left power-ful nicks in the carpet wherever she happened to walk. Fala didn't have much truck with humans, except for Ollie and the Boss, but he could smell another man on Anita's cotton blouse. The sailor stopped talking, and Fala lost him to the girl. They followed this strange human habit of crawling into bed without their clothes. The push of their bodies interested the dog. Oliver had a gentle hug. The ridges in his back deepened a lot as he bent towards Anita. Their mouths were stuck. They seemed to have too many tongues. Oliver's buttocks began to quail. The Pup never saw such commotion in-side the White House. Anita's hip shot into the air. Then all movement slowed. Their necks tightened, and the two of them let out a scream that raged around the pillows and roughed a dog's ears. The Pup hid under the bed.

Ollie had the devil of a time forcing him out of there. He got into his sailor pants and crept on his knees, calling to the Pup. "Fala, we're going home."

The Outlaw wouldn't move. He sat in a pile of dust balls, contemplating the erratic ways of men and women, their need to cover and uncover themselves, to lie down in a bed with their noses touching, kiss with their bellies, scream, and then fall apart.

"Lousy dog," Oliver said. "You'll have to stay with Anita. So long."

Fala waddled out with a grocery of colors on his coat; he was speckled with dust, tobacco, and Anita's gray hairs. Oliver had to spend fifteen minutes in Mount Vernon park, sneezing, glowering, and picking impurities off the Outlaw and restoring the shine to his coat.

SEVENTEEN

A Secret Service man brought Fala's basket up to Oliver's room. Without FDR, the Pup always slept in the attic. Ollie didn't mind, but the Pup had terrible dreams. He would growl into the night and whimper under the folds of his doggie blanket. "Fala, cut it out." Such admonitions failed to quiet the dog. He would stop and start again, and Oliver was resigned to noises coming out of a basket. How could he chastise the Pup for grinding his jaws in the middle of a dream?

Fala wasn't the only one who ruined his sleep. Ollie had a visitor at four a.m. It was Ethel Rosenquist. She marched upstairs from her switchboard in the West Wing to interrogate Oliver. Ethel hadn't been to Oliver's room since the lawn party six weeks ago, when she discovered him standing with Anita, and could tell from the burnished look on him that the cockeyed boy was having an affair with his sister and would marry no other girl. She nearly tripped over the dog in the basket.

"Oliver, are you being Fala's nursemaid tonight?"

"Watch yourself," Oliver muttered from his quilt; the month of September had settled on the mansion with an early chill. A wind howled through the attic when the sun was down, giving root to the worst of Fala's nightmares. So Ollie cautioned the telephone girl. "Don't badmouth the Pup."

Ethel wasn't seeking reconciliations with a barber and a dog. She would have liked to fillet Oliver Beebe. "Sailor, come down from that high horse. A nursemaid is what you are. A messenger and a scissors boy. And I'm not going to shush for a dog that's been spoiled rotten. He pees on rugs and steals food from everybody's plate."

"That's how a dog lives," Oliver said.

"And what about you, Mr. Beebe? I work downstairs. Couldn't you pick up the phone and say hi to a friend? Or am I less than that to you? Don't worry, if precious wakes up, I'll kiss him back to sleep. I know how to stroke a dog. I had my practice in this room. Where do you run to every day? Does your sister have a tidy mattress? You're a monster, Oliver Beebe."

She cried with her hands in her face. The awkward beat of her shoulders disheartened Oliver. He threw off the quilt and walked over to Ethel. Oliver wasn't profoundly naked. He wore his underpants to bed. "Ethel, I didn't mean to. . . ."

Still sobbing, she ran out of the room. Oliver remained in his underpants, baffled by the volatile nature of women. When something bothered him, he took to brooding; he didn't cry and shout and curse an innocent dog. Why was Ethel so interested in 'Nita's mattress? It wasn't lust that clapped the Beebes together. They existed on a different kind of glue. How could they rejoice in the strangeness of their bodies? His sister's navel, with all its convolutions, depth, and bittersweet musk, was more familiar than his own. When he lay with Anita, it felt as if he were falling down a coal shute into a beautiful slumber. It was akin to dying, Oliver imagined. He couldn't rest without his sister.

The Pup woke sharply at eight. He didn't try to jump on Oliver's bed. He plopped out of the basket in a hurry and whimpered with his nose against the door. Oliver understood. That dog could sniff the President more suddenly than any man alive. Oliver opened the door, and the Outlaw of Fala Hill rushed through the attic with wide swipes of his tail.

Oliver wasn't jealous. The Pup always abandoned him when Mr. Roosevelt was in the house. A Secret Service man would come in an hour to fetch Fala's basket. Ollie sat near the phone. The Boss might want his hair trimmed during breakfast. The smell of bacon began to rise up from the floorboards, but the phone didn't ring. The barber was in for another lonely week.

He didn't go out with the Liberty Club. He kept indoors, eating Baby Ruths and mashing cigarettes with the fat end of his telescope. The maids arrived at lunch time to clean his room. "Mr. Franklin's giving a talk tonight," they said. "From the Statler Hotel. Governor Dewey's been saying things about the dog, and Mr. Franklin's blowing mad. Gonna be an awful lot of Republicans chewed up inside that hotel."

The maids left after putting lavender sheets on his bed. The sheets were a gift from Madame Chiang Kai-shek, who slept at the White House in 1943. Madame Chiang couldn't tolerate ordinary linen. She brought her own supply of sheets from her palace, "Eagle's Nest," in Chungking. But she had no faith in American laundry rooms. She would use a sheet once, have it rolled into a ball, and donate it to the White House linen closet.

Oliver spent the afternoon in a bed of spotless lavender waiting for the Boss to go on the air. The maids knew more about a President's doings than a barber ever could. Ollie fiddled with his radio after seven o'clock, until FDR came on. The maids hadn't been wrong. The Boss was in one of his "Dutch" moods.

"The Republican leaders have not been content to make personal attacks upon me—or my wife—or my sons —they now include my little dog, Fala. Unlike the members of my family, Fala resents this. When he learned that the Republican fiction writers had concocted a story that I had left him behind on an Aleutian Island and had sent a destroyer back to find him—at a cost to the taxpayer of two or three or twenty million dollars—his Scotch soul was furious. He has not been the same dog since."

Oliver hoorayed in his room when the speech was over. You couldn't drop a blanket on Mr. Roosevelt's head. The Boss knew how to defend a dog. Even if he didn't have time for Ollie, he was still the greatest President in the world.

Mr. Dewey

There were grumblings outside the gates of the White House in September and October. Republicans were on the prowl. They would alternate the rhythm of their attack, using snarls and whispers on Grandpa Roosevelt. One day he was Franklin the First, who brought monarchy to the United States and built up the city of Washington to serve his own power-crazed image, and then he was "that tired old man," a pitiful wreck of a President, supervised by admirals and clerks.

The Dewey train would stop in Natchez, or Topeka, and the candidate would appear in his gray Homburg hat and talk in a grim monotone about the danger of kings in America, powerful squires who left their country homes to rule from a little house on the Potomac, with their wives, their sons, their sailors, and their dogs. He was Thomas Edmund Dewey, the crime-buster of New York, the governor and district attorney who walked into mobster dens and came out alive, the man who broke Murder Incorporated without firing a shot.

Only Mr. Dewey could end Roosevelt's twelve-year roost in the White House. Dewey would pull the royal curtains off the windows and let in a dose of fresh Republican air. The little governor promised to return Washington to the normal, thriving hum of a Southern town, a town that had been seized by war lords and tyrants of labor and turned into a squalid hippopotamus, Roosevelt, U.S.A., half country club, half lunatic asylum, a haven for crotchety admirals who were much better off as knitting partners for Mrs. Roosevelt.

Then the whisperers would come on, senators and Republican-minded captains in the Army, Navy, and Marines, who hinted at the feebleness of FDR. "A dying king," they said. "The old boy has to be shoved from room to room. He can't get through the day without his nose drops. The Roosevelt administration is run by a dog. The President couldn't stay awake long enough to sign one bill if Fala stopped barking and licking his shoes."

Roosevelt wouldn't answer the Republicans. He stuck to the mansion like a retired sailor, hid in his bedroom at Hyde Park, or escaped to Shangri-La, his Maryland retreat on Catoctin Mountain. The Navy ran Shangri-La for him. Its location was kept a secret to frustrate spies and fifth columnists. Reporters in the lobby grew obsessed with that place. They heard Fala scuttle on the second floor, but there were no signs of the man. The Big Boss must have gone into seclusion, and they couldn't figure why. Was it a case of bronchitis, or had the Dewey onslaught given him a nervous stomach? The key to it all was Shangri-La. If they could uncover Roosevelt's mountain, the mysteries would clear themselves.

FDR wasn't sitting on a mountain. He had an attack of malaise. Nobody could get him out of his pajamas. The Secretary of War had to use Roosevelt's bed as a conference table. The Boss wouldn't go down to the Map Room. You could find him with tweezers and a magnifying glass. He would hover over his stamp collection, spread a hundred cards on his blanket for a mammoth game of solitaire, jab a Lucky Strike into his cigarette holder without confessing his hunger for Camels. He rarely saw his grandchildren. He only had time for Fala and the boy.

After months of obscurity, Oliver was recalled from the attic. He didn't bring his barbering kit. The President wasn't eager to let Ollie root behind his ears. He wanted a sailor who wouldn't stare at a President's pajamas and ask about the campaign. The boy didn't have hooded eyes. The President had gotten balder since June. The pince-nez that he clipped on for games of solitaire had bitten into his nose. His neck was scrawny. He wouldn't touch the food that arrived on his servidor. Ollie suspected the President's fatigue had something to do with cigarettes. "Boss, I'll be right back."

Oliver sneaked out the basement and went to the soldiers' and sailors' canteen on Pennsylvania Avenue. He asked for Daniel Matisse. "I need a Camel," Oliver said.

Matisse squinted at him. "Try me tomorrow."

"I can't," Oliver said. "It's for the Boss. He won't eat without a Camel."

Matisse disappeared into the back rooms of his canteen and returned with a long box in a brown paper bag. "How much?" The barber only had a dollar in his pants.

"It's on the house. The President's a sailor, isn't he? He's entitled to his smokes."

Oliver hadn't seen a full box of Camels since 1942. He'd heard of black marketeers who retired to Barbados with their millions after trading in Camel cigarettes.

A gift like that could stun a President. "Child, where did you get the caboodle?"

Oliver had to protect the solitude of the Liberty Club. "I got it from another sailor."

The Boss wasn't unhappy. "Boy oh boy." He could smoke and become the good father, offering Camels to butlers, admirals, and valets, and sending two packs across the hall to his wife. When the Secretary of Commerce made glad tidings over the cigarettes, the President winked and said, "The child has his own source. Ollie went deep into the Navy Department to get them for me."

The Boss' appetite did improve. He would eat anything but spinach now, spinach and sweetbreads. He'd been feuding with the chatelaine Mrs. Roosevelt had brought into the White House. The chatelaine was in charge of menus. Wartime shortages were no hindrance to her. She could function within the boundaries of a ration book. Once, in 1943, when she'd overspent her allowance of stamps, she economized on the Boss by feeding him sweetbreads thirty days in a row. He had to scribble a note to her. "My Dear Mrs. Quentin, I do not want any more sweetbreads on my plate until 1946. Thank you. Your humble servant, Franklin D. Roosevelt." He couldn't get rid of the chatelaine. Mrs. Roosevelt ran that side of the house, and she admired Mrs. Q. "Franklin darling, Quentin is the best housekeeper we ever had."

Quentin be hanged, the President had his Camels! But he wouldn't campaign. Two weeks ago he went to the Statler Hotel on the arm of Kirkland Horn to deliver his Fala speech. Kirkland brought him to the dais and brought him home. Maddened over the unjust treatment of his dog, the President teased, gibed, and tore into Republicans for half an hour. He could make a whole country laugh. He turned the election into a case of Dewey vs. Fala. But he'd done nothing ever since.

His aides would bring their reports into his bedroom while the President was at solitaire. They told him about the Hollywood-for-Dewey Committee that was beginning to plague Democrats with the help of Ginger Rogers, Cecil B. De Mille, Adolphe Menjou, Leo Carillo, and Rosalind Russell. The Boss wasn't disturbed. He pulled a tally sheet out from under his pillow that revealed the magnitude of his strengths and weaknesses in Hollywood. These aides stood with open mouths as the Boss ticked off every name on the Hollywood Committee to Save the New Deal: Orson Welles, Lana Turner, Harpo Marx, Olivia de Havilland, Rita Hayworth, Katharine Hepburn, Walter Huston, Melvyn Douglas, Fanny Brice, and Baby Snooks.

"FD, you can't win the election sitting in bed. That's a fact."

The aides didn't enjoy being Roosevelt's aunt. They understood the cause of his malaise. The Boss would go to Quebec to meet with Churchill inside the Chateau Frontenac, but he wouldn't spend himself on Tom Dewey. He was sick of electioneering. He'd been President longer than any man, Wilson, Jefferson, his cousin Theodore, twelve years living in the rump of a wheelchair, unable to walk without leg irons and a harness around his waist that gouged his hip sockets, bruising him with every pull of his body. He thought he had the right to sidestep Mr. Dewey and campaign from the White House, only the Republicans were snipping at him like a gang of vicious geese. The Boss would have to get out of bed.

His sailor's chest burst through the pajama tops as

he started to bellow, "Children, where's my hat?"

His aides were mortified. No one had been thinking of a fourth term in 1941, when the President's old gray fedora, his lucky hat, was donated to the March of Dimes for its annual Hollywood auction. Jack Benny outbid Edward G. Robinson for the President's hat. His aides sent a telegram to Benny, imploring him to give back the old fedora. Benny agreed. The hat arrived in four days. Secret Service men pulled it out of an Army mail bag, tested it under their X-ray machine, and forwarded it to the President.

The Boss was ready to go. His aides decided on Brooklyn as the site of his first address. He wouldn't hide in any auditorium, where hostile reporters could say he was babbling to the woodwork, a sick man behind closed doors. The Boss was too wary for that. He would campaign in Ebbetts Field.

Ollie returned to the attic, expecting to fall into old routines while the Boss was gone: eating tootsie rolls and Baby Ruths, walking the Pup. Close to midnight a Secret Service man appeared in Oliver's room. "Get dressed. You're going with the Boss." It was the end of October, and Ollie still wore his summer whites. Couldn't they give you a half-hour notice in this place? He'd never been on the road with the Boss. What about a toothbrush, scissors, a Baby Ruth? The Secret Service man had to remind him to take his peacoat along. "Moron, it gets cold in Brooklyn."

A limousine waited for him outside the east gate. Ollie strode towards it with the peacoat dragging around his heels. It was a big gray Packard, the Boss' bulletproof car. Oliver got in. He had to sit next to Kirkland Horn. The President was hunched inside his Navy cape, with a lap rug on his knees. He stared out at Oliver from the wings of his cape. "Why so gloomy, child? Did Papa force you out of bed?"

The sailor rumbled a few words that were impossible to hear. Horn poked him in the ribs as a signal for Oliver to repeat himself. "Baby Ruths," Oliver said. "I didn't know how much food to bring."

The President laughed into the frogs on his Navy collar. "There'll be food on the train, child. You won't have to nibble."

Oliver leaned into the cushions with Kirkland Horn. There was an Army truck ahead of the Packard, holding a dozen riflemen from Fort Meyer, and two Secret Service cars in the rear. The Packard and its motorcade strolled down Fifteenth Street to a ramp under the Bureau of Printing and Engraving that led to a little railroad siding, where the President's train was docked. It was only six steps from his Packard to his private coach, the Ferdinand Magellan. The Boss wouldn't sit in a wheelchair for so short a ride. He hobbled up to the Ferdinand Magellan on his leg braces, with Kirkland at his elbow. Then two Secret Service men carried him aboard.

The facilities of the President's train confounded Oliver. The Packard wasn't left behind. A Secret Service man drove it onto a special baggage car near the middle of the train. Where was Oliver supposed to stay? In a sleeping car assigned to chauffeurs, barbers, Secret Service men, and cooks? Horn summoned him with his little finger. He was given a tiny bedroom of his own on the Ferdinand Magellan.

The sailor had a difficult time getting used to the Boss' coach. It had escape hatches on the roof like a goddamn submarine, to protect the Boss from drowning if the train ever fell off a bridge. The glass in each compartment was thicker than a man's nose. The furniture was riveted to the floor. A Filipino cook came out of the scullery with fresh orange juice for Oliver. He drank too fast and swallowed all the pits.

There had to be an intercom hidden in Oliver's berth. A voice piped at him from the hollows under his bed. "The Boss is looking for you, Mr. Beebe." He couldn't mistake the gruff calls of Kirkland Horn. Oliver went into the corridor. The train was rocking now. The lights blinked on and off in a dusty color. A red mustache frowned at Ollie from the rear of the Ferdinand Magellan. He tracked that mustache, hugging the car's mouse-green walls, and arrived next to Kirkland Horn, who jostled Oliver, took him into FDR's bedroom, and through another door. The Boss had a fullgrown tub aboard the Magellan, with a "saddle" built into it from wood that had been stripped off the seats of a canoe. He sat in this contraption, smoking a Camel. The ashes fell into the tub, swirled in the baby currents over the drain, and sank between FDR's spindly legs.

Ollie could tell from the new crop of bitemarks in the cigarette holder that the President was in some pain.

"Boss, is your lumbago bothering you again?"

Horn said, "Not today," and Ollie was chagrined. He couldn't understand why a red mustache had to speak for FDR. "Mr. Roosevelt's neck is killing him. It's from that harness he has to wear."

The Boss started to smile, but you could feel the tension in his face.

"Poppa's got the kinks."

Oliver stood behind that saddle in the water and

rubbed the stiffness out of the Boss' neck. The Boss didn't need a valet when Oliver was here.

Horn walked Ollie to his berth. You couldn't be comfortable around that old man. Kirkland dyes his mustache, the maids had told him. It's all rabbity hair under the dye. "I'll dress Mr. Roosevelt in the morning. You can stay in bed."

The bunk was short of bedclothes, and Oliver had to drape the peacoat around himself, or watch his ankles freeze. He missed Anita. But the excitement of his maiden trip with the President could soothe the boy's thickened heart, and he was ready to doze off. The land a train had to cross moved past Oliver in long black waves like any ocean. The boy could have been at sea. The Magellan had all the list of a good destroyer.

The Filipino cook was rolling him off the bunk when Ollie opened his eyes. "Get into your pants, Mr. Oliver. Late, late." Oliver brushed his teeth in coffee. The President had alighted from the train ten minutes ago. It was Horn's plot to leave Oliver behind.

"So long, Tom," Ollie said, grateful to the cook, and jumped off the Ferdinand Magellan, which was standing in Brooklyn, at an Army supply base. The ground had turned to mud. A wicked rain beat on Oliver's coat with the noise of hard pellets. Horn grunted at him from the Packard. "Get in."

Oliver sat in a wet coat. He wouldn't look at Horn. Two colonels from a nearby weather station squeezed into the back of the car, trying to familiarize the President with the properties of a storm. These colonels were erudite about the weather. The Boss was out of danger, they said. The storm that was biting into the Atlantic coast would weaken in Brooklyn. But it wouldn't go away until tomorrow. The cold air worried the colonels. The Boss might catch pneumonia in a damp car. They urged him not to speak at Ebbetts Field.

The Boss had always made his own weather. After crawling out of his woolen blanket at the White House, he wouldn't let a storm break into his campaign. He had his cape, his lap rug, his old fedora, and the warm bodies of Beebe and Horn to drive off the chill. The two colonels saluted their Commander-in-Chief and climbed down from the Packard.

"Kirkland," the Boss said, "I'd like a little sky." Horn signaled to the agent who drove the car, and the roof began to give way. The creaking of so much iron, leather, and glass threw knots across Oliver's forehead. But the knots disappeared with the first rush of wind into the Packard. The boy was in an open car. You could have come up to the President and touched him on the shoulder if Kirkland hadn't placed his strongest men on the running boards.

No rain could discourage the people of Brooklyn. They stood ten deep on the sidewalks to wait for FDR. Some with umbrellas, or paper tents, others with their mouths shaking in the wind. You wouldn't have heard a peep about Mr. Dewey. He was governor of the State, a former district attorney, the crime-buster whom Dutch Schultz had threatened to kill, and maybe he had the proportions of a future President, and maybe he didn't, but he was only a man in a Homburg, with a mustache under his nose, and that didn't make him Roosevelt. Did Dewey have Eleanor, or the Pup, or a sailor to ride with him in his car? They knew the President was an "IP," he had infantile paralysis, but none of them had ever seen him in a wheelchair. A cripple he was, but he could swim.

They went to the RKO like everybody else, and they watched the Movietone news, and there was FDR in the pool at Warm Springs, playing water polo with the Secret Service men, bobbing up and down, with a pair of flippers on him, shoulders that belonged on a whale. What kind of polio was that, when a man could attack with a rubber ball, and stroll in the pool, like me, you, and your uncle Moses? The guy was a magic cripple, vulnerable, imperfect, less than you, and more, a President with crooked feet, who slouched behind his desk in a bowtie and a shirt, with funny glasses on his nose, and could turn into a seal if you took off the bowtie and gave him a tank of water, a gentleman mermaid, awkward on land, powerful in the sea, Franklin Delano Roosevelt. They wouldn't have stood in the rain for no Tom Dewey.

The Boss entered Ebbets Field, his Packard bumping up the ramp of a long wooden platform close to second base. Then Kirkland got down on his knees, swearing at Oliver, "Get out of the way," and locked the Boss' leg irons. Mr. Roosevelt grimaced once, and throwing off his fedora and his cape, he slid to the edge of the car, raised himself with one hand on Kirkland's back, and walked to the speaker's stand that Navy carpenters had built for him in Ebbets Field. It was a slow, hobblekneed walk, and Oliver was afraid. The Boss could trip and die before he got to that Navy lectern. He was a man on a wooden horse, riding his own useless legs. The Boss didn't need the sun to make his "Roosevelt weather." He knew how to occupy a storm. He reached that lectern on the hump of the wind.

He said, "My friends," with the storm in his face. But Oliver couldn't listen. He saw the umbrellas twirling in the stands, and the steady sheets of rain that could hypnotize a boy who'd been sleeping in the White House for nearly six months. The President was in the car again before Ollie came out of his stupor. The Packard bumped down the ramp, with Kirkland under the Boss' knees, unlocking those damnable braces, and wiping the Boss' legs with two or three towels, while the roar in that ball park could have swallowed a hundred Dodger games, because Dixie Walker and Frenchie Bordagaray might chop a home run for you, but only FDR could walk on a pair of dead sticks.

They got him to the Coast Guard station around the corner from Ebbetts Field. Horn's men put him on a table and shucked off his harness, his braces, and his clothes. They fed him whiskey in a glass of milk, and twenty hands began to dry his body. The agents were squeamish about their work. It was odd for them to throw their hands on the President and towel him off. You could see the welts on his calves where the braces had plunged too far into the skin. A growl seemed to rise out of all those wiggling hands. "Where the fuck is Oliver?" It wasn't the President's voice. The Secret Service was looking for that little pest.

An agent found him sitting in the car. The boy didn't have enough sense to come out of a storm. Ollie had been dreaming by himself, trying to figure if there was a person in Brooklyn who didn't love the Boss. The Republicans wouldn't buy a vote around Ebbetts Field.

The Secret Service brought Ollie over to the Boss. The barber didn't have to squint. He knew what a naked President was. "Boss, how do you feel?"

"Grand," the President said, but he couldn't smile at Oliver. His body lay under the Secret Service men's hands like a fixture of lead. He didn't have the strength to put a Camel in his mouth.

NINETEEN

It didn't end with a rubdown across from Ebbetts Field, Oliver on a table, bestowing warmth to bloodless limbs. The boy was glued to Roosevelt. The Boss wouldn't campaign without him. But the obligations Oliver had weren't easy to declare. Sometimes he was a barber, sometimes a valet, sometimes a masseur, drifting through the Secret Service detail with the President's appointment book in his pocket, and also a package of dimes. Roosevelt never carried money. Oliver would have to tip a hot dog vendor in Chicago, a busboy in Duluth.

The President had a passion for ball parks. He appeared in the homes of the Red Sox, the White Sox, and the Phils. On Navy Day he went into Shibe Park with Oliver and excoriated Nazis, Japs, and Dewey Republicans. At Fenway Park he talked about putting Germans on a diet of pablum and potatoes for twenty years. "Pablum for breakfast, pablum for lunch, boiled potatoes before bed." The Democrats of Fenway Park worshiped the Boss' "potato" speech. They wouldn't have spent a good potato on the German people, unless FDR declared for it. They adored the cape, the hat, the Roosevelt smile, and that mum boy behind the President's chair. Admirals couldn't have moved them as much as Oliver Beebe.

They liked a common sailor near the Commander-in-Chief.

It was no boon to Oliver, all this adulation on the road. A boy could get weary shaking hands, delivering his autograph to a thousand pads. What could he write? "God bless you. Oliver Beebe." His identity didn't matter very much. Democrats preferred an unknown Oliver. How could the Republicans attack him? He was the mysterious seaman who traveled with FDR. His presence enlivened the Boss. Republicans were turning glum. They expected a crippled Roosevelt to sneeze out his last days in the White House, and the Boss was showing more energy than their man. He looked like a warrior in his cape. He talked about starvation diets. He had Oliver Beebe.

In Washington things got worse for Oliver. He couldn't rest, read a movie magazine, or make calls on Anita. Mount Vernon park was light years from Pennsylvania Avenue in October, 1944. Ollie couldn't have crossed that distance with his telescope, his brains, or his shoes. The White House had him shuffling around Fala and the Blue Room, the First Lady, the rose garden, the Secret Service, and Democrats on the Hill. He would go up to the Capitol with some messages in his pants for Mr. Roosevelt's favorite senators and congressmen. The Speaker of the House made a fuss over Oliver. The boy had to sip bourbon in the Speaker's rooms and guarantee his people that the Boss loved everybody in the House. "Oliver, what's the man's health these days?"

"Grand, sir. Simply grand."

He had to be careful about dinner invitations, since congressmen liked to pry. "Sorry," he would say, telling his standard little story. "I always eat with the Secret

Service." Then Oliver would run home and have his Baby Ruths and a can of beets in the attic. But one Thursday, at dinnertime, Kirkland Horn growled at him. "Beebe, come with me." They weren't with a pack of Secret Service men. Horn went with him alone to a seafood house on Connecticut Avenue, called Harvey's. You had to line up near the door and keep smiling at the headwaiter, because Thursday was Harvey's big night. The Vice President could drop in, or a party of ambassadors.

There was a picture on the front wall of William Howard Taft breaking a lobster with his teeth. The restaurant hadn't framed that picture out of any snobbish delight in itself. Harvey's didn't need a President on its walls to attract a clientele. It served as a reminder that this was 1944, and like other choice restaurants in the District, Harvey's would run out of lobster by eight o'clock.

Kirkland sat down with Oliver a few minutes before eight. He rushed to get Ollie's order in. The Negro waiters perspired in their black coats. They'd been out of lobster since a quarter to seven. They were also out of shad, bluefish, and smallmouthed bass. They could give you Chineoteague oysters and she-crabs from Tangier, one or two vegetables, and as much chowder as a man could drink. Harvey's was luckier with its sweets. The chefs had enough pecans to meet their quota of pies. Oliver had two enormous pieces, but Horn only played with his food. He kicked Oliver under the table.

"See that fellow with the pomade behind his ears?"

Ollie drank his chowder with a spoon.

"Do you know him, Mr. Beebe?"

Horn's kicks were growing savage. Ollie left his chowder to watch a man at a corner table scoop up peas with the edge of his knife. His eyebrows looked as if they'd been combed. His part was in the middle of his head. He had the pinkest gums in Washington, and perfect moons on his fingernails, but his nose was crooked; it flattened out across his dark face. He must have been fond of toilet water. The smell of lilacs arrived like a curse over Oliver's table. The man was dug into his corner, removed from Harvey's bustle, eating by himself. The waiters were careful with the guy, steering customers away from his corner, making sure no one interfered with him. He put down his knife and asked for another helping of peas. He was much more pugnacious with peas in his mouth.

"How come waiters trip over themselves to bring him some peas? Who is that guy?"

"The big G-man, J. Edgar Hoover."

Oliver had heard the Boss chat with Hoover on the phone. "Yes, Edgar, no Edgar," the Boss would say, without narrowing his smile. FDR seemed fond of the G-man.

A waiter stooped near Kirkland Horn as if he meant to eat off the old man's neck. It was nothing malicious. He'd come from Hoover's table with a message for the old man. You had to whisper at Harvey's, or the whole Free World would get to know your occupations. "Sir, Mr. Hoover would like to say hello to you and shake the hand of the President's sailor."

So Ollie and old man Horn went across the restaurant to sit with J. Edgar Hoover. The stench of lilacs nearly threw the boy off his feet. The hair was plastered thick on the G-man's bumpy head. In spite of the heavy jowls and flattened nose, he had a gracious smile.

"Kirkland, why do you keep all your friends away from me?"

"It wasn't my intention," Horn said. "We didn't want to ruin your dinner. Edgar, this is Oliver Beebe."

The G-man had a crisp handshake. He marked up your knuckles with the rings he wore. Ollie had never seen that much silver and gold on anybody's fingers.

"Oliver, Mr. Roosevelt couldn't win the election without you. That's what I'm told. You bring him luck."

"The Boss don't need luck from me," Oliver said, reluctant to drag FDR's campaign into Harvey's lobster house. "He's the President. He'll win. You wouldn't have a country without the Boss."

Hoover laughed gently at the boy. "We ought to tell that to the Dewey camp. We have to prepare them for defeat. Oliver, come to my office when you have the chance. I'll show you the FBI."

"He's too busy now," Horn said. "Edgar, your oysters are getting cold. Goodbye." He paid the bill and left Harvey's with a toothpick in his mouth.

"Mr. Horn," Ollie said, "did that G-man ever do something to you?"

"No. But he fucks the Secret Service whenever he can."

Dinner at Harvey's had only muddled Oliver Beebe. Oliver would stick to Baby Ruths and tootsie rolls, a sailor's meal. He couldn't understand the different twists a government had. The generals were warring with the admirals at the White House. You could hear them curse behind the door of the Map Room. Why couldn't the Army and Navy get along? Republicans walked down the aisles of Congress eager to bite Democrats on the ass. The Secret Service was having a feud with the FBI. Only the Boss could hold this crazy government together.

Ollie was invited to Hyde Park for election eve. It

was the first time the President brought him home to his estate in Dutchess County. It snowed. Oliver forgot his galoshes. Horn took pity on the boy. He dialed Washington, D.C. The galoshes arrived in the President's mail pouch on election morn. The President went down to vote in Hyde Park Village. The machine jammed. An official had to crawl under the curtain and go into the booth with FDR. He jiggled the levers and the machine fell into place.

The Boss fed bits of toast to Fala all afternoon. Later he was in the library with a host of Democrats, tallying up election scores while Mrs. Roosevelt scrambled eggs for everybody in the house. It wasn't a very long vigil. The Boss captured New York by half-past nine. Pennsylvania came in for him, and then New Jersey.

At eleven o'clock he wheeled himself out to the front porch and made his election night speech to the citizens of Hyde Park. Oliver wondered why the President bothered with such people. Hyde Park always voted Republican, Horn had told him. Then the Boss went to bed.

Oliver was given a closet near FDR's enormous bedroom. The closet didn't have a fireplace. It had once been Mrs. Roosevelt's room. Now she slept in her own cottage at Val-Kill, a few miles away. Oliver wasn't unhappy in his room. He had his galoshes, and the Boss had won. He wouldn't have to think about Dewey any more.

He heard footsteps in the rose garden. A Secret Service man must have been patrolling the grass. Where was Mr. Horn? Oliver pulled the sheets up past his neck. Fala had escaped from the Boss' room. He wasn't interested in any sailors. The Pup had come around to sniff Oliver's galoshes. "Let him sniff," Ollie muttered, and he dropped off before his sister or anybody could creep into his head.

Kirkland Horn

TWENTY

He was the old man of the White House, a babysitter to seven Commanders-in-Chief, poking into kitchens, bathrooms, bedrooms, state dining rooms, parlors, and broom closets since 1901. The maids called him "Moses" behind his back. His red mustache reminded them of the hairs on a bloody root. He could have been the devil. No one interfered with Kirkland Horn.

He was two years older than the President. But they remembered him carrying Mr. Roosevelt up a flight of steps, the Boss high on Kirkland's shoulders, that old man chuffing for air, his eyes squeezed shut, he could still feel a stray piece of metal jutting out of the wood. "He sure does know how to give a piggyback ride," the maids loved to tell. They wished he would retire.

"Mr. Kirkland, he beginning to creak," they said. "Just like the chandeliers." The agents under him agreed with the diagnosis of the maids. It was sheer drudgery working for "the Horn." That old man was addicted to strenuous exercise. He could squeeze blood out of a shadow, and have you sniffing into garbage pails for a possible fire. It was supposed to have been the glory assignment, District 16, the White House. You couldn't get close to it unless you performed like a wizard out in the field. They'd put you on the "crazy file" in Nebraska, Arkansas, and Illinois, and you'd have to track down all the lunatics who ever wrote a threatening letter to the Roosevelts, Fala, or that miserable Oliver Beebe, because anybody who wanted to harm the sailor and the dog might decide to kill the President too. So you broke your ass for the Secret Service. You gulped sandwiches in the rain, globs of mustard falling on your tie, until you had half the crazies of Nebraska tucked inside your folder. Then you got tapped for District 16. The White House and Kirkland Horn.

Major Colbert, the young chief of the Secret Service, would have liked to get rid of Kirkland, or push him into one of the field offices, where the old man would have a respectable senility, out of harm's way. Horn was an embarrassment to the Service, the relic of a simpler, gruffer age, when the raw power of a red mustache would have been sufficient to protect the Commander-in-Chief.

The maids swore he could spook a house. Windows opened without the force of any hand. Rubble would appear under a balcony. Green mold sprouted on certain walls. The maids borrowed that Hawaiian doll the Boss had given Oliver, and hiked through the mansion with the doll's forked legs sticking up in the air. They hoped to drive out any spell the Secret Service could impose on a hapless maid. Ollie didn't prevent them from using the doll, but he had little faith in the attributes of magic. The maids were gullible, that's it. He could clarify every instance of a haunting in the White House. Couldn't the wind open a few connected panes of glass? Cracked oyster shells in the mortar of the outer walls produced that rubble under the balconies. The green mold had come from faulty plumbing, not the evil slake of an old man.

Horn was tired, bloody tired, of policing the mansion. He would have liked to crouch on the Potomac seawall with a fishing rod and drag tin cans up from the water. 1944 was a dead year for fish. The Navy had strangled the Potomac with its destroyer runs. Oil spills from the knocking about of gunboats left a dark skin on the water that could turn a shoreline utterly gray. The only things that would spawn in the river were toads, pigfish, and aquatic spiders. Horn didn't care. He'd rather fish for toads than send in reports to his bratty superior, Major Colbert. They were putting boys over your head these days. Colbert was thirty-one, up from an Army war college. He had visions of the Secret Service gorging on the FBI. But he kept bumping into J. Edgar Hoover. The G-man knew how to quiet little boys. Edgar would go up to the White House, swallow a "horse's neck" (ginger ale and orange rind) with FDR, pose with Fala, and Major Colbert would have to retreat into a corner of the Treasury Building.

The White House was a dump to Kirkland Horn. The biggest deathtrap in the United States. Every foot of ceiling, every balcony, every wall, was a fire hazard. An idiotic civil defense chief rooted into the basement at the beginning of the war and dug a bomb shelter under the Boss' swimming pool. A great hollow of shit. It wouldn't have taken a bomb to bring down the White House. An elephant sitting on the lawn with its ass near the South Portico could have engendered a concussion strong enough to split the shelter in half. FDR would have drowned in the water of his own pool.

Horn conferred with the Army engineers. A second shelter was dug under the new East Wing. Blackout curtains were placed in all the rooms. Gas masks and fire shovels were given out. The Secretary of the Treasury, as lord and overseer of the Secret Service, appointed himself air-raid warden to the President. He decided to render the mansion invisible by painting it black. Horn had to discourage such crazy notions without offending the man. "Mr. Secretary, the Boss won't live in a black house."

He was sick of steering around jokers from the Treasury Department. Having to climb under a President's overcoat year after year had put a hump on his back. Besides, Horn was pissing blood. He had a pain in one kidney that obliged him to howl under his breath. He would talk to that kidney, mutter on the stairs to hide the wheeze in his neck. He'd grown subject to fainting spells in the last six months. He blacked out in the Green Room yesterday, falling into a Duncan Phyfe sofa table on his nightly tour of the mansion, with a cut over his eye. He kept the news to himself.

Kirkland wasn't going to wear a hospital gown while his President was in office. Kirkland loved that man. He wouldn't have spent thirteen years with any other President. The pomp and circumstance of a President's life bored him to death. Senators and party hacks squirreling in the vestibule, waiting for a nod from FDR. The press corps nibbling in your ear. "Kirkland, tell us a story. Was Cal Coolidge the dumbest man in the White House?" And Horn would mutter a noise that traveled down to his sandpaper kidney, a whistling pain in his side. "President Cal was smarter than you think." His grimace could frighten any reporter. You learned not to mess with that red mustache.

Then there were the kings, the displaced royalty of

Europe, who slept in the mansion for a night, had tea and cakes with Mrs. Roosevelt, sandwiches with the Boss. Horn had to inspect their luggage and their rooms. There could have been a false king among them, a saboteur out of Berlin with enough jelly in his shaving kit to tear a hole in the roof and deliver Mr. and Mrs. Roosevelt, Fala, Oliver Beebe, Harry Hopkins, and Kirkland Horn into the ground. He would catch them on the toilet seat or in bed with their kingly wives. The Secret Service didn't knock. No king could say how Horn got into the room. His head would peer at you from behind a blackout curtain. "Sorry, your highness, won't be a minute. Checking the premises, you know."

It was a filthy business, worse than a stab in the kidney, spying on kings and maids and Eleanor's guests and all the little barbers FDR tossed into the attic. Kirkland would have chucked it in for a fishing rod and eighteen inches of seawall, mud on his shoes, gunboats churning in their own oil, but he couldn't walk out on FDR. He didn't have to nose through doctors' reports, or trap the Boss' arm in a blood-pressure cuff. FDR was a dead man. The nose drops he inhaled for his "sinus attacks" was only a subterfuge. He would wheel himself into the ground floor clinic, offer his nostrils to the White House physician, saying "Spinach" (anything that disgusted him was always "Spinach"), because the drops would leak onto his chin. It was a show for the newsmen in the lobby. The Boss hates his nose drops, they would whisper to themselves, discounting Republican rumors about his health. Didn't you hear him bellow? And Roosevelt would disappear into his elevator car, a working President who took his nose drops like a dose of cod-liver oil.

But Kirkland saw the trembling hands that could only grasp an outsized coffee mug, the signature that had grown illegible, the blue-gray complexion under his eyes, the man who had to squint at each printed word, who couldn't squeeze a Camel into his cigarette holder on the first try, who would nod off while looking at his mail, slur in the middle of a sentence, his energy burning out before lunch. You could hide his condition from the admirals, not the maids. They called his death without turning macabre. "Mr. Franklin's sittin' in the dark."

The Boss wouldn't have opened to a feebleminded barber in 1942. He was a powerful, angry Dutchman in a wheelchair who could balance Democrats, Republicans, Eleanor, Stalin, Churchill, and Madame Chiang Kai-shek on the ridge of his thumb, play water polo with Kirkland in the basement pool. His signature had been firmer then. You couldn't fail to notice the "Roosevelt loop." He would enter the Map Room twice a day, avoiding the heels of Army and Navy men with the spokes of his chair, and watch the red and green pins on the wall with a terrible scrutiny. The admirals didn't have to lecture the Boss. He knew the position of any single pin. But he'd lapsed in two years. His memory couldn't hold. He'd wheel away from the Map Room with empty eyes. The fierce concentration would come and go. Fits of work, and then he'd fall into a sluggish reverie. Only Oliver and the Pup could bring back his smile.

Kirkland understood. FDR had no interest in Oliver's barbering tools. The maids could have stuck a pot on his head and clipped around his ears. The Boss wanted a sailor in the house, a boy who wouldn't involve himself in government intrigue, siding with this faction or that, or use his proximity to Eleanor and FDR to become chamberlain of the White House, dispensing favors, injuring one party, helping the next—no, nothing but a seaman who was loyal to a man and his dog. The Boss got Oliver Beebe.

Kirkland never liked the boy. It's the dumb ones that made all the trouble. Beebe arrived in a sailor suit, hugging his clippers and a candy bar, and the Service was thrown into a turmoil, because nobody had investigated the boy. The Boss sprung Oliver on them without a word. Through the gate, and up into the attic, Oliver Beebe, Seaman First Class. They broke into his room off "H" Street, their arms wiggling in his closets and drawers, feeling the lumps in his mattress for contraband. The barber was pure as gold. Not even a condom in the boardinghouse. Just movie magazines. Naval Intelligence put a copy of his records into Kirkland's hands. The records revealed one thing to Horn: the Navy was drafting idiots these days. They didn't have to worry about anarchism in Oliver Beebe. The boy couldn't hold an idea in his head. He had a sister in Milwaukee. A team of agents from the Milwaukee field office swooped down into her neighborhood and discovered that she wasn't married but she had a baby boy, and she was living with a draft dodger by the name of Phil. They could have passed this on to the FBI. But they didn't say a word. Edgar could do his own digging. Horn was only involved with Oliver Beebe.

The digging stopped. The Secret Service couldn't spend itself on one lousy sailor. Horn went to the Pacific with FDR and Fala in July. Beebe was allowed to rot in the White House. But the climate turned bitter in August. The Andrew Jackson tree began to molt vile pieces of bark. The south lawn stank like a sewer. Information was getting back to Horn. A few FBI men were smirking in the government cafeterias. Kirkland had to scratch under the ordinary jokes about the White House and Eleanor. Tales of Fala shitting in the Map Room seemed justified. It was an election year. Dewey people came out of the woodwork to slap at the Boss. But why were there so many mentions of Oliver Beebe in the cafeterias? Beebe and Eleanor. Beebe and the dog. Beebe on Massachusetts Avenue. Beebe in Mount Vernon Square park. The FBI was obsessed with the Boss' sailor.

Horn's men returned to the boardinghouse. "Sir, the laddy's sleeping with his sister."

Horn didn't like the hard grin on them. "Is that another cafeteria scoop?"

"No, sir. We had our binoculars in the park, sir, and we watched them in the act."

Kirkland might have grinned along with his men if that sailor wasn't living in the Boss' attic. He wasn't the inquisitor of Washington, D.C. Beebe could fuck his brains out if he could do it without hurting the Boss. The men of District 16 were aware that Ethel, the switchboard girl, was fond of climbing up to Oliver's room. Horn couldn't keep the world from copulating, inside the mansion and out. But incest was a bit too close. Republicans had eyes and ears. He could imagine them screaming about the tainted sailor under Franklin's roof. Still, he couldn't believe that Oliver's romance would preoccupy Edgar Hoover. There were choicer bedtime stories for the FBI to circulate. Kirkland would have to dig some more.

He didn't notify the Washington office, or that wonderchild, Major Colbert. The Major was too excitable. He would have put handcuffs on Oliver Beebe, after finding a D.C. ordinance that declared brothers and sisters couldn't lick. Kirkland took men off the White House detail to scurry across town. The men came to him with isolated scraps of news that Kirkland fit into a story: the barber had grown political since June. He was a member of the Liberty Club, an outfit of borderline fascists, run by Spain's naval attaché in Washington, the marqués de Estrella, a quack with mysterious war wounds, in love with Adolf Hitler. No one had bothered to suppress the Liberty Club. It had the sting of a dead mule. The marqués was D.C.'s pet fascist. He went to parties, kissed the sleeves of Washington matrons, and talked about the decline of manliness and democracy in the West. It wasn't diplomatic immunity that kept him in place at the chancellery. The internment camps in Oregon and Indiana could hold a remarkable number of naval attachés. The marqués had an exotic charm, an innocence of grace, that allowed him not to suffer for the excesses of his thinking. The Liberty Club bumbled through the capital without the ability to fright.

It couldn't lull Kirkland Horn to sleep. Horn had to stay out of the chancellery, but the men of his detail penetrated the marqués' apartment on Dupont Circle. They got around the marques' creole maid, who was napping in her room, and photographed his diaries, bankbooks, half the scribblings in his desk. Kirkland poured through the mess of pages. His opinion of the marqués didn't shift. The diaries were devoted to the ravings of a quiet lunatic. The marqués dreamed of a new democratic world under Adolf Hitler, where Negroes, mixed-bloods, and whites could live in terrific harmony. The new world depended on Oliver Beebe. Hitler couldn't come to the United States until Roosevelt was destroyed. Beebe was the requisite angel. The marqués swore to his diary that Oliver sang to him the latest Allied positions in the Map Room. It had to be crazy. The barber couldn't get near the Map Room without surrendering the teeth in his head. The Marine guard had little respect for unauthorized sailors, even if they belonged to FDR.

Kirkland mocked the diaries, but he wouldn't sit still. Forty years of trafficking with Presidents in a single house had made a recluse of him, taught him to trust nothing at all, neither intuition, facts, nor a President's word. He met with FDR's admirals. A precaution, he said. Against espionage. He was no more specific than that. The White House carpenters built a second Map Room behind the first. Horn stocked the outer room with Secret Service men dressed in admirals' uniforms, and put up fake charts that were maddeningly precise: stale replicas of the actual war, battlelines of a month ago, prepared by the admirals themselves. FDR never questioned this doubling of Map Rooms. Kirkland was chief of security at the White House, and you had to bend his way. The Boss wheeled through the old Map Room without glancing up at the phony alignment of pins. The admirals grumbled about such extravagance. Kirkland's playing catch-the-spy again, but they didn't interfere with the Secret Service men who went in and out wearing high Navy collars. There were enough admirals strolling in the lobby to populate half the armadas of the world.

Kirkland could order a room to be built, but he didn't know what to do with Oliver. Locking him in the attic wasn't any good. The Boss would scream for his Ollie. "Where's the child?" Horn did have a quick solution. Murder the boy. Lure him into a rowboat, attach lead weights to his feet, and drown him in the Tidal Basin. Nothing short of that would rid them of his presence.

The boy had created a scare in the White House, "the Franklin scare." He had compromised the Boss, made him vulnerable to attack from every conceivable point, known and unknown. Franklin Roosevelt, without being aware of it, had a multitude of wounds under his blanket, wounds that could rot away at him, turn an ugly black, and produce a stink with enough potency to deprive him of his job. The wounds had come from Oliver Beebe.

October was a ticklish month. You couldn't scratch out Beebe during an election campaign, or throw him in the Navy brig for having joined the club of a lunatic marqués. It would have made a lovely catch for the Dewey people if they could advertise how Oliver appeared in the marqués' diaries. Senators would be standing at the gates to see the spy who worked for FDR. You wouldn't have needed an election. Dewey could have brought his luggage to the White House and declared himself Commander-in-Chief.

The boy would have to stay on until November. After the balloting, Kirkland would find a box for Oliver Beebe. He'd return him to the Navy with his barbering kit and tell the Boss, "Oliver had a breakdown. He's been with his scissors too much. It's a case of loneliness. He couldn't adjust to that attic life. The sea will cure him, Mr. President. Destroyer duty, that's what the admirals recommend."

But Kirkland had his doubts, and they gnawed at him. Was he the only one with information on Oliver's link to the marqués? Kirkland and his men were infants in the espionage war that bloomed in Mr. Roosevelt's city. You could pick counterspies off any magnolia tree in Washington. Edgar Hoover must have had those diaries long before District 16 copied them out of the marqués' desk. Why didn't Edgar go right to the Boss and say that Oliver was climbing in too deep with the Liberty Club? Unless Ollie was related to the FBI?

He had his morning tea at the White House and walked to the Justice Department. No one welcomed him in the offices of the FBI, although Edgar's black chauffeur Bill did acknowledge that Kirkland was alive.

"I can't find your name in Mr. Hoover's book."

"I didn't make an appointment with him."

"Pity, Mr. Horn. The Director won't see you unless you're in the book."

"He can take care of all his appointments, Bill. I'll wait."

Horn couldn't squeeze a cup of coffee out of the Bureau. Secretaries shunned the old man. He had to occupy himself with John Dillinger's death mask, grinning out of a glass case with tunneled nostrils, cheeks, and eyes, and photographs of Edgar on the wall, Edgar in little exercises of glory. With Shirley Temple on his lap, with Gable, with Dorothy Lamour, or scowling at Gene Tunney.

The anteroom filled and emptied twice before Edgar's chauffeur smiled on Kirkland Horn. "The Director has a minute for you. I'll take you in." Kirkland got behind Bill and shuffled into the office on his rubber soles. The FBI had a sanctity and a whole shopping bag of rituals and taboos that reminded Horn of a nursery school. You whispered and crept on your toes inside the Bureau. Hoover was a little man, and it was smart to

make your height seem negligible around him. Bill said,
"Mr. Horn of the White House," and left Kirkland alone
with the FBI.

Edgar wouldn't kneel to any climate beyond his own
door. He held on to the seasons he liked best, enjoying
pale colors in February as much as he did in July. It was
October now, and he wore a white linen suit with a
handkerchief in his pocket. He didn't get up for Kirkland
Horn.

"Edgar, what's going on with Oliver Beebe? Is he
mixed up in the war games you're having with Major
Colbert? Who's been feeding him to the Liberty Club?
Edgar, was it you?"

"Nothing will happen to the sailor boy."

"You can hang Beebe out the window, and it
wouldn't bother me. But tell your men that I don't want
any shit from the Liberty Club landing on my roof. If the
President is hurt by this, you won't be fighting Colbert
any more. I'll come down to Justice with a cannon and
blow out every bit of glass."

The Director laughed. "I'll help you with your cannon. A bombardment might be healthy for us, Kirk."

"Edgar, the President is fond of that boy. He relies
on Oliver Beebe."

"I told you, nothing will happen to the sailor."

"Edgar, we're talking about FDR. The President
can be an angry Dutchman if you step on his face."

It was all trumpery. That little son-of-a-bitch in the
white suit had Congress licking out of his hand. Edgar
would go up to the Hill and sing about the exploits of his
men. He didn't have to smile and ask for money. The FBI
had three Pierce-Arrows for Edgar to use, so he wouldn't
have to worry about any of them sitting in the garage

with a broken chassis. And Kirkland had to beg and beg to get the President a new armored car. The old bus he had once belonged to Al Capone. The President of the United States rode around in a gangster's car.

Kirkland didn't wave to chauffeur Bill. He walked out of the FBI. He didn't think Edgar was scouting for the Republican party. If the Bureau had sent in reports to Governor Dewey, every paper in America would be howling for Oliver's throat. Edgar liked to sit on his files. Was he waiting to embarrass Major Colbert? Or watching if Dewey could win?

You heard Dewey, Dewey everywhere; people wore his buttons and gossiped about the doddering king and his bucktoothed wife, but Roosevelt climbed out of bed in October to campaign with the boy at his side, and Dewey crept away from the election with nothing more than his hat, coat, and his Republican skin.

Kirkland was too late with Oliver Beebe. He couldn't force the boy to disappear. What was the point of fetching him out of the attic, if the admirals wouldn't take Oliver back and hide him in some godforsaken ship. They were growing jittery around a sailor who was with the President mornings and afternoons.

So Kirkland had to scratch at Beebe by himself. The minute Oliver came down from the attic, a Secret Service man was assigned to cover him, even if Ollie went in to shave the President. Kirkland could fix a shadow on Oliver, but what else could he do? FDR was nuts about the boy. You couldn't tear Oliver away. The Boss would have taken to his bed, chewed toast with Fala, and locked admirals, country, war, and the First Lady out of his room.

Kirkland had another pest on his hands: Major Colbert. The Major had gone berserk over a pack of wild dogs. There were dogs in the alleys, everybody knew that. They would spill into the avenues from time to time, looking for food. They happened to forage close to the White House last week. The dogs entered Lafayette Park, overturned a few garbage bins, and peed on the President's gate. Fucking Colbert, he saw the fouling of the gates as a violation of government property and a threat to the President's life. He wanted to annihilate the dogs. But Kirkland wasn't going to lend him the White House detail to rush into the alleys and murder a pack of starving dogs. He refused to give any of his men to Major Colbert.

It was the middle of November, the mansion was dark, and Kirkland made his rounds. Mrs. Roosevelt was at the Mayflower with a group of female correspondents. Oliver was in the attic. The Boss was asleep. Kirkland was on the state floor, outside the East Room, with his flashlight. No memories knocked in his head. He didn't think of cotillions, Navy bands, quadrilles of ten, twenty, thirty years ago. He could smell nothing but mold in the walls. He didn't try to skunk out history from the corners of a room. He had little toleration for ghosts. Grover Cleveland never appeared in front of his eyes. Kirkland would only deal with one President at a time.

The maids had a different story. They were hearing the creaks again. "The devil's in this ol' house." Then it was a crash under the sewing room, a crash that whistled between the walls and sent the mice stirring to another district. The maids pleaded with Oliver. He had to give up his movie magazine, and a special item on Dane Clark. He got into his pants and jumper for the maids and went down to the Roosevelt floor. It was quiet. He wouldn't disturb the grand duchess who had the Lincoln Bedroom for the night. But he did peek in on the Boss. Fala was in his basket eating a rubber doll. FDR's eyes were closed. Oliver went down one more flight.

He didn't have to poke very hard. Kirkland Horn was lying in the East Room, near the big piano. Oliver ran upstairs for his pillow. He put it under Kirkland's head. The old man had dry lips and icy eyebrows. His ears began to twitch, and Oliver could tell that he was coming out of a funny kind of sleep. The twitching stopped. Oliver held his hand. He didn't ask silly questions about what Kirkland was doing on the floor.

"Would you like a glass of water, Mr. Horn?"

It took a while for the old man to answer Ollie. "I'm fine," he said in a wispy voice. "Thank you, Mr. Beebe." He stood up without Oliver, brushed off his knees, and walked away from the piano.

Oliver's
Pompadour

TWENTY-ONE

A fever struck the District in the middle of December. The streets cleared of government girls. It had nothing to do with the war. Sinatra was in town. He had three shows a day at the Bryant, and that was enough to bring pandemonium to any city in the Free World. You needed every available cop, and a contingent of marines, to control the mobs inside and outside the Bryant. But Frankie wouldn't sing without the President's wife: he wanted Eleanor at his first matinee.

It was a bitch for the Secret Service. You had to protect "Rover" (Eleanor's code name) without stepping on her feet. She despised an escort in public places. So Kirkland Horn planted female agents in the balcony for Mrs. R.

"Rover" arrived on the arm of Oliver Beebe. The boy was neutral about Sinatra. But he wouldn't refuse the First Lady. It took half a dozen marines to get them to their balcony seats. Oliver was the only male in his row. He couldn't believe the noises that women could make. They scratched, wiggled, snapped garter belts, chewed gum, waiting for Sinatra.

All they could see was a band in the pit, and a chorus of three male singers on stage. These men called themselves "Sinatra's Cavaliers." The government girls wouldn't listen to their crooning. The Cavaliers stood with hands on each other's hips and pumped their knees with each bit of syncopation. The garter belts killed their highs and lows.

Then a nervous current, like an electrical quilt, grabbed the auditorium and silenced the girls. Sinatra was on stage. What's so special? Oliver thought. A skinny guy dressed in dark blue. Cheekbones, padded shoulders, and a pompadour. He had more hollows in his face than Anita's scarecrow. What did he do for nourishment, this Frank Sinatra?

The girls recovered from that initial shock of Frankie on stage. They began to whisper and moan, "Frankie, Frankie Boy." Oliver was embarrassed for the First Lady. But Eleanor smiled at him.

Noises came from the pit. The band was striking up a song for Sinatra and the Cavaliers. The girls didn't know what to do when Frankie opened his mouth. Should they scream, bite their fingers, swoon under the seats? They would miss one of Frankie's syllables. He sang "Mairzy Doats," "Praise the Lord and Pass the Ammunition," and "Mr. In-Between." But the girls were dying for love songs. Frankie had to croon for them. Oliver could feel the shivers around him during "One For My Baby." That hollow boy had a voice that could cause insanity in a theatre. He sang "You'll Never Know (How Much I Love You)," with his eyes on Mrs. Roosevelt. He was serenading America's First Lady. But the words came like poison to Oliver Beebe. Sinatra had a murderous warble in his throat. He wasn't posturing on a stage. He couldn't have made Ollie and the girls shudder so hard with a neat, twopenny performance in the afternoon. The hollow boy had a way of clutching at you. He took your mind off the war, your fiancé in the Marines, butter shortages, movie stars. You let Frankie's voice stroke you to sleep.

It was a misery for Oliver to sit with Mrs. Roosevelt and hear "You'll Never Know." The crooning made him think of Anita. Did Sinatra have a song about brothers and sisters with no pajamas? Ollie began to wish he'd never come to the Bryant.

There was bedlam at the end of the show. The girls refused to let Sinatra off the stage. "Frankie, don't go!" He had to give them "The White Cliffs of Dover," and then lock himself in his dressing room, with the Cavaliers standing in his wake. The girls wouldn't look at any male chorus. They tried to storm the dressing room, but the marines held them off. You would swear you were visiting a battlefield. The girls had pulled strips of leather from the seats in their frenzy to get near Sinatra.

He wouldn't leave the theatre without shaking Mrs. Roosevelt's hand. The marines had to run upstairs and pluck Mrs. Roosevelt and her sailor from the balcony. The girls kept eying Oliver Beebe. They weren't really interested in him. It was the pompadour under his sailor hat. The pompadour reminded them of Frank.

The marines got Oliver and Mrs. Roosevelt into the dressing room. Now Beebe could spy on that hollow boy. He was skinny, so skinny, with suspenders hooked over his shirt, and a velvet bowtie sitting on his throat. The crooner was out of cigarettes. Oliver sacrificed his last two Camels for him. Frankie had Eleanor's blue-gray eyes. They talked about her grandchildren, radio, FDR, and the war. Frankie could tell that Mrs. Roosevelt liked his bowtie. Her husband, the President, was also fond of bowties. Frankie snapped the tie off his throat and gave it to her as a memento of her afternoon at the Bryant. The First Lady was shy about such things. She thanked the crooner with a kiss on the cheek. Then the marines escorted her and the sailor out of the dressing room.

Oliver didn't covet Frankie's bowtie. He had other souvenirs. He left the Bryant with the memory of love songs that ate into his guts. It was chilly on Pennsylvania Avenue, and Oliver didn't have anything warm under his peacoat. Navy men were supposed to wear regulation "blues" in December, with a double thickness of wool. But Oliver had his own sense of Navy gear. He despised the feel of wool.

Roosevelt didn't object to "winter whites" on the boy. FDR loved to joke about Oliver's dread of wool. "The child's as finicky as the Pup. All they ever do is scratch, scratch, scratch."

Laying in for winter, Oliver let his hair grow out. He had a pompadour that started high on his forehead and stood like a dark mop over his widow's peak. It would make his hat bob while Oliver was on the stairs. The pompadour was against Navy rules. A seaman's scalp should have resembled an onion with bristles on top. Ollie was no fucking crooner. You couldn't fight the Japs with a pompadour. But the admirals in the White House were loath to toss rules at Oliver Beebe. This barber was now the closest man to the President's ear. It was the first time in naval history that admirals and vice admirals had to genuflect to a seaman first class. They were the ones who whipped out their elbows as Oliver went by them in a dreamy state. Sinatra had given the boy a bad December. No mansion could comfort him, with its admirals and guest kings. He was lonely for Anita.

"Oliver?"

He didn't hear them, or notice the salutes. The boy was deep in thought. It wasn't always fun to board with a President. You couldn't invite your sister to the house.

The admirals had to curl their bodies out of his way. "Ollie, how's the Boss?"

"He's in his pajamas," Oliver said.

"Did he wake with a cough?"

"I don't remember. But Fala's hair got in his nose, and the Boss had to sneeze."

"Oliver, for God's sake, is he sharp this morning? Will he talk to us?"

"Wait until tomorrow."

Dressed in wool, with grave insignias on themselves, anchors, eagles, and silver stars, they set their clocks by Oliver's pompadour, because they couldn't grasp the Boss' moods without that bobbing head. The false Map Room, erected by Kirkland Horn, ran with a precision and clarity that mystified the White House clerks who couldn't have known about such a room. Horn's "admirals" developed an amazing jabber around their stale war charts. They marched in and out with briefcases, moved colored pins on the wall like no other human beings. The genuine, true-star admirals did nothing but bark. They bickered with the generals, they bickered with their own aides. And they needed Poppa Roosevelt to halt the rancor in their secret room. Poppa was upstairs in his pajamas. He had a head cold today. The admirals wouldn't knock on his door.

Oliver Beebe wasn't simply a broker for the admirals. Senators and bureaucrats from the East Wing relied on him. If he felt your cause was good, Ollie might smuggle you into the bedroom. You'd find the Boss in his pajamas and an ugly gray robe, sitting with Fala and the Secretary of War. A bathrobe didn't make an invalid of him. FDR had recovered enough from his head cold to take a Camel after breakfast. He would be biting on his ivory holder when he said, "Come in." Anybody would know he was the Commander-in-Chief. You could hear him lecturing on the dismal fate of the German people. "They'll have to live without cannons and gliders for fifty years. I don't want a man or child in uniform. They can tend lettuce with the women in the fields." Then he would smile, adjust his pince-nez, and say, "Ollie, get the Senator a chair."

The newsmen were also on Oliver's neck. Was the major theatre of the war going to be Roosevelt's mahogany bed? Would he come downstairs before Christmas? Without a president to enlighten them, they seized upon Oliver's hairdo. "That pompadour is FDR's weather vane. You have to watch how it dips and blows. Beware if it drops over Ollie's right eye. It means the Boss is mad at the world."

One of the Negro butlers, a beautiful man with an angry old-young face, didn't take his eyes off the pompadour.

"What's your name?" Oliver said.

"Me, sir? Sam."

"How long have you been here, Sam?"

"A month, sir."

"That's weird. I never saw you until today."

"I've been hopping around, Mr. Oliver. Tearing through the pantry for Mrs. Roosevelt and her friends."

Something about the butler's voice disturbed Oliver Beebe. It was mechanical, distant, as if an artificial larynx had been installed in his throat, a piece of exquisite machinery that could grind out perfect scraps of English under the butler's jaws.

"Why do you call me 'Mr. Oliver'?"

"Everybody knows about you, sir. You're the big man in the pantry. The cooks say the Boss is hopeless without Mr. Oliver. The bush on your head brings him luck."

"Are you sure your name is Sam?"

To escape reporters, admirals, and the significance of his own pompadour, Oliver went up to the roof. He could huddle with the machine gunners and not say a word. The machine gunners didn't have any use for a pompadour. They had to worry about chilblains and frozen ammunition. Oliver envied their peaceful days. The machine gunners were always quiet. Talking against the wind would have given them a case of blue lips. A raucous, inhuman bell shook the flooring of Oliver's hideaway. "Goddamn," he said, catching wind in his mouth.

A telephone rang under Oliver's feet. He could have ignored it. But suppose FDR was trying to buzz him? He wouldn't play hard to get with the Boss. So he climbed down to his room. He got the White House switchboard and Ethel Rosenquist. "Oliver," she said, in a somber tone. "Here's your party."

A man on the other end of the line asked Oliver if he would like to eat with J. Edgar Hoover at Harvey's restaurant.

"That depends," Oliver said.

"I beg your pardon. Depends on what?"

"The hour," Oliver said. "The Boss goes to bed at nine, and I have to tuck him in."

"Nine o'clock then, Mr. Beebe. We'll send a car for you."

Ethel Rosenquist sat on the wire and listened to Oliver talk. She told people about Oliver's date with the FBI. The maids were tittering at him by six o'clock. "Scared, Mr. Ollie? The FBI eats young sailors like you."

Oliver was glad to get away from the mansion for an hour. The pompadour was disrupting his life. He arrived at the north gate in his peacoat. It was ten after nine. A limousine brought him to Harvey's. The waiters bid with each other for the right to check his coat. It took four of those guys to seat him at Mr. Hoover's table.

The G-man was lord of the menu tonight. "Striped bass for me, Joseph, and lobster for the boy."

"Mr. Hoover, Harvey's doesn't serve lobster after eight. That's because our submarines keep bumping into the lobster pots off Tangier Island."

"Ollie," the G-man said. "I asked the chef to save a ten-pounder for you."

They had a feast that troubled Oliver because he couldn't reconcile it with the rationbook existence of 1944. The Boss ate sweetbreads for a month, and Oliver had ten pounds of meat and claws. The lobster's carapace covered the entire dish, and the tail bent over Oliver's lap. The chef came out of the kitchen to bone Mr. Hoover's fish.

Oliver was silent through most of the meal. The lobster-splitting was the only noise he made. Then he opened his mouth to speak. "Sam my ass! I know who that butler is. He's the wild man of Tangier."

And Oliver fell silent again. The G-man dropped him off at the White House. "Thank you, Mr. Hoover. Goodbye." He went down into the basement. The butlers stood with their collars open, shining Mrs. Roosevelt's teapots. "Where's Sam?"

"He's out, Mr. Ollie."

"Ask him how he escaped from the deaf and dumb school."

"We will."

"A butler's suit can't change a guy. He's Jonathan, the wild man."

"Mr. Ollie, who's that?"

You couldn't get much satisfaction from the butlers. Oliver climbed upstairs.

TWENTY-TWO

T hat mop of hair on Oliver's head was no divin-
ing rod. It couldn't help him ferret out Sam. He would
coerce the maids into a corner, badger them, trade tootsie rolls for news. The maids unwrapped the tootsie rolls
and bit off each little neck of candy. But their news wasn't
any good. "Sam?" they said. "You mean the colored
fella who wears the coat with monkey tails for Miss Eleanor? That varmint? He sneaks into the laundry room and
smells white folks' underpants. You don't want nothin to
do with Sam. Mr. Kirkland is looking to throw him out."

Ollie couldn't find the butler anywhere in the house.
The wild man was avoiding him. Oliver wasn't thick.
There had to be a pact among Mrs. Roosevelt's girls to
hide Sam's identity and keep the wild man under cover.
What were the First Lady's motives? Did she think Oliver
would snitch to FDR that a crazy nigger was bowing and
serving cocktails in the Blue Room? Hadn't the sailor
befriended Jonathan, taught him the fundamentals of civilized life? But Ollie could only brood at odd moments.
The President recovered from his head cold, and Oliver
had to get him out of pajamas and into the tub, shave
him, dress him, and wheel him to the oval office, while
Fala nibbled Oliver's cuffs. "Boss, tell the Pup to eat

somebody else's pants. I'm wearing government clothes."

FDR would throw his head back, clinch his eyes, and roar. "Don't you love it? Child, the Navy will buy you a new pair of pants."

That old, familiar laugh would bring reporters scampering behind the wheelchair. A roaring President couldn't be ill. Lads, they'd whisper to themselves, looks like we have a President today. The Boss is out of bed.

The reporters would crowd up to Oliver's elbows. "Mr. President, how do you feel?"

"Grand. Simply grand."

You couldn't believe the number of foreign diplomats, chargés d'affaires, gentlemen farmers, movie actors, and fallen kings who had to see the Boss. The sailor clocked every single visit. He would rush into the oval office after twenty minutes, and it didn't matter whether FDR was in the middle of a story. Oliver had the power to interrupt. "Boss, that's it for King Paul. You have ten more customers outside."

And FDR would play the victim. He was captive to a merciless sailor. What could he do? He gave his best wishes to the king's wife and let Oliver get rid of his majesty, King Paul. The chargés d'affaires soon realized that their own interests lay with Oliver. They would woo him in the lobby as often as they could. "Mr. Beebe, what about a Wednesday lunch?"

"Thank you. I have my lunches with the Boss."

"A Thursday dinner then?"

"Impossible," Oliver said. "I don't take any dinners without Mr. J. Edgar Hoover's advice."

The chargés d'affaires would nod politely and run. Oliver wasn't telling a lie. A limousine would come for

him almost every other night, after he put FDR to sleep.
They didn't always dine at Harvey's. The G-man liked
the snails at Aux Trois Mousquetaires. And if the owners
begged him often enough, Edgar might taste the bluefish
at the Occidental restaurant. Sometimes they would go
into the kitchen, so Oliver could watch the chefs stuff a
capon. He was amazed how far a human hand could
reach into a rooster's ass.

When dinner was over, the G-man would take him
to the "sky bar" on top of the Washington Hotel. It
wasn't a boisterous after-hours club for senators and
showy people. The "sky bar" was where the gentler
natives of the District could collect under a striped awn-
ing with sugar and lime in their whiskey and stare out at
a drab winter mist. Only the quietest "aborigines" came
to the Washington Roof. The G-man wouldn't be disturbed by autograph-hunters, rowdy soldiers, mean,
unescorted women, and abandoned wives. Two chairs
would be waiting for him at the southern end of the
lounge. The G-man didn't have to shake anybody's hand,
or repeat for the hundred, hundredth time how "Lepke"
Buchalter surrendered to him in New York. He could sit
with the President's sailor, both of them drinking a lime
concoction that couldn't have made Shirley Temple close
her eyes. The G-man wasn't holding court. He'd have
growled at any man who wanted to conduct business with
him on the Washington Roof. He liked to watch the
darkened White House across the road and complain
about the limes to Oliver Beebe.

Oliver wasn't listening. Airplane motors ground
over his head like disgusting metal teeth. The search-
lights on Capitol Hill threw great yellow beams over the
city that could pierce government buildings, wiggle like

mustard-colored worms, and bend away from the sky. But awnings, roofs, and miracle worms never got to Oliver. His psyche had been poisoned by a man and a woman a few chairs down from him. The dark bulbs in the wall probed very little of the couple, but Oliver could sense the fullness of their mouths, eyes, and throats. It was his sister and don Valentín's blond helpmate, Orlando Frayard. They weren't kissing or grunting in the chairs. Anita and Frayard were perfectly composed. They didn't have to bump on the Washington Roof to tell Ollie why Anita had closed herself to him. Anita couldn't sit still with a man for very long. The blond one, Orlando, was her new sweetheart.

A horrible nausea grabbed at Oliver's entrails. He pushed his body out of the chair, his face turning to chalk. He would have puked on half a dozen "aborigines" if he hadn't clamped his mouth with a fist. He crept over to the men's room, locked himself inside a stall, got down on his knees, and vomited into the toilet. The sailor should have stuck to a diet of Baby Ruths. He couldn't hold down lobster, capon, and Harvey's shrimp.

Oliver took care of all the amenities. He flushed the toilet, unlocked the stall, washed his face in wartime lavender soap, straightened his neckerchief, and rinsed his mouth in the sink. He couldn't explain why he should be sobbing now. What other sailor lived in the White House, and had his evening meal with the FBI? Lucky boy, and he was crying into a public mirror. Ollie fared better in a gunboat. He should have kept to the sea. On dry land Oliver was made to crawl. Here he was, rolling on the floor in the men's room of the Washington Hotel, his white blouse attracting footprints, ants, and two-days' dust. He saw the curled piping under the sink, the moorings of the toilet bowls. 'Nita and Orlando Frayard. He wasn't jealous of the scarecrow. Vivian's sunken eyes, the bitter, twisting words out of the slash in his face, belonged to a cadaverous man. Ollie didn't care if his sister fucked a corpse. But Frayard was much too pretty. 'Nita wouldn't lie down with Ollie any more.

J. Edgar Hoover found him in the men's room, balled up with his knees against his chin, crud on his uniform, smiling a cat's crazy smile. "Ollie, what's wrong with you?"

"Nothing, grandpa."

The G-man knew the boy was in a fright. "You must have swallowed too many limes. You'll recover. Just count to ten, and the fuzziness will disappear."

He put his own white jacket on Oliver's shoulders, helped him to his feet, and walked him out of the men's room. But he couldn't rearrange the pompadour. It hung over Ollie's left eye like a pitiful rag.

Jonathan
Roosevelt

TWENTY-THREE

A gloom fell over Oliver, a pallor that tightened his lips and gave him a godawful grin. It was a look that terrified the Pup and sent the maids scurrying out of Oliver's room. "Mr. Kirkland aint the only devil in the house." Bumplines developed in the sailor's forehead from so much moodiness. The swollen knobs were a sign of brain fever, according to the nigger maids. "Watch it," they said. "Oliver's boiling up." A vein appeared below the pompadour, with purple and red branches that seemed to live inside the knobs. The maids called it "Oliver's lightnin' mark." When the brain fever got bad, and the knobs stuck out, and the lightnin' ripped, the maids would clutch their bosoms and crawl to the ends of the attic. "Poor Mr. Ollie. The devil's in him again."

It wasn't meanness in Oliver that made his forehead "rip." His head bulged with grief. He wouldn't go into the basement any more to interview the butlers. He was sick of asking about the wild man of Tangier. Jonathan could hide from Oliver for the rest of his natural life. The sailor no longer cared. He had a sister who troubled him, and made the pompadour lie low on his widow's peak.

He found a bowtie, a shirt collar, and a pair of butler's underpants on the steps. It wasn't the first time

Ollie had tripped against a bowtie and BVD's. The wild man had a habit of undressing in the halls. The maids would pick up the various items of clothes long before Mr. Franklin was awake. They erased all of Jonathan's tracks, the pee stains on a rug, the wet patches where he had bitten into the wall, the globs of ketchup in the corner where Jonathan had settled down to eat, so that the wild man could remain invisible to almost everybody in the house. He was an uncommon butler, who could drop his britches without warning, serve a cocktail with slices of cucumber inside. Oliver wanted no part of him. He wasn't going to educate Jonathan again. Let the maids attend to the wild man's BVD's.

You could hear a bit of shrieking every night. It wasn't loud enough to disturb a President's sleep. The maids would mumble devil stories, but it was only a cover-up. They knew what Jonathan's shrieks were like. The wild man couldn't seem to rest in the dark.

Oliver had his movie magazines in case a bitter noise woke him at five in the morning. Or memories of Anita. He put on his pajamas, said goodnight to the machine gunners on the roof, and crawled into bed. His closet began to rumble a bit. He didn't run downstairs for the Secret Service. "Jonathan, get the hell out of there."

The closet opened, and a wild man fell out. He had nothing under his butler's coat except nipples, broad kneecaps, and a pair of balls that were tucked into his thighs. His toenails were fierce as a shark's teeth. He could have ripped off Oliver's face with them. But Ollie wouldn't capitulate to a butler's toes.

"If you say your name is Sam, I'll give you to the machine gunners for target practice. Who are you?"

"Jonathan Roosevelt, Franklin's other child."

"Don't get smart. Who are you?"

"Jonathan. Plain John."

That metallic purr in the wild man's throat still annoyed Oliver. "Who learned you to speak like that?"

"Like what, Mr. Ollie."

"Like a goddamn phonograph machine. Didn't they put you in that school for nigger mutes in Maryland somewhere?"

"They did, Mr. Ollie."

"Then why are you a talking butler now?"

"It's the Navy's fault. Three Navy doctors came to the school and looked down my throat. They said I was born with a flap of skin squeezing against my voice box, and that was the only speech impediment I ever had. It was lying there like a lazy knot, strangling my words. They didn't have the heart to leave me at school. They snuck me into their Navy hospital and cut that flap out of me."

"Is that all the Navy men did?"

"No, Mr. Ollie. They put a resonator in my throat."

"What's that?" Oliver said, picturing the wild man as a contraption the Navy had produced, half man, half metal, with a Frankenstein voice.

"It's an aluminum pin, Mr. Ollie, a baby tongue about a quarter of an inch high that makes an echo for me."

"A pin can't think out the right word. I asked you once. Who learned you to speak?"

"A voice technician. They locked me in a room with her. They wouldn't let me eat until I listened to her records. I had to pronounce cat and dog with her fingers in my mouth. She built up my vocabulary."

"Was she a white woman?"

"Yes, Mr. Ollie."

"Did she get funny with you?"

"How's that?"

"Did her fingers go in more places than your mouth?"

"No, Mr. Ollie."

Oliver frowned at the wild man. He'd never heard such a ridiculous story. "How did you get from the hospital to here? And no lies."

"They couldn't send me back to the school, Mr. Ollie, when I could talk. It might have disrupted the children, hearing me recite Shakespeare, which I got from the records. And I wasn't any good for the Navy, because they couldn't make a mess boy out of me. I had too much articulation for that, the doctors said. So they got in touch with Mrs. Roosevelt. They threatened to row me home to Tangier Island. Poor Mrs. Franklin didn't have a choice. That's how I became a butler, Mr. Ollie, swear to God."

"What's all this hiding for? And who gave you the name Sam?"

"It was election time, Mr. Ollie, and Mrs. Roosevelt's secretaries were afraid the Republicans would run all over Mr. Franklin if they discovered a wild man like me was mixing drinks in the White House. They kept Jonathan a secret and called me Sam."

"That's fine for other people, but you didn't have to sneak around Oliver Beebe."

"They told me to, Mr. Ollie. They said, 'Samuel, you'd better shun that sailor.' "

"Why?"

"Because you're Mr. Franklin's monkey, his personal ape. The secretaries are scared of you."

Oliver was perturbed. "They're cracked, those ladies. I cut hair. I take off the Boss' socks. I massage his back."

"They say nobody can get near Mr. Franklin without you. All his appointments are sewed up. 'Clear it with Ollie.' That's the formula of the month."

"The Boss likes to chat," Oliver said. "If I didn't kick out those phony kings, they'd be hanging on to his desk and asking about a lost princess in Hungary when Mr. Roosevelt has to watch out for the whole fucking world."

The wild man's ears began to prick. He rushed over to the closet and locked himself in. "Please, Mr. Ollie," he groaned through the door. "Don't let that devil lay his hand on me."

There were footsteps in the hall. Kirkland Horn came into Oliver's room. "Have you seen the new butler, Mr. Beebe?"

"I don't entertain butlers, Mr. Horn."

"I'm glad. Only he dribbled parts of his uniform on the stairs. And they lead up to the attic."

"Why don't you peek under my bed?"

"Not tonight. . . . Give my love to Edgar."

"I will."

The wild man wouldn't come out of the closet. "Jonathan, I told you, he's gone downstairs."

"Thank you, Mr. Ollie, but I'll sit where I am."

The sailor put out the light. He offered Jonathan a pillow, but the wild man preferred to sleep in a raw state. Jonathan's bitter cry woke him twice. Oliver didn't get out of bed. The wild man was safe in Oliver's closet. Shrieking was something Jonathan had to do.

TWENTY-FOUR

It was in and out of closets for Jonathan Roosevelt, the wild man who shed his underwear. Twice a day he would report to the basement, don crisp white sleeves and a dark coat, and carry up hors d'oeuvres to diplomats, musicians, actors, professors, and house guests of Mr. and Mrs. Roosevelt. It would be up again and down again with crackers and shreds of stinky fish. The cooks and maids and veteran butlers were constantly tugging on his coat. "Your tails are dirty, Sam. Let me scrub them with ammonia. And don't pick at your bowtie." He had twenty fathers and mothers to look over him, gracious servants in starched uniforms, to steer him out of trouble. If he sank a carrot in your vermouth, a nice butler would come out of the woodwork to whisk that glass away and get you another drink.

The butlers were in cahoots with Mr. Franklin's wife. The First Lady wanted to find a niche for Jonathan Roosevelt, a home where the wild man could exercise his vocabulary, chat with fellow humans, and stay alive. But old man Horn was alert to a butler with picky ways. How much of a check could he run on this Samuel? The boy had been recommended by surgeons in the Navy and hired by Mrs. Roosevelt. He was under Eleanor's cloak.

But if butler Sam became the least bit dangerous to the Boss, Kirkland would have to tear him off at the elbow and tie him to the dumbwaiter. Then Mrs. Roosevelt could keep him in the house.

Jonathan had to devote a good part of himself to the task of ducking Kirkland Horn and Detail 16. Kirkland's men would steal crackers off his tray and follow him into the lav. "How are you, Sammy? Looking swell?" The wild man could survive their taunts, but that red mustache would make him sweat in early winter. The maids, his guardians in the attic, had told him about the evil bend of Mr. Kirkland's mustache. "That's the devil biting his lip."

So Jonathan slept in closets and peed quietly on a rug. Oliver Beebe, the nigger deaf and dumb school, and the Navy voice technician had taught him to count, and to read the days and months of the year. The wild man had no past and no future until the oystermen of Tangier found him in July. He didn't know who had put him on Tangier Island. He woke with the sun in his face, crawled on his belly, speared fish in the shallows with his sharp toes. Does a wild man have a mom and dad? Jonathan couldn't remember. The knowledge of April or January, Christmas, Easter, and Mother's Day, would have been useless to him. He could slap open a gourd, scoop ants out of a tree with his tongue, squash a poisonous berry. But he'd fallen prey to a gang of drunken oystermen. They'd stumbled over Jonathan in the grass, jeered at him, called him "Jap, Jap," hung him upside down, paddled his buttocks, took him out of his timeless, dreamy life, and threw him into recorded history: Mrs. Roosevelt, the mayor of Tangier, Maryland, the District of Columbia, Shakespeare, and Oliver Beebe.

Jonathan didn't long for his earlier, purer state. He'd been a grubby wild man on Tangier, a mute rolling in the mud. He was neither happy nor unhappy, just an ignoramus with yellow mud on his back. He'd had earaches, chills, strong fevers, the shits. A maddened fox had bitten off sections of his heel. A huge, long-nosed bird nearly sucked out his eye. Bees drove him off a mountain for breaking into the wrong honeycomb.

His luck didn't improve away from Tangier. He had a benefactress in Mrs. Roosevelt. She was kind to him, the First Lady, lending him a surname, a house, and a butler's coat. He would go up to her sitting room and drink a glass of milk with the First Lady. She wasn't solemn with the wild man. She would laugh at her own creamy mustache and make a note to buy toothbrushes for Jonathan and herself. She didn't lay snares for Jonathan, trick him into revealing the weaker side of his nature. She only asked how he was. He would answer, "Splendid, ma'am," because he didn't want to burden her with the confusions of a wild man. The White House wasn't a satisfactory home for Jonathan Roosevelt. He lived in terror there. It was more than Mr. Kirkland and his detail of men. It was rubbing up against so many other creatures. The wild man had to distinguish between admirals, secretaries, kings, ambassadors, butlers like himself, the Secret Service, and a dog. He couldn't grasp the function they all played. Each of them had a particular dance, a particular costume, a particular smell, and it made the wild man crazy. He would howl at night, cry in his sleep, the resonator scratching his throat, as he dreamt how to say hello to an admiral, a chef, or Murray, the Outlaw of Fala Hill.

Humans filled Jonathan with an enormous dread.

His nose would twitch while he was in their company. Living around them put dandruff in his hair. And when they came up close without any warning, Jonathan got the urge to leap out of his puckered skin. He lost his job on account of that. One evening, just before Christmas, as Jonathan was dropping his shoes, socks, bowtie, and underpants on the stairs, a Secret Service man stole up behind him and shouted in his ear. "Boo!" Jonathan spun into the railing and flicked out his knee. It was nothing more than the reflex action of a butler trapped without his shoes. But the Secret Service man had begun to stoop with laughter at the prospect of a frightened wild man, and Jonathan's toes happened to sting him in the face. You could hear the rip of a man's cheek. A line of blood started at the Secret Service man's eyebrow and raced to the hollows under his ear. He clutched his head, looked at Jonathan Roosevelt, and wandered towards the infirmary downstairs.

The maids brought the wild man to Oliver's room. "Lord," they said, "Sam's destroyed himself. We should have cut his toenails. He scratched one of Mr. Kirkland's babies with his damn foot."

"I'm not interested," Oliver said, watching Jonathan shiver without his clothes.

"They'll arrest him, Mr. Ollie, if you don't help. Mrs. Franklin can't protect him now."

It was late, and freezing in the attic, and Oliver was numb with jealousy over Orlando Frayard. "What can I do?" he muttered from his blanket.

"Get him away from this house."

They threw onto the wild man's back whatever civilian clothes Oliver had in his closet. And a hat that held tight to Jonathan's skull. He looked like a gigantic child in Oliver's pants and shirt. Buttons popped on his chest. Oliver's cuffs met him at the elbows and wouldn't embrace his wrists. But enough of him was bundled for a winter night. Oliver led him into the basement and over to the south porch, the butlers peeking into the halls for Kirkland and his men. The soldiers on the lawn wouldn't challenge Oliver Beebe. "Me and the egg man," he told the sentries at the gate. It was an odd hour for an egg man to be on the grounds, but Oliver didn't care. He was Mr. Franklin's monkey, and he could say anything that came into his head. The sentries saluted him, and he pushed Jonathan off the President's grounds and into the nigger lanes surrounding New York Avenue.

They landed in Crawfish Alley. The only person Oliver knew that might accommodate a wild man was the cathouse lady, Odessa Brown. "Don't you tell me who he is, Mr. Ollie. I'll take him in. He's a cute one. He can sweep up for my girls."

Horn's men searched high and low for the butler who had wounded one of them. They blustered through the attic, stripping down Oliver's bed while he was still under the covers. They tore the bedclothes away, and Oliver had to lie on a pissy-looking mattress. He wasn't going to climb out of his pajamas to satisfy Kirkland Horn. They stood in Oliver's closet punching all his coats, in case Jonathan was lurking inside. They stepped on Oliver's movie magazines, took apart his telescope and splintered the glass. "Where the Christ is Sam?"

Then Oliver's phone rang. A Secret Service man clawed impatiently at the receiver. "Hello? Who's this?" His face turned a horrible ashen color. He handed the phone to Ollie.

"Yes, Boss, I'll be down in a minute . . . no, Boss.

It's the Secret Service. They're helping me decorate my room."

The Secret Service men picked up their hats and skulked out of the attic. And Oliver went to bathe FDR. The President sat on his bathtub board, conversing with the Secretary of War, while Ollie sponged those great swimmer's shoulders that were going to flab. The Boss had developed a thick curtain of flesh on his wings since Ollie had come to the White House. He would stop in the middle of a sentence and wheeze. But the wheezing meant nothing to him.

"Child, give Poppa a cigarette."

Oliver had hidden the President's Camels behind the toilet seat.

"Boss, no smoking in the tub."

The President chomped on the ivory holder in his mouth and winked to the Secretary of War. "Henry, did you ever see such an obstinate child? I'll give him to the Army if he doesn't watch out."

Oliver felt sorry for the Secretary of War. He was an old man in a starched collar who had to sit on the edge of a tub and soak up steam from the President's bath. Oliver couldn't make much sense out of these bathroom conferences. They would grumble about "Winnie" and "Uncle Joe." Would "Winnie" go for this or go for that? What would the "russkies" say? The boy fell into a stupor scrubbing the President's back. The pain of being without Anita had broadened that mad grin on his face. Oliver seemed disconnected, as if his guts belonged to somebody else.

He sat at Harvey's that night with "Uncle Edgar." The G-man's pockets were stuffed with Christmas gifts from his own men at the Bureau, and he was absorbed in snipping the knots off every little package. Waiters had to come over and remove the rubbish of paper and string. Edgar toyed with pen and pencil sets, neckties with his initials woven into the silk, handcrafted slippers, Hickok belts, figurines made of bone, and a profusion of cuff links and handkerchiefs. The G-man didn't have any lasting affection for the objects on his table. He handed Oliver a pen and pencil set, destroying the card that had come with it. The boy was confused. Anita had driven Christmas out of his head.

The G-man stared at Oliver. He pretended to scratch the tablecloth with his thumb. "Oliver, the pen has a golden nib. It won't break on you."

Oliver said, "Merry Christmas." But he didn't have a gift for Mr. Hoover. He was bad about holidays. Christmas in Weehawken had been nothing but a drunken father and a dwarfish tree, without wassailing or the exchange of trinkets, Anita in an end room, with a fresh suitor behind the couch, Oliver with egg nog going sour.

The waiters began to collect near "Uncle Edgar" like a troop of penguins that could smile and scrape their feet. Items vanished from the table. There was a ritual of handshaking as the G-man doled out cuff links, handkerchiefs, and Hickok belts. "Thank you, Mr. Edgar, thank you, thank you, thank you."

Oliver couldn't keep his mind on the pen and pencil set. What could he do with a golden nib? His eyes drifted over Harvey's main floor, which was reserved for junior and senior diplomats, government czars, and celebrities like J. Edgar Hoover. Untitled people had to sit upstairs. But the boy cursed Harvey's order of things. Anita marched into the restaurant wearing a new winter coat.

She clung to Orlando Frayard. The waiters took their coats and scarves and seated them in a choice spot, near Harvey's window. Men and women at the other tables were staring at Anita. It wasn't the plunge of her neckline that made so many people goggle. Anita was zippered up to her throat. She didn't have any fanciful coiffure. Her hair was almost slovenly. It sat on her forehead in rough bangs. But she had enough energy in her face to pull fixtures off the walls.

She was more beautiful to Ollie than she'd ever been. She could have turned a restaurant to mud without delivering one smile. There was nothing artful or deliberate in that deep flush on Anita. Her coloring was ruthless and pure. You could have spent a year of your life nibbling on the furrows along her neck. Anita had a rude animal grace.

Oliver had to look away from her. His cat's grin crawled to the ends of his face. The G-man was horrified.

"Ollie, should I get the car?"

"No," he said, with a napkin over his face. He was shuddering now. His ears were the most awful crimson Edgar had ever known.

"Sailor, what can I do?"

Oliver pointed to Orlando Frayard. "That man by the window . . . he's a lowlife at the Spanish embassy, and a member of the Liberty Club. Orlando Frayard. He's chasing my sister. Could you hurt him, could you take his job away?"

"Ollie, I can't meddle in Spain's affairs . . . but I'll try."

Oliver took the napkin off his face. The grin had narrowed down. The boy could chew his lobster and think about the pen and pencil set. Couldn't he write messages on his wall with that golden nib? Let the maids scream when they saw his room. Oliver could mark up the attic, scribble "Alan Ladd loves Anita Beebe" wherever he liked.

Orlando Frayard

Orlando was crazy about Anita, the little bitch. He had a novia in Madrid, a fiancée with pure Andalusian blood, who would inherit a castle, two foundries, and a smelting plant in Cadiz when her papa died. He had seen his novia once. She was as blond as Orlando, with a pretty nose and a bachelor's degree from the University of Córdoba. She could cook, sew, and recite the best lines of Cervantes and Lope de Vega. He'd been betrothed to doña Isabel since her eleventh birthday. Orlando had no choice in the matter. He was supposed to sit tight until the end of the war. Then he had specific instructions to take the Pan American Clipper and join his fiancée.

The house of Frayard had offices in London, Paris, Atlanta, Georgia, and Madrid. The original Frayard got out of Rouen a hundred years ago to make his fortune in Madrid. The Frayards bred into the Spanish mercantile class and seized hold of the leather business. Now their fingers were everywhere. Orlando was meant to bring the foundries of Isabel into the family line. The house of Frayard would starve him, force him to exist at the level of a clerk, until it had Isabel for his wife.

None of his father's spies knew about Orlando's

little bitch. He took her dancing at the Mayflower Club and the Pall Mall Room of the Raleigh Hotel. But he had to discontinue that. Packs of sailors would arrive off the street to leer at her. So he danced with Anita in Vivian's room at the Willard Hotel, without sailors or a live band, and felt the thump of her heart against his chest. Their eyebrows wrinkled and touched. He could kiss her until the teeth dropped out of his head.

Orlando had been an exalted stockboy for the Frayards, a compiler of inventories. Then his father placed him at the chancellery, awarded him to the Franco regime. Two weeks at the chancellery, and Orlando understood that it was a crazy house. The agents of half a dozen countries marched through the building disguised as clerks, cleaning ladies, plumbers, and radio repairmen. The walls were bugged. You couldn't even trust the flower pots.

It was 1941. Orlando's superiors were in a euphoric state of mind. They expected Hitler to dance on the roof of the White House by the end of the year. Orlando pulled his nose and came to a decision. It was more profitable to sell himself to the losing side. If the Germans got to hang Herr Roosevelt, Orlando would hide in one of the nigger alleys, or sink back into the house of Frayard.

Only the Americans were out of their skulls. The Army, the Navy, and the FBI had all penetrated the Spanish office, but with separate enterprises. The Army despised the Navy, and both of them were churlish to the FBI. Orlando might have gone with Navy intelligence, since it had the best rates, but its officers were gruff with him. So he picked the FBI.

Nothing changed. He rode the streetcar to the chancellery, did his paperwork, and collected twenty-five dollars a week from the Bureau. His contact was Mrs. Hutch, the cleaning lady, who didn't have a great liking for Orlando. He had to worry if his trousers were buttoned tight, if he had ink on his cuffs, or crumbs in his mouth.

Hutch watched over him like a murderous angel. Then she stuck a note on his chair. Two words. "Don Valentin." Orlando stared at Hutch's scrawl and destroyed the note. Did the FBI need a dossier on his boss? Don Valentin, the marqués de Estrella, was the crackpot of the Spanish office, but he couldn't be touched. He was the nobleman who suffered horrible wounds in the Moroccan campaign of 1925. He landed off the coast of Spanish Morocco with a complement of marines and swept down upon the rebellious tribes that had crossed into the Spanish zone to make war on Europeans.

A young admiral of thirty-two, don Valentin restored Spain's prestige in Africa with this pivotal landing of marines. But he was captured by the same tribesmen later in the year. No one knows what tortures he underwent. The sultan of Morocco was able to ransom him in 1927. He arrived in Málaga with a withered arm and purple splotches under his chin. He was much more popular than the king.

Unfit for regular service, he was sent abroad to act as naval attaché in Washington, a post that allowed him to wear a uniform and have a special seat at ceremonial dinners. A succession of governments, center, left, and right, kept him at the chancellery. The Franco regime loved his Nazi stance in 1941. Now it tried to isolate the marqués.

Orlando set out to explain don Valentin's eccentricities to the FBI. "The marqués de Estrella thinks Adolf Hitler is the ultimate democrat, the leveler of all men. He has not been to Europe in seventeen years. Hitler would save the American Negro. That is the marqués' fundamental belief. Hence, he formed the Liberty Club to bring Hitler's democracy to the colored race." Orlando left his memorandums in Hutch's coat. Hutch didn't get back to him. "My boss lives with a creole woman from Panama, mamá Salomé. She poses as his housekeeper, but she's his wife. The marqués is devoted to her. He's afraid the Americans would pressure my government into recalling him if they discover that our naval attaché is married to a woman of Negro blood."

His allotment from the FBI went up to fifty, then sixty, and seventy dollars a week. Mrs. Hutch became solicitous about him, even smiled. Then old Viv came to town, arriving at the chancellery in smelly clothes. Vivian de Vries, who wore an earring at The Citadel in Charleston, when Orlando was a shy cadet sent by his family to emulate the rough American boy conquistadors. He became Vivian's lackey and got kicked out of school. But that was twenty years ago. Now cousin Viv was a Trotskyite who talked about a paradise for workers and poets, and figured the Spanish office in Washington was a way station for Nazi Germany. He had information to sell, idiotic things about Roosevelt's barber. Orlando marched him out of the chancellery.

He sat Vivian down in a nigger cafe and let him babble about his "contact" at the White House. "Oliver Beebe . . . a stupid sailor. He'll do anything for his sister, and she's in love with me."

Orlando didn't care what hole he dug for Vivian and the barber. Couldn't he milk don Valentin and dispose of cousin Viv? Don Valentin still had his family estates in Asturias, and the income would have been enough to keep Orlando until the war was over. So he went to don Valentin with tales of Oliver Beebe. The barber was a true democrat, Orlando said. Oliver Beebe would damage Roosevelt for don Valentin and the Liberty Club. But it would take money. For the risk of spying on the emperor Roosevelt, Oliver would have to be paid.

The tribesmen in Morocco must have tortured the brains out of don Valentin. The old admiral, who was about to turn fifty, would have given up all his fincas in Asturias for Oliver Beebe. Orlando smiled to himself. Then he wrote to the FBI about Oliver's particulars. Agents didn't come running to him. He found a note on his chair after five days. He was told to wait for a man on Colorado Avenue, off Rock Creek Park.

It was July. The park was flooded with sailors and their girls. Orlando stood at the designated spot. An enormous boat, a dreadnaught with rubber tires, stopped for him. Orlando was swept into the car; its windows rattled with a violence that could have picked away at his sanity unless Orlando concentrated hard on the dollars he expected to earn. He was thrown onto the floor and had to look up at a man in a white suit, stuck into a corner of the upholstery. Orlando smelled a strange perfume. He had to sneeze. "God bless you, Frayard."

Orlando recognized that bulldog face, with its strong, tanned jowls. He'd seen John Edgar in the newsreels, shaking hands with Babe Ruth and pecking Judy Garland on the cheek. "Frayard, is the President's barber blond . . . like you?"

Orlando shrugged near the floor.

"What's his favorite cigarette? Luckies? Camels? Old Gold?"

Orlando shrugged again.

"How many times have you met Oliver Beebe? Once? Twice?"

Orlando's face was in the carpeting. He had wool hairs in his mouth. "Less, sir. Less than once."

"Then how did the barber crawl into your head?"

Orlando took the hairs out of his mouth and mentioned Vivian's name. "Beebe has a sister . . . she's in love with Vivian." He told John Edgar about Vivian's trip to the chancellery. "Insane. Haven't seen the slob in twenty years. And he wants to sell me things . . . things for Germany."

"So you thought you could make a piece of change for yourself by hyping Oliver to us and feeding him to don Valentin. Frayard, you're a thirteen-carat beauty."

"Mistake," Orlando said. "I'll tell Vivian to blow. I'll kill him if he ever says 'Oliver' again."

Orlando got off his knees and scrambled to the door.

"Frayard? This conversation never happened, is that clear? We didn't meet in my sedan. You didn't come to Rock Creek Park. If you see me anywhere in town, don't nod your head. Because if you do, Frayard, if you give the slightest impression that you know me, I'll have to close your eyes."

Orlando kept to his chair at the Spanish office. He wouldn't peek out at Mrs. Hutch. He would have to move from Georgetown and deal with the sidewalk merchants of "F" Street, picking all his clothes out of a barrel. He would starve without the FBI. Mrs. Hutch threw a hundred dollars in his lap. And the FBI began to build its own headquarters inside the chancellery. Orlando talked to agents in the men's room. He became a helpmate to the Bureau. He could milk don Valentin for as much as he liked. But he couldn't unbutton his trousers without informing the Bureau.

The FBI rented a room for Vivian de Vries at the top of the Willard, so he could scrutinize the White House and draw pictures of its walls for don Valentin. The agents marveled at their own doings. Hoover had a network of little spies under his thumb that he could batten or squash at will. The Liberty Club was run from an office in the Justice Department. It had grown into an appendage of the Bureau.

Orlando wouldn't disobey his many chiefs. He "handled" Vivian for the FBI, sucking him into a conspiracy that existed to glorify J. Edgar Hoover. Orlando couldn't tell when the Bureau would pounce on the Liberty Club and dismember don Valentin, cousin Viv, and cousin's girl. He'd been advised to send in a report on Anita. So he had a rendezvous in niggertown with Viv and the girl.

She wore an absurd dress with bunches of crepe that might have been good for a ballroom on Pennsylvania Avenue. It seemed macabre in a nigger cafe. She had the blackest hair Orlando had ever met on a girl. Her nostrils were wide. She kept her ankles crossed under the table. She wasn't much of a chatterer, this Anita. She let her "husband" talk. But she had a pulse in her throat that Orlando would have loved to grab with the edge of a finger. He wanted to bite her on the mouth. "She appears to be a stupid girl," Orlando told the Bureau. "Almost childlike. She's supposed to have a little son tucked away in Milwaukee. I can't imagine her as a mother at all."

He couldn't tell what was under that silly dress, but the contours of her mouth had gotten him crazy. He went to cousin Viv. His head was wooly from a lack of sleep. A few incomprehensible words puffed out of him.

" 'Lando, you asking for a piece of sis? Take it. She's yours."

Orlando came up to Vivian's room at the Willard and was handed Anita Beebe. The girl didn't seem to have much of an attitude about being alone with Orlando. She was wearing the same fluffy dress. Orlando heard a rumbling noise under his collarbone. He might have panicked in another minute. But Anita wasn't unfriendly. She wouldn't walk away from Orlando's first kiss.

He didn't know what to expect. Orlando had never experienced such biting before. He fell into Anita's body like a dying boy. The girl was unselfish. She fucked with a devotion that hurt the Spanish secretary. He wanted to sob against the pulse in her throat. It had taken all his thirty-nine years and a room owned by the FBI to stumble onto a fit of happiness in the arms of an untalkative, black-haired girl.

He would send Vivian out on worthless assignments, so that he could continue using the Willard Hotel with Anita. It didn't bother him that the bellboys and the maids on the floor probably worked for the Bureau. The girl's bitter eyes had more of a hold on him than Edgar Hoover.

But Anita didn't chase his luck away. The Bureau upped his allowance to a hundred and ten a week. The agents who convened with him in the lavatory had grown careful with Orlando. They called him *Mr.* Frayard. He must have gotten onto the Director's favored list. Mrs. Hutch left a cabbage pie on his chair. He prayed the war would go on for a hundred years.

And then he met Oliver Beebe. The Bureau had decided to lure Oliver into the Liberty Club. The barber came to don Valentin's. Orlando felt an ugly squeeze around his heart. Oliver had Anita's dark look. His hair was even blacker than hers. Their pout was too much alike to comfort Orlando.

He could barely control his hatred for Oliver. The idea of Oliver's mouth on Anita's made him sick. That little pathetic incest of theirs meant shit until Orlando saw the boy. It had been a game perpetrated by Orlando and the FBI, a means of securing Oliver, of getting a funny kind of hook into the White House.

The boy seemed sensual, sensual and depraved. Orlando wanted him out of Anita's bed. Could he clarify himself to the Bureau? "Dear Mr. Hoover, you'll have to find a different bitch for Oliver Beebe." The FBI would have set his desk on fire and burnt Orlando with all the wood.

So he didn't write a line about his distaste for the boy. Oliver's darkness was nobody's business but Orlando's. He couldn't imprison Oliver in the White House. He would have to nose Anita out of her room, make her unavailable to the boy.

He took her to dinner on FBI money, danced with her in Vivian's room, pressured her into staying at his flat in Georgetown. The girl had too many homes. She couldn't decide where to keep her nightgown. At the boardinghouse, the Willard, or Frayard's? Orlando rushed her from place to place. She never saw a man with so many fifty-dollar bills. He would thrust them into her sleeve and tell her to shop for winter clothes while he went to his chancellery.

Orlando had his independence from the Frayards, he made love to Anita as often as he wished, but he felt a sense of disorder creep around his ears. He heard stories about Oliver from agents in the lavatory. "That's no barber," they said. "That's the most powerful runt in America. Eleanor and Frank eat out of Ollie's fist. You don't have a President in '44. You don't have a First Lady. You have a sailor who wheels Frank in and out of offices and says who can meet with him and who can't. Dewey might have beaten Frank. But he couldn't outfox the sailor. Don't kid yourself. That's one hell of an Oliver."

Orlando dismissed such crazy talk. Oliver? The boy had his problems putting three words together. The agents weren't through. They swore to Orlando that Beebe ran the FBI. Orlando stuffed a finger in his mouth in order not to laugh. Then he saw them at Harvey's lobster house. John Edgar and the boy! He didn't dare turn his eyes. He hunched into his seat and watched their reflection in the window. Anita didn't even know her brother was there. She bit into a carrot and touched Orlando's leg under the table. Orlando spilled chowder in his lap. Hoover smiled at the boy during every course. They sat with chunks of lobster in their faces. " 'Lando," Anita said, "what's wrong with you?"

There was a savage knocking in his legs. Orlando had to grab his own knees; somebody had him by the tail. He couldn't say who. All of a sudden he was glad to have a fiancée in Madrid. Maybe don Valentin was right to love the Nazis. The Nazis wouldn't feed you money and tear out your guts. It would have been one or the other.

"Drink your soup," he told Anita. "I'm getting out of here."

Edgar, Otto, and the Major

They sat in Edgar's limousine, making polite little burps from all the lobster and cherry pie they'd had tonight. "Sailor, what would you like to do?"

The sailor said, "Ox." And Edgar was stuck with a boy who lived in an attic and went into reveries. It was time to take Oliver home.

"Uncle, what ever happened to the Tuskegee Ox?"

"Him? He had to retire. Baseball was like a disease to Otto . . . it made him want to kill."

"Did he become a farmer again?"

"No."

"Uncle, where is he now?"

Edgar muttered something to his driver, and the limousine swerved away from Pennsylvania Avenue and brought Ollie to a wooded area with a big old house and a gang of cottages. The sailor wasn't blind. He'd been here before, with Mrs. Franklin. It was the crazy farm, St. Elizabeth's, where Oliver had met the wild man of Tangier, in a cage.

Edgar didn't have any trouble getting onto the grounds. Gates were unlocked for him. No attendant or hospital trustee had to walk them to the cottages behind the big house. Edgar whispered to the sailor.

"Don't call him Ox. Anything to do with baseball gets him violent. Talk about FDR if you want, but no batting averages."

They were let onto a screened porch. Ollie saw the Ox. He was sitting on a bench in wide, sloppy pants that were pretty close to baseball knickers. His energies were gone. It wasn't the man who had slapped doubles and triples in July. He sucked on tootsie rolls, like Oliver Beebe. The Ox didn't remember Ollie. He never asked about FDR.

They left St. Elizabeth's. The boy was morose in Edgar's car. "Uncle, who took away his plow?"

"He's better off where he is. He didn't have much of a family around Georgia. His people are dead. Now he has his own nurse. He's better off."

The boy said good night to Edgar and chauffeur Bill and crept into the White House. Edgar didn't run home. He could have gone to a rooftop club and sat with sports writers and gabbed about Joe DiMaggio and Billy Conn, and the fate of the Senators without their Tuskegee Ox. Edgar drew a crowd wherever he went. He was a local boy, born and raised in the District. He wasn't like that Roosevelt, who hid in his bedroom, or vanished to Shangri-La. Washington had to survive without a President in its streets. If it couldn't have Roosevelt, at least it had the FBI. You could always read a good Edgar story in the *Star.* He wasn't afraid to talk. You got Edgar's views on draft dodgers, parole boards, Japs, and Joe DiMaggio's swing. Edgar only had one taboo: Eleanor Roosevelt. He hated that witch and her pinko friends. But he wouldn't attack the Boss' wife.

He wasn't in the mood to talk about baseball with the boys from the *Star.* Chauffeur Bill took him to the Washington dog pound. He had been going there ever since he was nine or ten. The Director couldn't get along with cats. They were too independent for him. None of them could have a fierce devotion to a man. But he loved all kinds of dogs. Mongrels, bitches, animals with valuable blood in them. He would visit the pound, stare into the cages, consider adopting a dog that struck his fancy.

The attendant didn't mind that it was close to midnight. He could unlock the works for J. Edgar Hoover. Edgar liked the acrid smell of dogs living in iron rows, on piles of wet straw. He traveled from cage to cage, peeking at the crop that had been captured this week: a toy poodle, abandoned or lost, half-breeds with yellow eyes, a sick collie, a schnauzer that wouldn't leave off staring at Edgar, a lady chow with scars on her neck. Was she a warrior from the alleys, or a stray dog scratching for food?

The back room of the pound was open. Edgar could see a man with a silver belt buckle and sandy-colored hair harangue the dogcatchers. His trousers were pressed in the military way. It was young Colbert of the Secret Service. He was trying to get the dogcatchers to join his crusade against the wild dogs of the city. Colbert was obsessed. He'd gone into the alleys with a small citizens' army. Colbert found starving children, rats, whores, dead alligators, but no dogs. He went back in again with a team of Army engineers and mapped the zones of Nigger Lane. Major Colbert was preparing himself for the dogs. He knew every trail and hovel. Now he conspired with the dogcatchers for his final crusade.

He must have spotted Edgar near the cages. He said, "Shit, bloody shit," and slammed his door shut. The

G-man didn't have to worry. Two of the dogcatchers "belonged" to the Bureau. Edgar would have Colbert's plans by tomorrow morning.

He thanked the attendant, touched the schnauzer's nose, and signaled to chauffeur Bill.

Triskaidekaphobia

He was a President who didn't invade the District. You wouldn't find FDR at the Occidental, or The Three Musketeers. The President always ate at home. It was Eleanor who went into the city for luncheons, or rode her horse in Rock Creek Park. You learned to wave at her, shake her hand. You could touch the President's missus, stare into her horsy face, but it wasn't like meeting with Frank.

The emperor was eating toast with his dog. He didn't have any of the Roosevelt boys around him. His children weren't at home.

It wasn't Elliott, John, James, and Franklin, Jr. Poppa and his boys. You couldn't talk about their radio stations, their business deals, their actress wives. They were in the Army and Navy now. Mr. Frank only had one more male child: his sailor, Oliver Beebe.

When the Boss wasn't in Casablanca with Mr. Churchill, you'd catch him in bed. He thrived on cigarette smoke and a homey kind of magic. You couldn't tell where you stood with the old squire. He would pick you up, stroke you, be your Poppa for a while, and then cast you down for the next bureaucrat. It wasn't that you were out of favor. Poppa didn't scream or chew off your leg, but he might not see you for another year. Look at poor Harry! Harry Hopkins, the Boss' hatchet-faced assistant, used to be an indispensable man. There was a time when FDR wouldn't turn his head without Harry the Hop. Churchill and Stalin were always polite to Harry. He was the czar of war supplies. Harry moved into the White House after his first wife died. Mrs. Roosevelt gave him the Lincoln Study. But Harry was too busy to sleep in one place. He napped on whatever couch he could find. Ushers often had to go into twenty rooms looking for Harry. Then he decided to live in Georgetown with his little daughter and his second wife. Harry took sick. He was in the Mayo Clinic now with a rotting stomach. The ushers had already forgotten him. New aides discovered Harry's napping places; they would snore on an old couch until FDR needed them.

There were no other Harrys: only the Pup and Oliver Beebe. The Boss was at odds with his missus. She'd been hectoring him too much about the absence of Negro officers in his Navy. He wasn't deaf to the policies she described. But how could he revolutionize the Navy in the middle of a war? "Lily-white," she said. Mr. Franklin's Navy was lily-white. It had been a service for gentlemen since the Navy began. If the Army had Negro pilots and combat troops, why couldn't the Navy?

The Boss would have to signal Ollie to wheel him away from Eleanor. He would smoke a Camel in the presidential toilet, take out his stamp collection and ponder over a commemorative issue from Hong Kong, or work on Fala's mail. He loved to answer letters addressed to his dog. He would scribble a few lines in Fala's name. "Dear Johnny Temple. Thank you for writing and telling me what your dog Sebastian eats for breakfast. I usually have scrambled eggs, bacon, toast, and coffee with Mr. Franklin Roosevelt. He eats faster than I do, so I have to gobble my food if I don't want to stare at an empty plate. It's either heartburn or hunger pains when you eat with Mr. Roosevelt. Sincerely yours, Murray, the Outlaw of Fala Hill.''

If it was Friday the thirteenth, the Boss might not get out of bed. He suffered from triskaidekaphobia, a morbid fear of the number thirteen. Ollie had to go through the Boss' calendar and check off unlucky days into 1945 and '46. The Boss wouldn't travel on the thirteenth of any month unless it couldn't be helped. He wouldn't sit down with thirteen correspondents, meet thirteen ambassadors on his stairs, or have his thirteen grandchildren together in a single room.

His dread could carry over to any particle of thirteen. Secretaries in FDR's house learned not to light *three* cigarettes with the same match. The third light was anathema to FDR. It could bring horrible misfortunes, like setting your hair on fire, burning out your windows, or raising boils on your ass.

Oliver was soon infected with the Boss' triskaidekaphobia. He wouldn't go around with thirteen Camels in his pocket, or remove the thirteenth pencil from FDR's pencil cup. He allowed the machine gunners to warm themselves in his room, but whenever they were chintzy and tried to get three lights out of a match, he would push them up to the roof and watch the tobacco freeze in their mouths.

Oliver became a tyrant about the number thirteen. The attic fell under his influence. The maids couldn't iron thirteen blouses in a row, store thirteen pillows in the closet, fold a stack of thirteen handkerchiefs. Ex-

Empress Zena had eighteen candles in her room to remember all the dead princes of Bulgaria, her nephews
and sons, whose nothingness had made the royal house
extinct. Bulgarian writ forbade Zena to light her own
candles. So Ollie had to do it. But he would pass over the
thirteenth candle and leave it unlit.

The maids were sure that Ollie's "fever" was a sign
of devilry. Mr. Kirkland, he must have bewitched Ollie
and the Boss. They burned incense to counteract the
devil, and drive this number madness out of Ollie. Ollie
didn't change. But the incense caused such a stink in the
attic, he had to run downstairs and read his movie magazines in Mrs. Roosevelt's sitting room.

TWENTY-EIGHT

It was going to be another military Christmas, with a darkened White House, machine gunners tramping on the roof, and the Boss vacating his bedroom for Hyde Park. The mansion emptied on a Saturday, December 20, because neither the zero nor the two of "twenty" was a dreaded number, and the Boss was fond of Saturdays. FDR took his missus and his Pup, secretaries, assistants, maids, Secret Service men, and the princess regent of Norway, who had a bigger entourage than Mr. Roosevelt. Altogether a band of forty motored to the secret railroad dock under the Bureau of Printing and Engraving, and boarded the President's train. Ollie was left behind.

Even in a darkened house, the Boss' schedule never stopped. Ollie had to interview all the grumblers and malcontents who wanted to see the Boss, and find out who had a legitimate gripe and who did not. It wasn't easy. The sailor had his intuition and nothing else. How could he test the worth of a Navy captain who believed his superiors were starving him to death? An inventor who needed a hundred thousand dollars to produce the ultimate camouflage, rayon that turned invisible on a soldier's back? An alderman out of Buffalo who felt FDR owed him a favor since 1923? Ollie would look in your eyes. God help any man if he happened to blink more than once or twice. It was the mark of a dissembler to Oliver Beebe.

The day after Mr. Roosevelt went to Hyde Park, don Valentin appeared outside the basement closet Ollie stole from the chief usher in order to conduct his interviews. The Secret Service men who remained here for Christmas were in a fury. They would have liked to stomp on a Nazi marquis. Oliver had to restrain them. But he couldn't understand why the Liberty Club had come begging to FDR. Oliver was blunt with the little marquis. "The Boss will see you on June 13, 1948. It falls on a Sunday. I can't give you anything earlier than that. FDR is getting busy."

"I'm not interested in FDR," don Valentin said.

Was every little marquis going to pester Oliver Beebe? The boy had work to do. There were generals crouched on the basement steps with petitions for the President. They felt the Army was being assed out of the war. Oliver was no military strategist. He'd never been to the Map Room. He couldn't have read the huge green charts of the Pacific Ocean, or located the outline of France on the wall. But he knew FDR wouldn't put his admirals on top of the generals. That wasn't the Boss' way. He would let them bitch and growl, and then they had to come to Poppa to get themselves untied.

Don Valentin coughed into his handkerchief. He was paying Oliver Beebe five hundred a month through Orlando Frayard. Frayard warned him about the boy's finicky nature. You could drag him into the Liberty Club, but you couldn't talk politics to his face. The boy never acknowledged the money he got from don Valentin.

Such were the spies of 1944. Rifi tribesmen had torn out the marquis' fingernails, and then relieved him of the fingers themselves, but they didn't have as many psyches as Oliver, or carry ten thicknesses of feeling under their shirts, make a pauper out of you, and then snarl. If the Rifis decided to scratch your heart, it would have been simple, direct, not the jumbled, cheerless maneuvers of a sailor boy. "The Liberty Club needs you," don Valentin said. "We're having a rally in Lafayette Park."

"What's it for?" Oliver asked, with a doubtful look.

"To protest the miseries of black servicemen . . . Oliver, can you help us? Will you ask Mrs. Roosevelt to attend? We can't have a rally without her support."

"Who's this *we*?" Oliver muttered.

"Odessa Brown and myself. She's co-sponsor of the rally."

"Why is Odessa going partners with the Liberty Club?"

"She has three sons in the war . . . they're messboys and shoeshine artists, all of them."

Ollie turned glum. "I thought whore ladies don't fix themselves with children. They're supposed to be smarter than that."

The generals were becoming impatient. They knocked on the closet walls. Oliver yelped at them. "Hold your horses. I'll be with you in a minute." Don Valentin couldn't extract any promises from the boy. He had to step between an arcade of Secret Service men. They stared at his withered arm and pulled on their lips, like monkeys in the White House. The little marquis wasn't disturbed by it. What could you expect? America was a land of white baboons, where FDR was king of kings, and Oliver his idiot prince.

Oliver had to reserve his princedom for the attic. He'd come upstairs, with only a tootsie roll to succor him and break the monotony of constant gripes. Slave for a President, and you don't even get a phone call to ask ya how you are. The Boss had his stamp albums in Hyde Park. He could forget about Oliver Beebe.

Then, like a game of magical wires, the telephone rang, and the operator, who wasn't Ethel Rosenquist today, told him, "Ollie, Hyde Park is calling you."

He picked up the phone and started to blabber. "Boss, I saw General Talbert, General Lyden, General Armstrong, and General Taylor . . . I gave them next Thursday at two-forty. But they have to be out by three. You're having orange juice with Margaret O'Brien at three-oh-five."

"Oliver dear. . . ."

Mrs. Roosevelt was on the line. And he'd given the Boss' news away. "Merry Christmas," she said. Only Christmas was tomorrow. She wished Oliver could have his turkey at Hyde Park. The sailor would stick to tootsie rolls. Turkey thickened his head. He could sleep in her cottage at Val-Kill if he liked. Oliver thanked the First Lady. "Got to work," he said. It was almost a lie. Complaining generals couldn't get onto the grounds during Christmas. Oliver could shut his closet door. But he wasn't riding up to the Boss' country home without an invitation from the squire himself. And he didn't say a word to Eleanor about don Valentin and that nigger march. He wasn't going to poison her holiday.

Ollie had nothing to do on Christmas Eve. He couldn't go to Harvey's with the FBI. Edgar had planned his Christmas away from the capital. He was sunbathing in Miami. Oliver put on his peacoat and went down into

Lafayette Park. The wind was fierce. It nearly blew him into the cannons at the base of Andrew Jackson's Monument. A man rasped at him from a bench behind the rump of Jackson's horse. Oliver had the urge to run. But the wind brought him closer to Vivian de Vries. The scarecrow loved to celebrate in an empty park. Oliver had to dig with his toes to keep from sliding into Vivian's lap. "Don't you have a warm room to sit in?" he said, with the wind rising up his coat.

The scarecrow smelled of cooking wine. "Aint none of your business, Ollie boy."

"The niggers might grab you out of the park. Didn't you know? Marquis is organizing a rally."

"Let him organize," Vivian said. "Nobody's chasing me off this bench." He wore a hat that knifed down over his eyes, and his collars were up against his ears; all Ollie could find was a slit in his face that breathed.

"Come on," Oliver said. "We're going to Odessa's house."

"Bullshit. I'm not spending Christmas Eve with Mother Brown and her twitchy girls."

Ollie couldn't budge him. The scarecrow gripped the bench with flintlike hands and told Oliver to shove off. What could Ollie do? He left Vivian to suck wind behind Andrew Jackson's horse.

Odessa fed him hot rum cakes and a mulberry wine that blackened Oliver's mouth. He asked about her newly acquired stepson, Jonathan Roosevelt. "Him, Mr. Ollie? He's awful nice to my girls. Never saw a man who took to fornication the way Johnny does. Where'd you say he lived? On an oysterman's island? Those oysters must have settled in a good place. My Johnny goes from morning to night. Nothing like that to get a girl through the winter solstice. Whores turn freaky in December, didn't you know? It's the Christmas shakes. And Johnny sweats that rawness out of their hides."

Then he asked about her own natural sons, the three servicemen that don Valentin had mentioned to him, and the scars near Odessa's eyes began to ripple out. She patted her face with an enormous handkerchief, but she didn't blubber to Ollie. She told him a bitter story: her sons enlisting to fight in the war, and being humiliated at boot camp; thrown into the nigger brigade, forced to shit in separate latrines, trained to wash trucks and cars for Uncle Sam, pick weeds out of the commandant's garden, polish the colonel's spoons, bake pies for the admiral's wife, like a maid's service in the Army, Navy, and Marines. "Mr. Ollie, it's not right for a mama to hear her boys crying on the telephone . . . they didn't put on a uniform to live like chickens in Mr. Roosevelt's backyard."

Oliver was too disheartened with the history of Odessa's sons to walk through a whorehouse looking for Jonathan Roosevelt. He said goodbye, touching Odessa's handkerchief. But he couldn't hop out of Nigger Lane. A hundred feet from Odessa's cribs he heard a steady, muffled roaring in the mud and grass. The ground under him began to sway. Was Crawfish Alley splitting apart? Then, in the shadow of a broken fence, he noticed a thick party of dogs. These animals squeezed their long bodies between the pickets, their bellies scratching wood. Their noses seemed incredibly long, as if Ollie were watching a pack of swine. They leered at him with open mouths. But they didn't jump on Oliver. They swarmed past him, ruffling their backs. The sailor couldn't tell how many dogs were in the alley. Their swollen backs made a kind of endless bumping train. The dogs left and Ollie returned to the attic.

He found a note on his bed. A machine gunner must have climbed down from the roof to answer his telephone. "Somebody named Anita called. If you don't want her, save her for us." He got into his peacoat again and walked to Mount Vernon Square. The light was on in her window. He went up to Anita's room.

She didn't make trouble for Ollie. She let him take off all his clothes. He snuggled up against Anita, going dizzy from the nearness of her skin. He loved to smell his sister's body. It was more familiar to him that the juices in his mouth. He would die without that smell. It brought him away from attics and presidential closets, into a zone that had nothing to do with Weehawken, mother, father, or any recognizable past. Anita was everything. Loving her, buried in her smell, he had a warmth that couldn't be touched by a President or the navies of the world.

Afterward they smoked Ollie's Camels in bed. She didn't try to explain her disappearances from the boardinghouse. Oliver was the one who babbled first. "Your scarecrow's moved to Lafayette Park." He saw bewilderment in her puckered face. "That journalist of yours. He thinks a statue's the next best thing to a house. He's living under a horse's ass."

"I don't care about him," she said. "Vivian deserted me. He can live where he likes."

Anita wouldn't talk any more. He'd gouged her forehead with mentions of de Vries. She didn't prevent him from looking for his pants. He stood near the door in his peacoat. She stuck his nose in her mouth. That's how she kissed her brother goodbye. Oliver moaned softly and shambled down the boardinghouse stairs.

She'd called the White House that evening and asked for Ollie out of a crazy impulse. She wouldn't have thought of her brother if Orlando hadn't grown obsessed with Ollie. "The sailor is king man at the FBI. Edgar Hoover feeds him lobster and salaams to him. That little boy whips Franklin Roosevelt every night. Admirals shake because of him. Girl, you'd better be nice to your brother."

So she became curious about the "king man" who whipped Franklin Roosevelt. Who was this Oliver? Had he learned to eat fire in the President's attic? Would he scald her with his tongue? She developed an ache for him, a twitch that ran along her thigh and left a rash on her belly. And then he was outside her door, a boy in a sailor suit, the same old Ollie, gaping at her with his weasel eyes. She could have ripped his ears out, and the great man of Washington wouldn't have done a thing. . . She slept with him, sucked his nose, and sent him back to the White House.

Yalta

TWENTY-NINE

Anita never paged him again. Oliver's forehead crinkled with evil lines, and his pompadour fell another quarter of an inch. He was the wild man of the attic. He barked at the Secret Service men who liked to follow him on the stairs. "Tell Mr. Horn to scratch himself. I don't need a chaperone in this house." The machine gunners learned not to whistle at him from the roof. He would knock on the ceiling with his telescope and shout, "Don't you bother me."

He hadn't cut the Boss' hair in weeks. Roosevelt was closeted with his aides. Ollie bumped into Kirkland Horn and the generals who rushed between FDR's bedroom, toilet, and oval study like well-bred mice. All this scurrying was for the Boss' itinerary. Oliver heard talk of bedbugs and the Black Sea. FDR was going to sit down with Churchill and Stalin somewhere in the Crimea. Roosevelt had a daughter, Mrs. John Boettiger, and he was taking her along; but he had no room for his missus, his Pup, and Oliver Beebe.

That red mustache appeared in Oliver's door. "Beebe, you have five minutes to pack. You won't need a toothbrush. The russkies are fond of sour breath."

The sailor could only give a dumb stare.

Horn growled at him. "Pack, you idiot. Mr. Roosevelt wants his barber to meet Uncle Joe."

Ollie threw white blouses into a suitcase. He scribbled a message to the Boss' wife. "Dear Mrs. FDR, Odessa Brown is a good lady. Her children suffered in the war. Nobody will let them fight on account of they are colored boys. Odessa is having a rally. Maybe you could say hello to her in the park. Sincerely, Oliver Beebe."

Oliver left with Kirkland Horn, and the message was delivered to Mrs. Roosevelt. It wouldn't have made much sense to the First Lady, these pencilings of Oliver's, if a committee of Negro mothers hadn't visited her in the Blue Room and told her about the Mothers March on Lafayette Square. The First Lady understood the politics of war. She could criticize the treatment of black soldiers and black sailors, petition her husband with a list of grievances in their behalf, but she couldn't attack Franklin's Army and Navy in the open and help these mothers organize their march. Yet she was a mother herself, and she couldn't ignore their plea. Mrs. Franklin would come to the park, not as mistress of the White House, but as a war mother showing her sympathy to the aims of the march.

Doris Fleeson discussed Eleanor and the committee of Negro mothers in the *Washington Star.* Stories began to circulate about "that mansion of niggers" on Pennsylvania Avenue. The President was on his way to the Crimea. And Eleanor had to suffer nasty looks from the Washington "aborigines" and a number of senators' wives.

Vivian de Vries noticed Eleanor's name in the *Star* and rang up the Spanish embassy. It took him five nickels

to get Orlando on the phone. The Spaniard was uneasy.
"Cousin, I told you not to call me here."

" 'Lando, I have to see you . . . *now.*"

They met in a nigger cafe north of the chancellery.
Vivian seemed to have a chill in his eyes. " 'Lando, how
much can you offer me for killing a Roosevelt?"

Orlando didn't stop eating his banana cream pie.

The scarecrow uncurled his lips, and you could see
the raw spots in his mouth. "Mama Roosevelt is planning
to sit with the niggers in Lafayette Park. A man could
plunge a knife into her chest and walk away from there.
The government would think it's a nigger plot."

Orlando scrutinized that tight, bony face and decided cousin Viv had to be bent. The planet was in a
turmoil over Mrs. Franklin Roosevelt. Half the world
hated her, and the other half would have kissed the
threads on her dirty white socks. But who would want to
kill that tall lady with the buckteeth? "Vivian, what's she
done to you?"

"Nothing," the scarecrow said. "She's Franklin's
ally, isn't she? The palace queen. She takes the pressure
off the old man. Fondles the niggers, so Franklin can
chew up Republicans and win his war. But you cut her
heart out, and the old man won't have hands, head, or
feet. He'll dangle in his wheelchair like a chump from
Dutchess County." The scarecrow had a rabbity smile.
"He'll have to borrow some brains from Ollie boy."

Orlando finished his pie and got up from the table
without guaranteeing much to cousin Viv. "Speak to you
tomorrow," he said. He buttoned his coat and paid the
bill, leaving Vivian stranded in the cafe with murderous
thoughts. The scarecrow could have gone to his room at
the Willard, bathed, and ordered custard, chicken, and

wine. But his room smelled of Anita and Frayard. Her hair was on the pillows. She kept her perfumes in the medicine cabinet. And 'Lando had his Trojans in the drawer. So the scarecrow took to living behind a statue in the park. The statue blocked the wind, but when the cold bit through his shirt, he would sneak up to the Willard for an hour, warm himself on the rug, and return to his bench. He'd been abused in Washington, D.C. He'd handed the President's sailor over to Frayard and the Liberty Club, and his girlfriend gets stolen away. They give you a room that Anita uses to clutch another man, and Vivian has to winter in Lafayette Park.

Roosevelt. He's the guy who keeps poets on a park bench. The Charleston de Vrieses were as pure as any Roosevelt. Vivian should have been the squire. But he didn't want to be king. He would touch the emperor on the nose, topple him by getting to Eleanor. Then you'd have an America where poets could breathe, and Vivian would spread the gospel of that little Russian Jew, build a cadre of artists and workers that would trample on the White House and murder every king.

THIRTY

It was a thin presidential party: Roosevelt and his daughter Anna, Harry the Hop, who had climbed out of a sickbed to be with FDR, four Secret Service men, the new Secretary of State, FDR's physician, a naval aide, and Oliver Beebe. You could fit them all into the two American Packards that the NKVD supplied. Kirkland Horn and most of the military chiefs had gone ahead. The palace where FDR would stay was flooded with generals and boys from the State Department. They smoked, flirted with the Russian sentries, who were fifteen-year-old girls with bayonets, mittens, and lovely round cheeks; the generals tied and untied their shoes, and sucked on American candy, waiting for FDR.

The Boss was carried off his plane, the Sacred Cow, at a hidden airstrip in the Crimea, and he rode down to the Black Sea in the same car with Anna, Ollie, and Harry the Hop. FDR had his old gray fedora, with the brim tight on his forehead to protect his eyes from the glare of mountain snow. He wouldn't have come to Yalta without his lucky hat. His face was hollow; he'd lost his "swimmer's neck," the benign thickness under his ears that often gave him a look of power, even in a wheelchair. Hopkins sat inside a blanket, his head tucked into his shoulder, like a gigantic sleeping bird. The NKVD agents along the road saw two sick men, a sailor, and a girl.

The Boss hadn't come to a beggar's house. The Soviets lent him Livadia, the summer palace that Czar Nicholas had built for his family on a hill overlooking the Black Sea. It had fifty rooms. Its ground floor wandered over a maze of corridors and rooms that could have swallowed up twice the boundaries of Lafayette Park. Livadia had yew trees, towers, gardens, sun porches, and lice. These were Nazi lice, according to the NKVD. Hitler's generals had sat in Livadia until the Red Army drove them out. But you couldn't get rid of all the lice.

Roosevelt had the czar's own austere little bedroom on the ground floor. Anna would sleep in a different wing, at the opposite end of the palace. Ollie was midway between FDR and his daughter. Bathrooms were scarce at Livadia; generals had to line up outside the palace's five or so facilities if they expected to wash and shave in the morning. But the sailor had executive privileges; he and Anna could use the President's john. The British and Soviet officers who hiked through the tall, barren rooms of Livadia looking for their American counterparts were struck by Oliver Beebe. None of them could figure out the sailor's function in the Crimea. He wasn't among the party of Americans that entered the great ballroom of Livadia for meetings of the Big Three. He would accompany Roosevelt to the ballroom door and then retire to some passageway with his Camels and his tootsie rolls. But he was always there when the plenary sessions were over at eight or nine o'clock, so he could wheel Roosevelt into the czar's bedroom, and scowl at any man who tried to impede the Boss and engage him in a knotty talk about Russia, Poland, or the fate of Germany. He would give the Boss a rubdown, help him into the tub, mix cocktails for him, and arrive with him at the Russian compound for a banquet in Churchill's honor.

Who was this boy that no one dared exclude from a dinner list at Yalta? You could disinvite a general, shuffle diplomats around, but you didn't tamper with Oliver Beebe. Churchill's closest aides were suspicious of the boy. They felt he had an undue influence over FDR. Rasputin is what they called him. The Prime Minister would grumble in Oliver's presence and bite on his long cigar. Yet he was reluctant to say a bad word to Roosevelt about the boy. The British team came to accept Oliver as a kind of necessary evil. He was the lad who revived FDR after a hard day in the ballroom.

The P.M. also grumbled because the russkies were fond of Mr. Roosevelt's sailor. Marshal Stalin took a liking to Oliver that seemed perfectly sinister to the "Prime." Were the russkies playing up to Oliver because this was the clearest route to FDR? NKVD men would beg Camels off him by shaking their huge, jug-handled ears. The boy thought he was surrounded by a league of elephants. Did the Russians grow "jugs" on a man's head the way you dropped a cabbage in the ground? Still, he enjoyed the NKVD men, and he gave them whatever Camels he could spare.

He had tootsie rolls for the Red Army guards, Russian boys and girls who were like infants around a twenty-three-year-old sailor, infants with chocolate sugar-tits in their mouths. Oliver's tootsie rolls and Baby Ruths arrived from Sevastopol (a U.S. communications ship was anchored there), in a pouch together with the Boss' mail. FDR hadn't come to Yalta to neglect Oliver Beebe.

The sailor would have been lost in the czar's palace without his tootsie rolls.

Oliver was lonely in the afternoons, while the Boss sat with Winnie and Uncle Joe. The P.M. had also brought his daughter. Sarah she was, Sarah Churchill. She would take Anna away from the palace on sightseeing trips, and Oliver was left with Kirkland Horn. Horn stared at Oliver with such virulence in his eyes, the boy had to turn and face the window. Horn had an antic look at Yalta. He was blistering mad. The sailor shouldn't have been here. FDR decided at the last moment that he couldn't exist in the Crimea without his "child." So Kirkland had to protect a President, clear the palace of NKVD men (they were dressed up as servants in white pants when Kirkland arrived), and watch over that little spy with the pompadour.

Oliver couldn't drop his pants in the Boss' john without seeing eyes wink at him from selective holes in the wall. Oliver stayed in his room. He would look out at the soft, inky pull of the water and conjure up his sister's face. He wished he was inside the boardinghouse with 'Nita. They didn't have to cuddle. 'Nita could stick to her clothes. He would smell the dark roots of her hair, and the rest of the world could tumble away into nothingness.

It was while mooning over Anita that he met Youssipev. The sailor was on the porch outside his room when he discovered a man on the palace lawn with two NKVD's. The man was wearing a mustard-colored uniform with two stars on the shoulder boards. He was short and stout, with Stalin's mustache and pockmarked face, thick knuckles and tiny feet. But it couldn't have been Uncle Joe. He inspired no terror in the NKVD's. They smirked at him as if they were guarding a trained bear whom they could have dragged across the lawn by some invisible rope around his neck. He was Youssipev, Stalin's double.

Stalin had five doubles along the battlefront to confound his enemies. This Youssipev was yet another double, who was meant to draw out any fanatic or anti-Soviet agent that might want to kill Uncle Joe. He'd been shot at eleven times. A mad Ukrainian nearly bit off his chin in the streets of Kiev. Oliver called down to Youssipev from the sun porch. The boy had learned how to ask a man his name in the Moscow dialect.

Youssipev cocked his ear. Then he smiled. "Youssipev," he said. With a few simple shrugs he got Oliver to understand that in spite of the shoulder boards he was a prisoner of the NKVD. Oliver pointed to the Secret Service men whose heads would appear every few minutes at both sides of the porch. Youssipev smiled again. He bowed to Oliver Beebe. He must have understood that the American sailor was also a captive. A different kind of Youssipev. One of those expendable persons that great men like to keep in their pockets so they'll have something to bark at, something to squeeze, something to throw away. Youssipev pulled out a cigarette and shambled across the lawn in boots and shoulder boards, the NKVD's tugging at him with their invisible rope.

And Oliver was left with images of Youssipev, the man who was and wasn't Uncle Joe. But he had to suspend his thinking on the subject of doubles. The plenary session would break early tonight. The Boss was due at Churchill's villa. Ollie went down to wheel FDR from the ballroom. FDR was haggard and blue in the face. His neck had grown scrawnier and scrawnier near the Black

Sea. He was hollow under the eyes. He barely had the strength to clamp that ivory holder into his mouth. It had something to do with Poland. They'd talked and bargained and scowled inside the ballroom, but nobody could budge Uncle Joe. Now the generals sat in the czar's bedroom with Mr. Roosevelt, who was naked under a towel. The generals bragged and schemed, while Oliver rubbed his body. FDR listened to each of their arguments, and shrugged them off one by one. The Red Army had crossed the Oder. Stalin was in Poland to stay. It was a fact the generals would have to live with. The Prime Minister and FDR could mutter little stories about "free elections," but Stalin wouldn't move over for any Polish government-in-exile that was housed in London in 1945, its generals peacocking in British uniforms around Leicester Square. Stalin would pick a government for the Poles. And it sickened FDR.

He would wear nothing but his old gray suit at Churchill's party. The Secret Service had to shake Harry Hopkins out of bed. Harry got into the Boss' car with pajamas under his coat. And they went to Vorontsov, Churchill's villa by the sea. It was Oliver, Harry, and the Boss who came into the dining room, with the Boss' interpreter slouching behind the wheelchair like some uninvited guest. The British team was at the table with Stalin's generals. Uncle Joe hadn't arrived.

Churchill welcomed Harry and the President, and made a grudging hello to Oliver. The British team felt they were looking at a dead man. Churchill's own physician was convinced that FDR had no more than a few months to live. His bluish complexion and palsied hands were apparent to everybody in the room.

The British team glowered at Oliver. He was the

boy who massaged the President of the United States, this Rasputin in a seaman's blouse. Did he blow a crazy fever into the President's dying limbs? Were America's wartime strategies determined by a glum boy with black eyebrows and dark, dark hair? How could they test Oliver's views when they couldn't get the boy to talk? He would mind the President with a dumb expression on his face. But the eyes were shrewd. The boy wouldn't make himself vulnerable to the British team. They could glower until their noses dropped off. They couldn't scratch Oliver Beebe.

The Russian generals sat with their thumbs inside their sleeves. They were like a pack of outlandish toys in military clothes that could fart and breathe and gaze into their vodka glasses, and give nothing beyond a tight, silly smile. Then the clack, clack of boots was heard in the corridor, and the toys livened up. You could watch the dread creep into the generals' eyes. The doors opened with a wretched whine. Red Army guards poured into the room. They weren't uncivil to the Americans or the British. They smiled at Roosevelt and the P.M., and searched under the dinner table. They left without overturning cups or shattering a plate. Stalin walked into the room with his two monkey men, Molotov and Gromyko, and two bodyguards from the NKVD. The Russian generals rose up out of their seats with a huge hysterical shiver. And the party began.

Stalin didn't sulk in his chair. He moved around the table to clasp Churchill's hand and inquire about the President's health. He stopped in front of Ollie with one of the generals, who acted as his interpreter, and asked the boy how he liked the Black Sea. "It's beautiful," Ollie said. "But the dolphins make too much noise outside my window. I can't sleep." Stalin gave a soft chuckle as Oliver's words were whispered in his ear. Then he muttered three short sentences that Roosevelt's interpreter picked out for Ollie.

"The dolphins are party members. I can't chase them away. But I can tell them to go swim in somebody else's window."

There were polite titters around Winston Churchill, to satisfy Uncle Joe, but nothing to do with Oliver could have roused the British team. They despised Stalin's attention to the boy. The dolphins got FDR to roar. His blue-gray pallor disappeared. He tossed his head back, and Churchill was amazed. It was the old Roosevelt, vigorous, alert, with that powerful lion's head and a laugh that could have taken in a whole continent of things: men, women, chairs, palaces, and trees. It was like an infection that beat down all resistance to it. Roosevelt could charm the world.

The roaring had to stop. The head slumped forward, and the grayness returned. You were with a dying man again. He was the youngest of the Big Three, but he couldn't walk into a room, like Uncle Joe. He had to be carried, or wheeled, or get close to the ground and crawl, an infant who had just turned sixty-three. The mind was there. He could be the old horse trader, bending to win you over to his cause, but in the Crimea he had to bargain with a scrawny neck and hands that wouldn't stay still.

Thirty-seven toasts were drunk that night in Churchill's villa. The P.M. took his vodka straight. Thirty-seven times he leapt off his chair to drink with the russkies and Roosevelt's little party. Neither the Russian generals nor Stalin himself could compete with Winston's thirst. Uncle Joe had to keep a jar of water beside his vodka glass. By the tenth or eleventh toast he was drinking mainly from the jar. Roosevelt didn't have any vodka at all. He and Harry nibbled on their water glasses. But Oliver played the fool and tried to drink with Winston Churchill. Soon he was leering like a fox. Churchill's waiters could have wrung a pint of vodka from his blouse. The sailor was loose enough to glower back at the British team. Churchill gave him a cigar. Ollie and the Prime Minister smoked across the table and destroyed two vodka glasses with the clench of their teeth. Churchill began to admire the crazy American boy. Rasputin had his pluck. He wouldn't dive under the table no matter what you put in his mouth.

Oliver wasn't in any trouble. His knees were firm. He could spoon up lentils or lick caviar off the handle of a knife. The fumes in his eyes hadn't gotten him to hallucinate. He did see another Stalin in the room! The sailor was staring at Youssipev. Stalin must have had his double trundled in to amuse Churchill and FDR. Youssipev didn't even have a table seat. He sat alone, in the corner, wearing his marshal's uniform. Here, in front of the Allies, he was allowed to mimic Uncle Joe. He lit cigarettes, wiped his mustache, watered his vodka with a jar. Youssipev made everybody piss. FDR was roaring again. Hopkins came out of a light sleep to start his brittle, sick man's laugh. Winston almost swallowed his cigar. Stalin was laughing *and* crying. He had a handkerchief over his face. He mumbled something through the handkerchief. The interpreter tried to smooth Stalin's twisted speech. "I'm an old man . . . I'm an old man . . . I'm an old man."

Throughout his impersonation, Youssipev had looked at Oliver Beebe, as if a special kind of charity existed between them, the comradeship of fools. But

Stalin's handkerchief talk bit into Youssipev. The uniform seemed to tighten around his neck. He looked away from Ollie, watched his own feet. The double had committed the grievous sin of making Stalin cry. An NKVD man touched him on the shoulder, and Youssipev went out of the room.

Stalin wiped his eyes with the handkerchief and delivered the next toast. Was it to the king of England? Harry the Hop? Youssipev? There was too much whistling in Oliver's ears. The room shrank around him. A British general had to leave his side of the table to poke Ollie in the ribs. "Get up, get up. Mr. Stalin's drinking to you."

The general grabbed Oliver by the elbows and raised him off the chair. Otherwise they couldn't have finished the toast. The boy noticed bedbugs in the chandeliers. He had vodka in his mouth. No Englishman would dare remove him from the table. He was held in place while Churchill could think of a new person to toast. Then the sailor fell into his chair. He didn't hurt his arms. The drop was soft. He slept with a cruel leer on his face until the party was over.

The First Lady
of the
WesternWorld

Oliver didn't wake to the beat of dolphins under his window. The Secret Service rolled him out of bed. The boy had to catch a ride. He was going home on the Sacred Cow with admirals, generals, and the Secretary of State, but not with FDR. The Boss would sail from Sevastopol this afternoon for the Middle East. He had an appointment with "three Arabian kings" to talk about a homeland for the Jews. Oliver couldn't even say goodbye. The Boss was locked in a room with Marshal Stalin. So Oliver gave his last Baby Ruths to the Russian soldiers, took a military car up into the mountains over the Black Sea, and stepped aboard the Sacred Cow.

The boy was hit with a tragedy when he got to the White House. Ex-Empress Zena died in her sleep while Oliver was on the Sacred Cow. Mrs. Roosevelt had gone to lecture in Los Angeles, and none of her aides would assume the responsibility of burying an ex-empress. The task fell to Oliver. Nobody had ever told the sailor how to put people into the ground. He had to start from scratch.

Zena couldn't get out of the attic. She lay in a box that the White House carpenters had built for her at the instructions of Mrs. Roosevelt's secretary. This temporary coffin could scatter the maids, who had liked Zena, but wouldn't go near her room. Oliver wasn't afraid of a carpenters' box. He knew that Zena's children had been murdered in the war. Still, he had to look through her belongings to find out if Zena had any relatives in the world. All he uncovered were pamphlets from an order of begging friars near Buffalo, New York. The boy didn't hesitate. He called the friars on the telephone. They would bury Zena in their graveyard if the sailor could get her to Buffalo with a proper death certificate. Oliver lacked the authority to put Zena on a train. He went down two flights and cornered the first admiral he saw coming out of the Map Room. The admiral cringed at the bleak lines in Oliver's forehead.

"There's a lady upstairs. She used to be the empress of Bulgaria. Now she's dead. The Boss isn't here to cry for her. He was her friend. He's going to be mad as shit if the Navy doesn't help. I can't find her death certificate. Send for a Navy doctor and tell him to fix another one up. I'll need a chauffeur and a truck to get her to Union Station and the right papers to ship her out, so the conductor won't scream at us. Admiral, if there's any flack, the Boss will piss on the Navy and piss on you."

There was a furor in the mansion when Mrs. Roosevelt got back from L.A. Her people tried to cover up their lack of devotion to the ex-empress. They presented her with a niggardly list of details. A death in the attic, they said. Poor Zena. We had to force that Oliver Beebe to take charge of her burial. The First Lady could sense a hollowness beneath the shrill talk of her aides. She didn't bother shouting at these women, but she glared at them with frozen husks in her blue-gray eyes. The women figured they would have to watch out. Eleanor was on a tear. The First Lady wouldn't fire you, or slap your cheeks. But if you stood outside the range of her mercy, God forbid. Eleanor didn't have the power to forget.

Her aides broke down under the terrible scrutiny of Eleanor's glare, and they began to cry. They let out the story of their own neglect syllable by syllable. With blubbering faces they mentioned Oliver's goodness to Zena. Eleanor told them to powder their eyes.

The girls marched into Eleanor's closet to groom themselves. They shut the door. They puffed on Chesterfields over the sink. The girls knew their Eleanor. She hadn't been close to Franklin's bed in thirty years. It had nothing to do with the ravages of polio. Franklin shunned her long before he became a paralytic. He'd had this love affair with her own social secretary while he toiled for the Navy Department under President Woodrow Wilson. He might have run away with that deepchested Lucy Mercer if his mother hadn't promised to cast him out of the Roosevelts. Mother Roosevelt made herself quite clear. Franklin wasn't to see Lucy again. But Eleanor couldn't forgive. She guarded her righteousness and wouldn't sleep with Franklin after that. The mistress of Albany and Washington, D.C., had her private quarters. Franklin didn't object. He built a cottage and a swimming pool for her at Val-Kill. As far as Frank is concerned, said the girls, giggling in the closet, Eleanor can soak her head.

The girls were only human. How could they keep up with Eleanor? She had all the energies of a disappointed woman. She could push from cause to cause, from Negroes to miners to motherhood. It was better than staying in an empty bed. The girls believed in the very same causes, but *they* could rest half a minute, stop for a sandwich, file their nails. They didn't come at you like a hurricane.

Eleanor went to the basement. She sat with Oliver and apologized for her girls. The sailor was already blue in the head from hearing so many admirals' complaints. But he listened to the First Lady. Removed from squabbling secretaries and superstitious maids, they could mourn an ex-empress in peace. They would ride to Buffalo in the spring, Mrs. Roosevelt said, and visit with Oliver's friars. There's no First Lady like this First Lady, Oliver thought. She would have rushed home from Los Angeles to touch a dead empress' hand, if her girls hadn't hid the news from her. Now she had to prepare for the nigger rally. She would occupy a bench tomorrow in Lafayette Park with a gang of Negro mothers, field their questions, and speak to the crowd. "Oliver," she said, "will you stand next to me in the park?"

"Yes'm."

The boy closed up his tiny office in the basement after Mrs. Roosevelt left, grabbed his peacoat and a supply of brittle candy, and hiked to Mount Vernon Square. It was bitter cold in February, and Oliver thrust his hands deep into his pockets. His sister's shades were down, and the lights were off in her room.

It was the Spaniard who obliged Anita to lower the shades. Orlando lay on her bed with that smooth groin of his. The Spaniard had magnificent calves. He was scared to death of Ollie. "Honey, can't I go downstairs and tell him not to wait for me? His ass will freeze in the park."

The Spaniard jerked across the bed. His calves tightened, and Anita saw the beautiful hooking muscles under his knee. "Girl, stay where you are. I don't want Beebe getting any ideas. He might decide to come up. I'm not going to play clap-hands with your brother. He could tear my arm off."

Orlando couldn't take Anita to Vivian's room right now. The FBI had warned him to keep away from the Willard until after the nigger ladies marched up to the edge of the White House and kissed the President's ugly wife. Then he could have Anita in Georgetown, the Willard, and on the chancellery floor. Orlando Frayard was the Bureau's good little boy. He'd fingered Vivian de Vries, told the Bureau about the plot on Mrs. Roosevelt's life. "That skinny son-of-a-bitch intends to stab her in Lafayette Park and blame it on the colored folks." Orlando couldn't figure it out. The Bureau hadn't swiped cousin Viv off the street. The scarecrow was still dancing around with a bottle of wine in his pocket. And Orlando had to crawl on his knees in a boardinghouse if he expected to rut with Anita Beebe.

Both of them heard a timid knock on Anita's door. Orlando reached for his pants. His lips were white. But he couldn't lose all that blondness over his eyes. "Is that Oliver?" he said, wondering how fast he could shrink into Anita's closet.

Anita put on her gown. "Who is it?" she rasped from her side of the door.

"It's me. Phil."

Her "husband" from Milwaukee had come to her in rags, with a pathetic growth of hair on his chin. "Where's my baby?" she said.

"I left him in the Catholic nursery for a couple of days."

Anita had visions of Michael in a big church basket with other abandoned two-year-olds.

"Anita, the FBI's been following me . . . couldn't

take Michael for a walk . . . always two men in brown overcoats . . . I had to get away. Your brother works for the President . . . I thought Oliver could help me . . . when I got off the train, two more guys in overcoats . . . they're downstairs in the hall."

Philip tottered into Anita's bed. He threw the covers over himself and shivered underneath. "Maybe Oliver can kick them out. . . ."

Anita turned around. The Spaniard had climbed into his embassy shirt. "Stop worrying," he said. He walked out of the room to parley with the FBI.

Anita chewed on her fingers. She could swear a fat possum was moving in her bed. "Philip, can't you act like a human being? Get out of my sheets."

He tore into the sandwich Anita prepared, his mouth thick with mayonnaise. "Are people starving in Milwaukee?" she asked. "Phil, if my baby gets malnutrition on account of you, I'll bust your head."

"Baby's fine," Philip muttered, with a bulge in his cheeks. God, you couldn't look at men! If they weren't stuffing themselves, you could be sure they were stuffing you. Was her Spaniard taking a holiday on the boarding-house steps? She was stuck with crazy Oliver, a boy who loved to brood, and a husband who gobbled tuna fish, and Orlando Frayard. 'Lando returned with a smugness on his face. "Kid, they won't bother you. Just go back to Milwaukee fast as you can."

Didn't he have any respect for the father of her child? 'Lando was clutching her tits before Philip had the chance to run into the street. Frayard was delighted with himself. He'd gone down the stairs on crooked, trembling knees. But he was tough with the overcoats in the parlor. "Call the Bureau," he shouted into their lapels.

"Tell them you're playing with Oliver Beebe." It worked. The agents used the landlady's phone. They dipped their hats to Orlando and left the boardinghouse. And he was hugging that dopey girl again.

Anita stayed quiet under him. She wasn't dazzled by the press of his body. She just didn't understand how he could negotiate for a draft dodger like Phil. "Honey . . . what did you do to the FBI that they had to let Philip go?"

"I mentioned Oliver. That's all."

Anita couldn't relax with mysteries grinding in the walls like the bump, bump of mice. This was Oliver's room. This was Oliver's pillow. This was Oliver's bed. *Oliver.* Could that name absolve Phil, get him out of trouble? When you muttered "Oliver," was it like saying boo? Her neck was arched. She could peek through a corner of the window shade. Her eye was in Mount Vernon Square. The peacoat hadn't dissolved. She wished she had a tongue, a long sturdy tongue, that could stretch out the window and say hello to Oliver. She wanted to suck his face, scoop him into her mouth and hold him there. She would taste his gristle, and then she would know how much magic Oliver had.

But you couldn't keep your head straight about your own brother. Sometimes he disgusted her, sometimes he didn't. She'd scrubbed his prick when he was four and five. A soft snake with soap bubbles on it. Is that where the magic comes from? Her neck hurt, and she had to push her forehead away from the window. Would Oliver spend February waiting for her and go into March? Why shouldn't she have a brother outside her window? Who else would have scrubbed his baby prick?

THIRTY-TWO

Oliver wouldn't roost in Mount Vernon Square park. He stood three hours with his fists in his pockets. Then he started for the White House. The scarecrow waylaid him on Thirteenth and "G," jumping out at Oliver from a dirty yard. "Give me all your tootsie rolls," Vivian said, menacing the sailor with a pocket-knife. You couldn't have opened a chicken's neck with that blade. It was eaten through with rust. Oliver was too disheartened to laugh. He plucked a ten-dollar bill out of his wallet. "Take a room," he said. "You could die in this cold."

Vivian scoffed at the ten-dollar bill. "I don't want your charity. I got a room in the biggest hotel. The heat comes up twenty-four hours a day. But there's scum on the bed. I'd rather sleep with the niggers."

The scarecrow shambled away from Oliver. "It's hopeless talking to you. All you're good for is yessing First Ladies. You grab her hand tomorrow at the nigger show, hear? And you give it the best squeeze you can. Because you'll have to get by without her."

Oliver went home. He lay in his attic bed with the light out and pulled on his lip. Vivian hadn't jumped on Oliver for his tootsie rolls. The scarecrow was trying to tell him something, and Oliver couldn't say what. A tail was beating on his door. Fala had come for a visit. Ollie had to crawl out of bed and let the little pest in. The Pup took to the attic when FDR was away from the house.

The sailor didn't come out from under his pillow until the sun climbed up the wall. It was Sunday morning, and six o'clock. He had Ethel Rosenquist ring the FBI. "Oliver, you must be out of your mind. Don't you believe in Sundays?"

"That's all right," Oliver said. "Mr. Hoover works seven days a week."

The girl who ran the switchboard for the FBI was huffy with Ethel Rosenquist. "Who's calling, please?"

Ethel said, "Oliver Beebe . . . at the White House."

The girl routed the call to Edgar's home near Rock Creek Park. The Director wasn't aleep. He was about to have breakfast with his two dogs, and he invited Ollie over. The sailor had to dress in a hurry. Edgar's limousine would be at the south gate in ten minutes. The Pup watched Oliver wrap his neckerchief. He rolled in the blankets and made an awful whimper.

"Bullshit," Oliver said. "You're not going with me."

He got into his peacoat on the stairs. The sailor didn't have to ride to Rock Creek Park. Kirkland Horn had returned from the Middle East ahead of Mr. Roosevelt, and Oliver could have told him about the scarecrow. But he didn't get along with the Secret Service. Horn would have mocked him, made him feel that he had no more brains than a cow. So Ollie had to depend on J. Edgar Hoover for advice.

They had breakfast in Edgar's kitchen. It was a red brick house with copper gutters on its gray roof. Bill prepared the food. He was Edgar's bodyguard, chauffeur, gardener, and cook. He could poach an egg like no other man. The egg arrived perfect on your toast. It was still hard to eat at Edgar's table. Ollie had two Airedales in his lap, "G-boy" and "Franklin, Jr." They must have sniffed the Outlaw on Oliver's clothes, and they wouldn't stop nuzzling him. The sailor had to live with two bony heads near his groin.

Franklin, Jr., was the puppy of the house. Edgar had gotten him from the dog pound in October as something of a talisman to help FDR shellac Governor Dewey. G-boy was older and stronger, and tyrannized Franklin, Bill, and Ollie. He left a blue mark on Oliver's thigh with each swipe of his head. He would have eaten Bill's trouser cuffs if Ollie hadn't been around. But he couldn't look Edgar in the eye. The Director didn't have to scream at his dog. One twitch of his jowls, and G-boy would slink out of sight.

"Uncle, there's a guy named Vivian who's been saying some crazy things about Mrs. Roosevelt. Could you watch out for her at the mothers' march? Vivian's carrying a knife."

Bill drove Ollie back to the White House, and Edgar had the two dogs to himself. He fed them pieces of toast and rubbed their wet mouths with his fist. Why should Ollie become a godmother to Mrs. Roosevelt? The sailor didn't belong to her flock of hens. You had to be a sob sister or an ugly girl to stay with Eleanor. Edgar couldn't stomach that long-faced witch without a corset. She drew all the pinkos to her, the old-maid liberals, the intellectual granddads, the Negro philosophers who loved to tell you how the world would come into its own soon as the armies and navies and police departments disappeared.

He didn't intend to be at the mothers' march. His agents could handle rabble-rousers and cockeyed Trotskyites. Edgar had been following the career of Vivian de Vries since 1938 when that Charleston baby began to put out *Contempo* magazine. The G-man read all the pinko sheets. The Bureau had to scrutinize everything, even the drivel of Vivian de Vries.

It wasn't always like that. The Bureau had been the drowsing arm of the Justice Department until Edgar woke it with a kick. He was the boy wonder, appointed to head the Bureau in 1924, at the age of twenty-nine. The Bureau had dingy quarters in the old Justice Department Building at Fourteenth and "K," where Edgar would arrive in a white linen suit. The professionals inside the Bureau, agents who were often twice as old as Edgar, poked fun at their new boss. They saw his briefcase, his index cards, his shiny pencils, and his white suit, and they dubbed him "the Boy Scout" and "Sherlock, Jr." They ignored "the Boy Scout" and slept in their cubicles, on a Justice Department chair. Edgar didn't back off. He rid every cubicle of its chair and forced the agents to resign.

He brought lawyers and accountants into the Bureau. He established a fingerprint unit and a tiny crime lab, and got machine guns for his accountants. But Edgar wasn't happy. Agents in the field were calling attention to themselves as they smoked out rats like Alvin Karpis. Edgar loved anonymity for his men. He would boil when he came upon photographs of a special agent hugging a machine gun as if it were some erotic device. It was the fault of the journalists. The papers had turned the FBI into a wild west circus. Edgar didn't exist to glorify Alvin Karpis. It took hundreds of hours of field work, turning in affidavits, checking files and fingerprint cards, stroking the right informant, to trap one lousy crook or saboteur.

A wandering Trotskyite named de Vries, in Edgar's files for six years, stumbles into Washington last summer. He visits one of the Bureau's own informants, Orlando Frayard. De Vries tries to "sell" Franklin Roosevelt's barber to German sympathizers at the Spanish embassy. The Trotskyite is keeping company with the barber's sister, who has tremendous influence over this Oliver boy. The Bureau could have arrested de Vries and warned Roosevelt to sack his barber. But this was too easy. Edgar would have to sit on his index cards for a while. The cards weren't ripe.

He was warring with Major Colbert of the Secret Service. The Major had enormous hopes for himself. He wanted to scrap Edgar's Bureau and operate his own FBI out of the Treasury Building. So Edgar kept quiet about Beebe and Beebe's sister and Vivian the Trotskyite. He could embarrass the Secret Service whenever he chose. He built up a phantom network, a hoax of spies, that moved in and out of a fascist club run by an imbecile marqués.

The FBI read every piece of mail in the Spanish diplomatic pouch. There were enough microphones in the chancellery walls to create a little orchestra for the Bureau. Half the Spanish couriers owed their livelihood to Edgar Hoover. But these were only precautionary measures. The sailor wasn't a spy, and the Bureau always knew that. Oliver's awareness came out of a barbering kit. His talents were limited to his tools. He was loyal, dumb, and good. He had one liability, a diseased slut of a sister, a depraved bitch, who seduced Oliver and tried to smear him in Vivian's moronic shit.

No harm would come to the boy. Edgar saw to that.

He wasn't doing Oliver a favor. He was protecting the President of the United States. Roosevelt was sacrosanct in Edgar's principality at the Justice Department. Agents wouldn't have dared utter a word about "that cripple in the White House." You could find Roosevelt on every Bureau wall. But this idolatry didn't carry over to FDR's retainers. It was safe to hiss at the pinkos surrounding the President, the bleeding hearts who were out to infect the country with Soviet ideas. FDR was a prisoner to their yakking music. The only comforts he had were his dog, his stamps, and a quiet boy like Oliver Beebe.

Then the old man of the Secret Service, Kirkland Horn, introduced Edgar to the boy, brought him into Harvey's restaurant, and Edgar had his first look. He scrutinized Beebe in that white sailor suit. Now he could understand the President's attachment to Oliver. The boy had the blissful face of the dead. He didn't plot with his eyes. They were beautiful and dark. He had nothing to reveal under his pompadour. No wonder Franklin let the sailor live in his house.

Edgar got to like the boy. He would steal him in the evenings from Kirkland Horn and dine with him at Harvey's. People would stare at them, thinking the Director of the FBI was in collusion with the President's mysterious aide. The boy must have seemed foreboding in his Navy collar. This was America, where a seaman first class ate with the most powerful men in the world.

Edgar rose up from the breakfast table. His two dogs scattered to the ends of the kitchen. The G-man had to get dressed. He wouldn't have time to watch Eleanor the witch and her band of Negro mothers. Edgar was going into the alleys in his white suit to check that rotten Major Colbert. Washington had to be a desperate town, when the head of the Secret Service dreams that a pack of mangy dogs was plotting to kill FDR and take over the District.

Colbert had no understanding of a dog's mind. Did he believe animals could develop a sense of politics in Nigger Lane? How many of those renegades listened to Roosevelt's fireside chats? The country was short of food. You had to bring your own butter to the restaurants. People were hoarding carrots in their homes. The wild dogs of Washington had come into being on account of the war. They didn't intend to run a flag over Massachusetts Avenue. The dogs were starving in the alleys. They herded together to scratch for something to eat.

Colbert organized a citizens' army. He had vigilantes to fight the dogs. Grocers, retired firemen, off-duty cops, led by the Major himself. It was holy warfare scheduled for Sunday afternoon. Colbert would wait until the alleys emptied of mothers, infants, and old men for the march on Lafayette Square. Then he would seal off every exit and murder the dogs. Edgar would be there, alone. He couldn't send his agents in to challenge Colbert's army. The press would crucify him for having the Bureau take the side of renegade dogs.

He hadn't forgotten the witch in the park. He'd arranged a tiny picnic for Mrs. Roosevelt. His men would surround the First Lady without identifying themselves. When that Trotskyite got within ten feet, they would grab his puny knife and hustle him out of the park. The First Lady would yak, yak, yak to the mothers and never know that the Bureau had turned an assassin away from her. Edgar would close shop at the Spanish embassy, pitch that whoregirl Anita out of D.C., and the sailor could go on cutting Roosevelt's hair.

THIRTY-THREE

The White House had gone mad with activity when Oliver returned from Rock Creek Park. The maids drifted in and out of attic rooms pulling magical signs from their feather dusters while the Pup groaned on Oliver's bed. Secret Service men were clumping everywhere. They took over the north side of the house.

The old man was getting nervous. His kidney flared again. He would be pissing blood before the afternoon was over. He had to work around Mrs. Franklin's obstinate streak. Eleanor wouldn't tolerate an escort in Lafayette Square. So Kirkland grew sly on an ailing kidney. He shipped agents into the park dressed as peanut vendors and recruits from the forestry service. They were supposed to form an invisible ribbon around the First Lady.

They had plenty of time. The square wouldn't fill until the niggers got out of church. It must have been an odd Sunday. Oliver could hear a constant mewling sound before eleven o'clock. Fala crawled under the bed. Secret Service men tilted their binoculars over the White House roof to deal with the whimpering from the park. The noise wouldn't go away. Its lilt would reach through the walls and set a chandelier to shivering. The quietest spot in the house was the little row of dressing rooms near Mr. Franklin's indoor swimming pool. The butlers locked themselves inside these closets. It didn't help. That drone could turn a man crazy.

Mrs. Roosevelt left the White House with Oliver and her husband's dog. Oliver had to carry the Pup. The dog was petrified. He wanted to dig both ears into Oliver's coat.

Ollie couldn't understand the nigger ladies. Their whimpering stopped once Mrs. Franklin was outside the north gate. Was it the boundaries of the White House that had made them cry? They had reason to dislike the different armies of the Commander-in-Chief. Their sons had been turned into woolen-headed boys who couldn't be trusted to hold a rifle or a gun. So they collected in front of the President's house and cried for the indignity of black soldiers and sailors.

Mrs. Franklin lived in that house, where the generals came to visit, but she wasn't part of Mr. Franklin's military machine. And when they saw her leave the grounds with no one to protect her except a young sailor and a dog, and cross Pennsylvania Avenue into the park, without hat or gloves, her long face quivering in the cold, they didn't have to cry. She was the First Lady of the Western World. She could have walked on any primitive road, entered any shack, and she would have been recognized, the tall, marvelous woman with white hair who wouldn't turn a soul away. She'd rather sit with colored mamas than go to clambakes with the matriarchs of the city. She didn't ignore the alleys like earlier Presidents' wives. It wasn't tokenism with Mrs. FDR, pats on the head for the nearest pickaninny. She'd come here to cry with the mothers. She knew the dread of having sons in the war, but her sympathies went beyond the details of a mother in the White House. That horse's face she had, puckered and long, with wild teeth, could suck up the pain in every eye around her. You couldn't avoid the First Lady, even in her baggy suit. Her awkward concentration would win you over.

She was welcomed up to the speakers' platform at the southern end of the park, with Odessa Brown and the other members of the steering committee. There must have been ten thousand mothers in Lafayette Square, together with FBI men, peanut vendors, black sailors, city cops, sightseers from second-class hotels, the Secret Service, government girls who'd come to watch the niggers, a squad of generals in mufti who were slumming at the march, Fala, and Oliver Beebe. The sailor wedged himself as close to the platform as he possibly could. He meant to block the scarecrow, to deflect the path of Vivian's knife, with his coat, his hand, or his mouth. He had to stuff the Pup between his legs, so he could have a good shot at Vivian.

There was a curious nigger up on the platform, behind Mrs. Franklin and Odessa Brown. He had a wooly beard, a cane, and a wooly head of hair, but he didn't prowl like any old man. That was Mrs. Franklin's lost son, Jonathan Roosevelt, under the cotton wool. He was camouflaged that way to fool the Secret Service. Kirkland Horn would have pulled Jonathan off the platform for ripping up one of his agents, if he could have seen through the beard. Odessa still had her wits. She decked out the wild man and brought him to the rally to guard her and Eleanor from crazy white men and crazy niggers.

People began to point at Ollie and the Pup between his legs. Roosevelt's sailor and Roosevelt's dog. But Oliver wasn't giving autographs. He stuck out his lip and stared at the wild man's toes.

His sister found him like that. She was at the rally with Orlando Frayard, thirty feet away from Oliver, and she spotted his coat and his sailor hat. The boy didn't like to move. He was frozen in a particular attitude, and not even an army of mothers could have taken him off his spot. Anita was glad to spy on her brother, to catch his pompadour and the volatile bumps along the edges of his face. What was Oliver brooding about? And why did he seem so handsome in the company of tourists, vendors, cops, and old mamas? Her brother was adored in Lafayette Square. All those eyes on Ollie, as if he were a piece of Roosevelt that people could touch with a pinkie.

A lump of metal scraped her arm. Anita let out a little scream. Orlando was hovering over her ex-boyfriend de Vries. "You're jabbing the wrong lady. Cover that knife."

Vivian leered at Anita. "Might as well have sis too . . . 'Lando, lemme mark her up."

They were wrestling, those boyfriends of hers, but it was like a slow, deliberate game, where you had to hide your moves from everybody else. Orlando rasped between his quiet lunges at the knife. "Cousin, you're going to miss your fat chance. . . ." He had reddish lines on his knuckles from Vivian's blade. "The cops don't like children who play with knives . . . Viv, you'd better lay off. Franklin's bitch might not wait for you. She's got speeches to give."

Vivian straightened his shoulders with a twitch at the neck and slipped away from Orlando. "Honey," Anita said, "what the heck is going on?"

Vivian seesawed between the niggers, shoving with

an elbow while he listened to the mothers on the platform address Mr. Roosevelt's sorry queen. He couldn't make sense of their shrill talk. Sons? Army? Navy? Kitchen hands? Latrines? These weren't Vivian's grievances. Roosevelt was the man who bowed to Stalin and helped murder Leon Trotsky. He was the emperor and king who strangled America and devoured human blood. His queen was babbling now. Her squeaky voice wasn't unpleasant to Vivian. She mentioned hearts and sacrifice, the unfairness of war, her husband's plan for a new world body that would fight racism, hunger, neglect. She called it the United Nations. Vivian smiled. This was the emperor's way of parceling out bits of the planet for his greedy kinsmen, Churchill, Stalin, and Chiang Kai-shek. Vivian would also do a little parceling. On that big-lipped queen who loved to jabber in a field of niggers. He began to whittle at the air with his knife as he mumbled over the mothers' backs. Miss Eleanor, here Missy, Missy, Miss.

Oliver heard scatterings of Vivian's song before he ever noticed the scarecrow's bobbing head. Where were Edgar's boys? Two men in brown overcoats pushed into the moving screen of tourists and black mothers, but they couldn't get to Vivian. Oliver was going to shout up at the platform, *Mrs. Franklin, please run away,* when he felt the blur of a cottony beard riding over him. Jonathan Roosevelt had the eyes of a wild man trained on Tangier. He couldn't have missed the colors of a rusty blade in that clean February light. The blade might have been meant for either of his two mothers, Mrs. Roosevelt and Mrs. Brown. Jonathan had to leap.

Washingtonians had never seen a wild man in the air. Could shoulders fall out of the sky just like that?

Vivian was knocked off his feet. Jonathan had the lazy, driving kick of a demented mule. But his beard came off, and the Secret Service men recognized the butler who had scarred one of them for life. Jonathan climbed over Vivian and shrank into the crowd of black mothers. Tourists shrieked at him. Vivian lay twitching on the ground. His forehead was turning green.

Anita had a visceral devotion to that son-of-a-bitch. She wanted to run up to Vivian. The Spaniard clutched her arm. She could sense a bitterness around his eyes, a disappointment that gave a nasty curl to his mouth. "You can't do a thing for that boy. Come on."

Fala couldn't have stayed alive under the sailor's legs. He was bumped in the crush of heels and soles until Ollie remembered to pick him up. Fala had clots of fur in his eyes and two bloody paws. Oliver stuffed him in his peacoat, and searched for Jonathan Roosevelt. The wild man scrambled out of the park at Madison Place. The Secret Service and the District police weren't quick enough to grab his tail. Was Jonathan heading home to Crawfish Alley? Oliver had to warn him. Mrs. Brown's whores couldn't help the wild man. The Secret Service would pluck him off the steps of any cathouse in Nigger Lane.

The sailor couldn't follow Jonathan with a dog in his coat. The Pup was slowing him down. He had to spill Fala onto the mud floor of Nigger Lane. The wind had a horrible bite in the alleys, and Mr. Franklin's dog wouldn't budge from the convenient little tent of Oliver's sailor pants. "Shove off," Oliver said. "How can I run with your ass in my way?" And Fala had to keep up with the sailor's churning legs.

It was a lunatic chase, from alley to avenue and alley

again, Oliver pacing himself by that head of cotton wool. He couldn't gain on Jonathan Roosevelt. The wild man gave Oliver a lesson in geography. You could succumb to a powerful schizophrenia while pursuing Jonathan Roosevelt. The sailor's mental climate couldn't absorb the sudden switch of things. A starving goat at the rear of an embassy house on Massachusetts Avenue caused Oliver to blink. He stopped and fed the goat a tootsie roll, and then stumbled after Jonathan. He fell over a baby lying in a patch of alley grass. The baby was dead. Oliver hunkered in the grass. The chase had exhausted him. He could swear he was in Weehawken, playing in a lot. He began to cry. The wild man stood near him when Oliver got back on his feet.

"Don't they bury babies in this part of town?" Oliver asked Jonathan Roosevelt.

"What for? The wind's as good as any shovel. It'll make that child a comfortable grave."

"There's dogs in the alleys, wild dogs. They eat rats. Won't they eat a dead baby?"

"No sir, Mr. Ollie. These are nigger dogs. They're loyal as hell. They wouldn't eat a nigger child."

Jonathan stared at his old mentor, the sailor boy who'd taught him the manners of this world: toothbrushes, toilet seats, and comb your hair. He still had some affection for Oliver Beebe. "Why'd you come after me, Mr. Ollie?"

"To tell you to stay away from Mrs. Brown's. The Secret Service isn't blind. They saw you on the platform. They know you belong to Odessa."

"Who says I'm going to 'Dessa's place? Those suckers wouldn't have a chance at catching me if they didn't have you and the dog."

"Jonathan Roosevelt, what are you talking about?"

"All they have to do is follow the peacoat and Roosevelt's Pup. . . . What happened to the dog, Mr. Ollie? Where's that Fala?"

Oliver patted the bottoms of his pants. The dog wasn't in the pants. Jonathan had to say goodbye. "The alley's filling up, Mr. Ollie. You can always smell a sucker coming upwind."

The wild man crouched against the walls of the shacks and plunged ahead, his left shoulder sliding off the rotten alley wood. The sailor couldn't resist a final shout. "Jonathan, you ought to hide in Rock Creek Park."

"I wouldn't know how to get there, Mr. Ollie. Thanks."

Oliver heard the tap of bone on wood, then the tapping died, and the wind howled in his face, and the boy was utterly confused. His feet made little pushes in the grass. He couldn't have gotten out of Nigger Lane. An older man had to rescue him.

It was Kirkland Horn who came trundling up the alley in rubber-soled shoes. Kirkland must have sensed that he'd fallen upon a bewildered boy. He didn't try to shake revelations out of Oliver. He winced at the baby on the ground. He was sixty-five years old. He couldn't walk away from a dead infant. He stooped and picked it up, the skin like bark against his gloves. He stuck the baby under his coat and signaled to Oliver with his head. It was fifteen paces and a single turn, and they were in a garden plot that brought them out of the alley. Oliver stood on Vermont Avenue. Nothing outside the attic would ever be a home to him. He couldn't function away from the President's roof.

THIRTY-FOUR

The Pup didn't flounder in Chicken Bean Row. Long-bellied rats, a bearded goat swallowing the paper on a tootsie roll, crafty wood lice, slippery rocks, dolls without heads and toes, wild carrots, and human shit couldn't frighten the Outlaw of Fala Hill. His paws healed over with cakes of mud. He learned how to run with hair in his eyes. He joined a pack of mongrel dogs that owned Nigger Lane.

The dogs didn't resent his pedigree. They were willing to forage with the Pup. But they were seasoned animals, with all the advantages that mixed blood could bring. They had broad foreheads, tight pink eyes, fat on their throats to protect their jugular veins, lumpy withers that would have been hard to grab, genitals that could be tucked under in a fight, strong flews, smelly brown teeth, and a range of scars on their crests that they would exhibit to an enemy.

These dogs had a specific line of attack. The ones with the most scars made up the perimeters. They were supposed to inspire dread. Weaker, smaller dogs would hold to the center of the pack, and reinforce the perimeters whenever a lead dog fell out. The Pup didn't have much of a battle station. Fed on a rich man's diet of coffee, sugar, and toast, he lacked the raw desire to bump over a trash can and dig with his nose for some edible thing. And how could he scatter an alien dog, when he had no scars on his soft black coat? He'd been around human beings too long. Pampered at the White House, petted and photographed, he stank of milk and Camel cigarettes.

He was the newcomer, the vulnerable dog who occupied the centermost spot. He ran with the lame and the one-eyed, dogs who were of little use to the pack. They were the last to eat, the first to look for a safety zone in times of war.

The Pup didn't chafe over his rank at the bottom of the pack. He was happy to be with the one-eyed, to assist the lame, to lean into a fellow dog and help mend the pack's lines with his own meager body. These dogs had the socking power of a baby storm. The pack would flood through an opening in the alleys and raid a choice avenue. It moved with the lightning of hungry dogs, its energy concentrated at the edges, as it smashed bottles of cream, overturned spice racks outside a vegetable market, stole offal off a butcher truck, ripped into bags of groceries left on a porch. Raid and run. Raid and run. Or else the police and special dogcatching posses would have skulled them with the long poles they carried.

The pack couldn't keep to one or two coveted areas inside Nigger Lane. There was almost no nutrition in the alleys. Bitter carrots, bugs, and shit. So the dogs had to risk meeting a posse, and other mongrel gangs who were scavenging for the same limited supply of food. Rival gangs would desolate each other. Perimeter dogs might lose an eye. Ears and tails were bitten off.

The Pup had to endure seventeen assaults, from

posses and competing dogs. Blood spouted over him, but he was cushioned by members of the pack, and he still had his tail. There were strange goings-on in the alleys. Men in gray butcher's smocks had come in to hunt nigger dogs. This was no ordinary posse. The men in gray smocks had knives, clubs, and scatter-guns. They crouched near an exit and fell upon an entire pack of dogs. The scatter-guns boomed like cannons in Nigger Lane. It was Major Colbert and his vigilantes, organized in combat groups.

The Major was up to his nose in filth and guts. He'd never been happier in all his life. He was saving Franklin Roosevelt from the mongrel hordes, and taking his vengeance on the alleys. Nigger Lane couldn't swallow up mongrels any more. Colbert had his maps. He could reach into any cave or hidden corner, pinpoint a dog on a mound of nigger trash. Then one of his scouting parties spotted a man in a white suit, and the Major's joy was gone.

His men wouldn't kill dogs with Edgar Hoover breathing on them. They were only butchers, grocers, and off-duty cops. The FBI could scare the smock off a vigilante's back. Colbert went up to Edgar in a blinding rage. "Hoover, the alleys aren't your bailiwick. Get the fuck out of here."

Edgar's jowls didn't flame up. He didn't sputter at the Secret Service. He held his calm Virginia accent. "Major, I think I'll squat in the grass for a spell. Don't mind me, son. Get on with your work."

The Major rushed to different outposts, trying to rally his men. But word of Edgar had already reached the outposts. The butchers laid down their scatter-guns. Colbert was left with a small band of grocers and stalwarts from the Secret Service. The vigilantes prepared to fall upon a new pack of dogs. They could feel a shuddering in the ground. The mongrels were running again. The Major held up his arm. The vigilantes would strike when the arm went down. The sign didn't come. The Major's teeth were rattling in his head.

Colbert had recognized a little Scottie in the pack. Fala was running with these nigger dogs. Now the Major understood where the mongrels got their intelligence. It came from the Pup. Roosevelt's dog had been living two distinct lives. White House mascot and leader of the renegades. The Major called off his men. He couldn't fight Edgar Hoover, Roosevelt, and the Outlaw of Fala Hill. Colbert's men trudged out of the alleys, stepping on the bodies of dogs they had slain. The mongrels had beaten them.

The Pup had no memory of Major Colbert. He ran with the dogs to a hummock in Bloodfield Alley. The pack attended to its wounds and had to rut for carrots in the earth, or starve. Fala's stomach began to growl for coffee and toast. During the quietus, when a majority of the dogs were asleep, he abandoned his center spot and slipped out of the perimeters.

The Pup had an instinct for Pennsylvania Avenue. He was at the gates of the White House ten minutes after he left the dogs. The sentries were appalled. They had never seen the Outlaw of Fala Hill with blood and shit on him. A Secret Service man arrived to fetch in the dog. Something was amiss. No one fussed over the Pup. Butlers and maids collected outside the chief usher's office and barely said hello to Fala. The maids had amulets under their shirts, tiny rattles that sounded horrible when squeezed against their bosoms. Fala barked and jumped, but he couldn't get through the butlers' woeful looks. So he sneaked into the usher's office to find out what could be more important than the reappearance of Mr. Roosevelt's Pup. A dead black thing was lying on the usher's table in a little torn blanket. The Pup darted under everybody's knees and hid upstairs in the Blue Room.

The Secret Service, the household staff, and Mr. Roosevelt's ushers were in a funk. The maids wouldn't let go of their amulets. That devil, Mr. Kirkland, he brung a dead chil' into the house. Prayers and incantations didn't help. Mr. Kirkland wouldn't get rid of the child. His own men hinted to him about sealing the child in a pillowcase and sending for the police. Horn said no. "I found that child. And I'm not letting any fool throw him in a grave without any marker on it. *No.* The child stays here."

They had to figure that the old man was deranged. Whoever heard of a nigger baby in an usher's office? The maids went up to the Roosevelt floor to tell Mrs. Franklin what that devil Horn had done. Only Mrs. Franklin had the power to clear the usher's office and dispossess that chil'. Mr. Kirkland wouldn't budge without her. The men of District 16 sniggered behind his back. They grew bold the longer Kirkland stuck to that deathwatch of his. Their sniggers fell closer and closer to the child. Kirkland wasn't worried about the opinions of his men. They could see all the gray bristle under the mustache he had to redden every week. He was an old man with a piss-poor kidney, who'd given over his life to guarding Presidents. He'd gone to the Crimea, felt his guts jiggle in an airplane, parried with the NKVD, picked up lice on his ankles and in his ass, for the love of FDR. And he'd become a handmaid to Oliver Beebe. Kirkland wasn't giving up the child.

A long, wrinkled face with smoky eyes observed

him from the door. Mrs. Roosevelt had come to the usher's office in her peignoir. The maids got her out of bed to reason with the devil and also chastise him. "Kirkland," she said. "Kirk . . ." She stood over the dead child with a look of such deep pity, Kirkland lost his grimace.

"Ma'am, I wasn't going to leave that baby in the grass. I'm from West Virginia, where you don't abandon the dead."

The maids peeked into the room. A pudgy fist stirred under the blanket. The maids said hallelujah and clutched their rattles, or they might have swooned. Mrs. Franklin breathed on the infant, and it moved a fist. Sweet God, it must have thawed out like a fat mud pie. Mrs. Franklin had the gift of healing in the webbed pockets around her cheeks. The dead chil' began to wail. One of the maids ran upstairs for cookies, soup, and Oliver Beebe.

Horn couldn't be swayed. "Makes no difference, ma'am. I won't orphan the baby to a hospital. It needs a mother right away."

Oliver walked into the room. Seeing the baby wail narrowed his heart. Were they raising black Pinocchios under the Boss' roof, dead things that could learn to cry?

"Ollie dear," Mrs. Roosevelt said, "can you think of a mother for Kirkland's baby?"

Oliver looked from Mrs. Roosevelt to the baby to Kirkland Horn. " 'Dessa Brown," he said, without a bit of hesitation.

Mrs. Roosevelt crinkled her mouth and telephoned Crawfish Alley. The Secret Service had to venture into a whorehouse, find Odessa, and bring her through the north gate. Mrs. Roosevelt served a midnight tea for Odessa in the West Sitting Hall. The butlers clanked up and down the stairs with fresh pots of tea. Their pride in Mrs. Franklin had begun to shrink. The First Lady ought to have met Mrs. Brown at the gate and passed her the child. But Mrs. Franklin didn't have the butlers' snobbish ways. She talked to 'Dessa Brown in old wooly socks, with crumbs and dregs of tea on her pegnoir. There was no consternation between them, no brittle remarks. 'Dessa agreed to take the child.

Then, after the chief usher got his office back and Kirkland's child was no longer in the house, a maid discovered Fala snoring in the Blue Room. The dog was rushed to the attic. The maids drew a bath for him. He was scrubbed until his eyes rolled with pure delight. "Well, I never . . ." the maids said, as the water turned black from all the blood and shit on Fala's body. But they had to finish the job. Mr. Franklin would be home in two days, and the Boss, he couldn't live near a shit-cluttered dog.

Inside
St. Elizabeth's

Vivian didn't know a thing about wild butlers with wooly hair. He couldn't have told you who kicked him in the head. He remembered a squeezing sensation around his eyes. He thought he'd ripped through the empress' skirts with his knife. He smelled blood while he was blacking out. He woke in a hospital shirt with the sleeves knotted behind his back. They hadn't robbed him of all his wits. He was in some kind of violent ward. He shouted at his male nurse. "Kiddo, did I get the emperor's lady? Did I total Eleanor?"

The nurse asked him to shut his fucking mouth. He lived like that for a week, with both arms tucked under the shirt. They fed him cod-liver oil and jello with a big spoon. They escorted him to the craphouse, freeing one of his arms so Vivian could unroll the crap paper by himself. Then they took him out of the violent ward. The hospital shirt came off. And the nurses gave him a companion. A giant in farmer's pants.

They would spend afternoons on an enclosed porch, Vivian and the grim-headed giant. The nurses warned Viv not to mention baseball in the giant's presence. Baseball would stir him up. He'd already broken five or six porches. "That's Tutmiller," they said. "The Tuskegee

Ox. He used to wallop them for the Senators last June, July, and August. Rookie of the year until he went berserk. You call him Otto.''

So Vivian had the baseball player who couldn't talk baseball any more. It made no difference. They passed the time chewing tootsie rolls that the hospital provided for them in a special bin. The male nurses had little conspiracies against Otto and Viv. No baseball. No news of Eleanor and FDR. Vivian developed a pocket in his left cheek for securing tootsie rolls inside his mouth.

The Ox had a visitor who didn't bother with visiting rooms. He came right onto the porch, this gentleman caller in a white suit. "Who is that guy?" Vivian mumbled to the Ox.

"Shit, I don't know. That's my Uncle Ed."

Edgar didn't tease the Ox, or pout at Vivian the Trotskyite. He wasn't there to gloat. He brought comic books, a hairbrush, and packs of bubble gum that only the Bureau could get. You couldn't buy bubble gum in a store. He sat with the Ox, shared silences with him, because the G-man had his own sense of loyalty. He could have sent an agent over with the hairbrush. The agent would have smiled obediently at Otto. But Edgar wasn't crude. He wouldn't forget the Ox.

The looks that passed between the farmer and Uncle Ed were making Vivian jealous. How come no one visited him on the porch? Why couldn't he have Oliver Beebe?

"Uncle, how's Mrs. Roosevelt? Is she dead or alive?"

Edgar didn't stall the Trotskyite. "She's breathing, son, breathing hard as ever."

Viv started to cry. He was considering injustices, not

feeling sorry for himself. The queen was in her White House, and Viv was captured on a porch. It wasn't an age for poets. That much he understood. Edgar distributed the bubble gum and the nurses let him out through an opening in the porch screen. The Ox waved goodbye. Vivian contemplated the indignities of grown men blowing bubbles in a madhouse. Still, he was glad to have the gum. The noise of chewing seemed to annihilate the fact of Mrs. Roosevelt's life. He and Otto molded the gum between their jaws. There was a smack of exploding bubbles all afternoon. Vivian wasn't worried. He'd survive. He had his nurse, Otto, and Uncle's next visit to dream about. But he wished the nurses would tell him the name of this goddamn place. Was he going to leak out his existence on a porch that didn't have a name?

Deuces
and Kings

He might have been a skeleton in a sack of clothes. His neck had disappeared. His skin was like paper under the dull blue sheen. What on earth had happened to FDR? He'd met with Haile Selassie, Ibn Saud, and Farouk of Egypt, expecting to have a good chat with three kings. They smiled at Roosevelt and traded gifts, but they wouldn't talk about the Jews. Roosevelt could do nothing for the Zionists.

He had his hat over his face when a Secret Service man carried him into the house. Excuses were given to the press. "Watch it now. The Boss is asleep."

FDR formed a barricade around his bed. It wasn't the first time that he'd ruled in his pajamas and a tattered gray robe. The President saved his mornings for Anna, Ollie, and his dog. He wouldn't see another soul before eleven o'clock. He shunned long interviews with his wife. The missus could have ten or twelve minutes, like the rest. He didn't have to leave his bed for lunch. Lunch would arrive in a rolling hot-table. His daughter would have to peek under the servidor. FDR had lost his nose for food. He would stare at a baked potato and yell, "It looks like spinach. Take it away."

He would forgo an afternoon nap to play solitaire,

work on his stamp collection, and lead Ollie into frightful games of poker. The Boss loved wild cards. And he made all the rules. He wouldn't tell Oliver which cards were wild until the middle of a game. "Deuces wild," he would announce. "Deuces and kings." The old smile would reach under the pale, lifeless mouth, the jaw would grow thick again, as he watched Oliver sweat. Ollie had no luck fishing for deuces and kings. The most worthless cards in the deck would always land on him.

The Boss seemed to revive after his games with Oliver. He began to invite admirals into the room. His bed became the nearest thing to a war office. You could glimpse the edges of a chart under his pillow. He was losing the urge to isolate himself in a bedroom with his sailor and the Pup. On his fourth day home from Suez, he got out of his pajamas to have lunch in his oval study with J. Edgar Hoover. The lunch was off the record. Edgar sneaked in through the south gate. He didn't want to parry with reporters. There were too many "Edgar watchers" at the White House, men and women who interpreted his every sneeze.

They had corn soup that tasted like a purée of mud and yellow starch. You couldn't blame the President. The White House cook was a notorious bitch who worked for Eleanor and wouldn't have been unhappy to poison FDR and his guests. FDR had one spoonful and bellowed, "My God! Edgar, this is terrible stuff. Don't drink it."

And they laughed. FDR wouldn't let a cook spoil his lunch. They fed on crackers and cheese. A butler arrived with bottles of warm ginger ale. "It's a conspiracy," Roosevelt said. "They'd like to drive me out of here, so they can have the place for themselves."

He was going to Georgia in another week, to the

Little White House at Warm Springs. First he had to address Congress on his Crimean trip. His enemies were saying that Grandpa Roosevelt had done a pathetic dance at Yalta to appease the Russian bear. FDR had a war to win. He didn't go halfway across the world to bite the necks of his allies. It disturbed him that he couldn't bring about a "democratic" Poland, but did Congress expect him to join up with the Nazis and slap Uncle Joe out of Warsaw, and back into the Ukraine?

They drank the tepid ginger ale, and Roosevelt asked Edgar about the ruckus in Lafayette Park. It was nothing, Edgar declared. A harmless Trotskyite. A mental deficient who had his own silly magazine. He couldn't have gotten near Mrs. Roosevelt. An impetuous Negro started the commotion, a whore's boy. The special agents Edgar had in the park surrounded Mrs. Roosevelt and sealed off the platform once the whore boy made his leap.

The Boss thanked Edgar for helping out his missus and muttered something about a game of poker. He shook Edgar's hand, and a Secret Service man wheeled him into his bedroom, with Fala sticking close to the Boss' pants. FDR wore the same pants in 1935. Edgar noticed that the cuffs were frayed. He avoided all the "Edgar watchers" by using a tradesman's exit under the South Portico. A reddish mustache leered at him from inside the exit door. He had to swerve his shoulder or bump into old man Horn.

"John Edgar, how come you didn't go up to the attic and visit with Oliver Beebe?"

"Because it's not my day for a haircut."

He left the old fool with his mustache twitching, passed the Jackson magnolia tree, and hopped across the south lawn.

THIRTY-SEVEN

T he FBI had already moved out of the Spanish office. The cleaning lady, Mrs. Hutch, was gone. And there were no agents in the lavatory to meet with Orlando Frayard. Orlando himself had been erased from Edgar's "active list." A few checks would miraculously appear on Orlando's desk. That was Edgar's doing. The G-man wasn't erratic with his accounts. He'd pay a man exactly what was owed to him, and then shut him off forever.

Orlando blamed his disaffection from the Bureau on Oliver Beebe. Oliver was getting even for what Orlando did with Anita. He would have to give up the stupid bitch, throw her back to Ollie. Orlando didn't have much of a career in the United States. His secretaryship at the chancellery would soon dry up. Orlando still had a fiancée in Madrid, a girl of many properties. It was time to marry her. He would raise cattle in Asturias, manage one of her father's mills, if only America could hurry up and win the war.

His boss, don Valentin, had become an "undesirable." Edgar Hoover must have sent the Justice Department down on him. Don Valentin was being recalled to Spain. But he couldn't take his whore along. Mamá

Salomé didn't have the right identity papers. She was an illegal alien who had been smuggled out of Uruguay by a steamship company that supplied domestics for the United States. Even if the don could get mamá into Madrid, she was a criolla, and she wouldn't have been welcomed at the Spanish court as the "wife" of an ex-naval attaché.

The little marquès was disconsolate. He begged Orlando to look after mamá. This was no country for criollas. They would force her out of Dupont Circle when the marqués left for Spain. Orlando would have to find rooms for mamá. Don Valentin offered his secretary a monthly stipend to become mamá's caretaker in America.

Orlando nodded to the little marqués. He didn't intend to sit through the war holding mamá's thick hand. He would donate her to Mrs. Brown. Mamá could count pillowcases in a whorehouse and have philosophical discussions with Odessa.

He took the trolley down to the Willard Hotel. The Bureau had forgotten to close him out of Vivian's room. He would take advantage of the lapse to "court" Anita one more time. The bitch was waiting for him. She sat on Vivian's bed in a white terry cloth robe from the Willard.

" 'Nita, did anybody stop you in the hall? Ask you questions about Viv or Ollie boy?"

"No," she said. "The maid let me right in."

Orlando got out of his clothes. He wanted the bitch to ogle him until her eyes split with blood and fever. But she had grooves in her head that didn't come from looking at Orlando. She sucked her lip with deep concentration and fingered the metal curls on a hotel corkscrew.

He'd tear her nose off with that thing if she didn't have a brother in the White House. "How come you're playing with a corkscrew when I'm here?"

" 'Cause you said you were bringing a bottle of wine."

"Don't fret. I can always steal wine from the hotel."

Anita stared at him. "I'm not drinking wine in a missing man's room. I called the police . . . I asked them what happened to the guy from the park, and they said, 'Sorry, ma'am.' They didn't know of any Vivian de Vries."

"Girl, you didn't have to call the police. You should have asked ol' Frayard. This is Edgar Hoover's town. The FBI can snatch a dummy out of the park whenever it feels like it."

"Honey, who told you so much about the FBI?"

"God damn," Orlando said, "don't you ever wake up? How do you think I got you all your winter clothes? I work for the Bureau."

He dug under Anita's robe with his blond hands. She didn't pull away from him. He was such a pretty man without his shirt, pants, and shoes. Her robe was on the floor. Orlando licked her body with that Spanish tongue of his. Anita wished she was with her brother now. Ollie would shudder in her arms. His need was so very great. He was all dark eyebrows and brooding gums. He wouldn't smile until he slept with Anita.

The Spaniard could drive Anita crazy with a push of his thumb. But he only waxed the surfaces. It took Oliver to twist her guts, to make her believe she was giving birth again. It was Oliver she hated and loved. Not Orlando Frayard.

She couldn't forgive the Spaniard. He threw money

at Vivian, manipulated him, helped make him vanish from the park. Orlando had safe-conduct wherever he went. He could walk out of embassies, Garfinckel's, the Liberty Club, the Willard, Harvey's restaurant, don Valentin's house, and the FBI. Orlando had used Vivian and her. Did the FBI own 'Nita's body? Was she their little incest girl? Why were they out to hurt her brother?

She was on top of Orlando, loving him, pressing into his smooth blond groin, watching the satisfaction on his face, the purled skin over his squeezed-together eyes. Edgar Hoover's secret agent. She jabbed the corkscrew into the side of his neck. 'Lando didn't scream. His head didn't rise off the pillow. His blondness didn't run away. His nostrils wrinkled once. Blood squirted onto Anita, as if she'd put a blowhole in his neck. She twisted the corkscrew far as it could go. His calves tightened, but he couldn't throw Anita off the bed. His eyes stayed shut. The blowhole seemed to disappear. Orlando fell asleep.

Anita left him there. She opened the window and went out onto the roof. She wouldn't bring her robe. The cinders mashed under her feet. It had the packed, slippery feel of a bed of frozen moss. The wind blew under her tits. The coping stones knocked with a sneaky rhythm that could have been the voice of a man sobbing on a roof. Anita wasn't sensitive to ghosts. The dead could cry to her and Anita wouldn't listen. If she blinked very hard and kept the cinder dust out of her eyes, she could see the White House, with its porches, windows, and machine guns on the roof.

Which was Ollie's window? She scraped her toes in the cinders and danced for Oliver Beebe. She could get by without a piano. The wind churned music in her face. Under its dull, persistent roar she could hear the slap,

slap, slap of "Mairzy Doats," America's favorite song. It had been the rage of 1944, nonsense syllables to calm the home front. "Mairzy Doats" lasted into 1945. No one seemed to tire of it. Anita sang it every day. Shirley Temple danced to "Mairzy Doats" in the Movietone news. Mrs. Roosevelt hummed it in her parlor. Why couldn't Anita serenade her brother with it?

Mairzy Doats and Dozy Doats and little lamzy divey
A kiddley divey too, wouldn't you?

She must have sung that song fifty times for Oliver. Her legs were weary. It was hard dancing to "Mairzy Doats" on cinders, without your shoes. Why didn't Ollie wave to her from his window? The White House wouldn't stir for Anita. She had an infant in Milwaukee, baby Michael, with poop in his underpants. Couldn't she sing the poop away? She was everything a woman could hope to be. Mother, sister, daughter, cunt. Fuck your brother, abandon your child, leave your father's house. She'd been the little lamzy divey to a hundred men. "Mairzy Doats" made perfect sense. It was the song of a girl who learned to talk and breathe with a prick in her mouth.

'Nita had an audience. A man was crouching next to her. He had wavy black hair and gold on his fingers, and he didn't peek at her tits. Funny guy. He had Oliver's dark complexion. Was he a goddamn talent scout, looking for Shirley Temple and Fanny Brice? Or a hotel manager, up from the office to read her the Willard's regulations about singing in the nude?

"Mister, what do you want? I'm busy. Can't you tell?"

The guy began to stutter. He had fat lips for a man.

"Jesus, you want to take my picture? Bring a camera next time."

He must have been scared of high places. He wouldn't give up his crouch. He had to hug the cinders, eat a whole lot of dust. His socks were getting dirty. The wind blew his white pants up to the middle of his calves and exposed the garters he wore. They were silky and black. His mouth was open. She couldn't hear his quiet barking in the wind. She had to read his lips. He was saying, "Miss Anita, I'm your brother's friend. . . ."

That was Edgar on the roof. His agents at the hotel had spotted the crazy, dancing girl, but Edgar wouldn't allow them to retrieve her. He'd come down from Justice to save Anita Beebe. His men were waiting for him in Vivian's room. They kept pointing to the corkscrew in Frayard's neck. The Director wasn't blind. He could tell where the metal bit. A whistling sound came up from Frayard's throat. The Bureau was prepared for a contingency such as this. They wrapped Frayard in blankets and sheets and picked him off the bed, without disturbing the corkscrew. The Bureau had its own "hospital" in Arlington, Virginia, a convalescent home for sick operatives and informants. They would get him there while Edgar climbed out the window.

He'd looked at photograph after photograph of Anita Beebe, dressed and undressed, standing, sitting, snuggled in someone's lap, indoors and out. Teams of special agents had broken into walls, dug under mirrors with a periscopic device, to shoot Anita in bed with Oliver, Orlando, and Vivian de Vries. The photographs were vile. They filled Edgar with disgust. He'd locked them away in his drawer.

It took a roaring wind, a weak pile of coping stones, and pebbles in his shoes to educate Edgar Hoover. The photographs had minimized Anita Beebe. The girl was much less of a whore in her real skin. He could find nothing purient in her dance. Anita wasn't shaking her limbs at Edgar. She shouted over the roof. He didn't understand what she was warbling about. But her kicking thighs couldn't embarrass him. She was gorgeous with shreds of sunlight going down her back. She had lovely hooks in her spine that wavered with each kick. Her ass was tight and perfect. It didn't seem strange any more that Oliver should have loved this girl. Edgar couldn't account for accidents of birth. She might have been anybody's sister.

Her dancing made him forget corkscrews and spies. He could have spent the afternoon in 'Nita's company, but she was getting closer and closer to the crooked edge of the roof. She shattered chunks of coping with her heels, and Edgar grew worried. He crouched, so that he would be in position to grab her feet if she started to slide. He called to her. "Miss Anita."

She didn't spurn his overtures. She moved back from the crooked edge, smiled, and got off the roof with Edgar. He had to dress the girl. His agents had fled to Arlington with Orlando Frayard. The newspapers would eat Roosevelt alive if they discovered that Oliver's sister had skewered a minor diplomat inside the Willard Hotel. Anita would have to be Edgar's ward for a little while.

Two FBI men accompanied her to the boarding-house. She couldn't brush her teeth without her new escorts. They helped her pack, saying "Yes'm" and "No'm," and sat with her on the train to Milwaukee. They woke her "husband" Phil out of a vague, draft-dodger's sleep. Phil rubbed his eyes and stared at the two brown coats. He was going crazy. It had to be a merry year when the FBI brings Anita to your door.

Something wasn't right with 'Nita girl. She kept wiggling her toes. And she didn't ask about her baby. The FBI men went into the parlor with Phil and nodded instructions to him. Anita wasn't to leave Milwaukee, they said. Neither was Phil. If he tried to get on a bus, they would throw him in an internment camp, with prisoners of war. They told Phil not to put a corkscrew in Anita's hand. It would be smart to sleep with the lights on, they said. The girl had picked up a rare fever in Washington, D.C. She might turn delirious from time to time. Phil was to make sure she didn't get in touch with her brother Ollie. If any letters arrived from Oliver, Phil wasn't to open them. The letters were to be sent in their original envelopes to the FBI. It's Oliver Beebe, Phil muttered to himself. Oliver gave Anita whatever sickness she had. America belongs to Ollie and J. Edgar Hoover. They're the guys who drag FDR by the nose. After Germany collapsed and Russia exhausted itself, Oliver Beebe was going to take over the world.

The two brown coats returned to Washington. They couldn't catch Edgar in his office. The G-man had gone to the convalescent home in Arlington to watch Orlando mend.

The corkscrew had lodged in a sensitive spot, in the webbing around Orlando's esophagus. The doctors wouldn't dig it out before they consulted with surgeons from another clinic. Orlando had to lie three days with the corkscrew in his neck. Then the doctors went in with their knives. They cut around the corkscrew and unstuck each twist of metal. They had a special plastic cuff designed to fit under Orlando's ears. The cuff took his jaw away. His face was incomplete. The doctors gave Edgar their best prognosis. The neck would heal in a month. There was nothing to worry about. Orlando would only have one small souvenir. His voice would be hoarse for life.

The doctors wouldn't allow him to talk with that cuff on his neck. But he managed to squeal two words at Edgar. Mamá Salomé. Edgar didn't react at first. The fascist marqués was already out of the country. What did the FBI have to do with don Valentin's housekeeper-wife? But Orlando's squealing cuff began to trouble him. He sent a man to investigate the affairs of mamá Salomé. The fat old cow was in difficult straits. No one wanted her. The landlords and tenants of Dupont Circle conspired against mamá. They couldn't let a creole inherit don Valentin's flat.

Young lawyers from the Justice Department showed up at the landlords' place of business. They didn't say very much. They whispered something about mamá, Edgar, Eleanor, and Frank. The landlords dropped their eviction order. They wouldn't have hesitated to fight Mr. and Mrs. Roosevelt, and all their nigger-loving friends, but the landlords couldn't afford to grapple with the FBI.

The men closest to Mr. Hoover were amazed at the pleasure he took in thwarting the landlords of Dupont Circle and rescuing mamá Salomé. You couldn't tell where Edgar's generosity would fall. He could be Caligula, or Robin Hood, depending on the day. It was always much easier for Edgar to act when the White House was deserted. FDR had taken his sailor and his Pup to Warm Springs. Only Eleanor was around. And that witch with the long face couldn't hamper Edgar's Bureau.

THIRTY-EIGHT

He wasn't President Roosevelt in that little peck of Georgia on Pine Mountain road. He was the lord of the mountain, who could bring a village back to life. He'd arrived there in the 1920s, a hopelessly crippled man, to bathe in the magical waters. It was a broken-down resort, with an old, impossible inn and cottages that had been entertaining field mice for a hundred years. Nobody came to Warm Springs except for the mice.

Mr. Franklin fell in love with the goddamn place. He took that old inn and turned it into Georgia Hall, a center for the treatment of infantile paralysis. When certain townsmen grew afraid that the IP's would contaminate their swimming pool, Mr. Franklin built his own small pool for the children of Georgia Hall. He played water polo with them. He established a polio foundation at Warm Springs. He wrangled fresh businesses into town. He had a cottage put up for himself on a hill above Georgia Hall. After he assumed the presidency, that cottage became the Little White House, Mr. Franklin's Georgia retreat.

It was the end of March, 1945. Half the village had come to the railroad station to greet the master of Georgia Hall. The mayor was there; the manager of the Warm Springs Hotel; the blacksmith who had designed the levers and pulleys of Mr. Franklin's hand-driven Ford; the barber who used to work on Mr. Franklin's scalp before the days of Oliver Beebe; the twins who ran the grocery shop; the village undertaker; the marines who would help guard the President's compound on the hill; and the patients of Georgia Hall. But you couldn't say "howdy" to a lord with a hat over his eyes.

Mr. Franklin descended a tiny elevator at the back of the Ferdinand Magellan. A row of Secret Service men kept him apart from the villagers. He was carried into a limousine that had just been wheeled out of a special baggage car aboard the train. The limousine drove him to the Little White House.

Mr. Franklin retired to his narrow pine bed. The Secret Service stood outside his door. Horn's men could nap with their noses against a wall and gobble lumps of cheese without dirtying the President's rug. Horn would rouse them with blows on the arm. "Look alive. I don't need a bunch of sleeping beauties." The Boss stayed in his bedroom sixteen hours. Then he called for Oliver Beebe. His admirals had made the trip with him. But he wouldn't see any of them. He wouldn't see his doctors, his secretaries, or his masseur. He wouldn't examine the pouch that arrived from Washington. He wouldn't give his signature away. He wouldn't drink coffee with the Pup. He wouldn't telephone his missus. He only wanted to play cards with the "child."

Deuces and kings. Deuces and kings. Roosevelt turned half the deck into wild cards. Oliver was stumped. He fell prey to the Boss' lust for poker kingdoms of flushes and straights. The sailor couldn't husband his wild kings. The hands he held came to nothing. He would ponder over the king of diamonds and other one-eyed cards, while Roosevelt beat him to death.

Poker with Ollie always revived the Boss. He would sign papers now, see his admirals and his doctors. He went down to Georgia Hall and had lunch with the staff. But he couldn't play water polo with the children any more. His scrawny neck was obvious to the men and women at lunch. He could hardly break a roll for himself. His knuckles wobbled against the butter knife. But he could still smile and tell a story. He didn't withdraw behind his rotten blue-gray color. He was the master of Georgia Hall and the President of the United States.

Suddenly the Boss stopped playing "deuces and kings." He wouldn't go near the card table. Oliver drifted through the compound. The child had nothing to do. There were marines scattered in the bushes. The Secret Service had its own sentry boxes. Horn's men wouldn't chat with Oliver. He noticed a tall, dark lady in the guest house. She'd come to Warm Springs with Madame Shoumatoff, the artist who did the watercolor of Roosevelt in his blue cape. You could find it in every barber shop. She'd painted the Boss without a wrinkle or a mole. That wasn't Roosevelt. It was some touched-up doll's face of a President for the barber shops of America. Madame was here to execute another "portrait" of FDR.

The Boss had to sit in the living room while Shoumatoff measured his nose with a little sliding ruler. Why didn't the Boss yell at Shoumatoff and throw her out of the cottage? It had something to do with the tall, dark lady. She had a long neck, Mrs. Lucy Mercer Rutherfurd of Baltimore and New Jersey, and beautiful pieces of gray in her hair. The Boss posed for Shoumatoff and looked at the dark lady.

He took Mrs. Rutherfurd for a drive in his old blue

Ford convertible, and he didn't invite Shoumatoff, the admirals, Ollie, or the Pup. The Boss could get along without a chauffeur in his car. The special pulleys allowed him to shift and maneuver the brakes with his hand. But he couldn't be utterly alone with the lady. He had to go up Pine Mountain with the Secret Service in his lap. Two of Horn's limousines sandwiched the old convertible.

Horn sat in the rear limousine. He was only a cop paid by the Treasury Department to guard the President's life. What right did he have to comment on Mr. Roosevelt's thirty-year romance? The Boss didn't have a chippy. The woman was devoted to FDR. Horn was aware of that. He had to engineer all her meetings with the President. She attended his inaugurations in secret, staring out at the ceremonies from the window blinds of Horn's limousine. It was Kirkland who found a way to get her into the President's oval office for a two-hour lunch, Kirkland who closeted her in Hyde Park when the missus wasn't around, Kirkland who mapped their automobile rides through Rock Creek Park.

Roosevelt's car reached the top of Pine Mountain. Horn didn't peek. He wouldn't allow his men to watch a President kiss. But even with their eyes in the trees, they couldn't avoid the hugging in the car, the gentle embrace of a President and his Lucy. It was a pathetic, murderous job to be head of District 16. The Boss had no privacy. The world ran to his heartbeat. The Secret Service was always ten feet away.

The presidential caravan returned to the Little White House. The Boss wasn't in the mood for wild cards. It didn't matter. The child had gone down to Carver Cottage, where he was billeted with two of the admirals. The admirals gave Oliver free run of the cottage. They were uneasy in the presence of his scowls and his pompadour. They decided to use the toilet at Georgia Hall. They would rather undress in front of crippled children than look into a sailor's eye.

Oliver learned to play water polo with the IP's. The children were much more aggressive than Oliver. They scored points off him at will, diving between his legs, grabbing his trunks, hiding the ball in the crook of an arm, dribbling it into Oliver's chest. He wasn't confused by the miraculous buoyancy of the IP's. You could have floated a team of sick elephants on the salty skin of Mr. Franklin's pool. Infants and hysterical old ladies wouldn't have drowned at Warm Springs. Oliver was enjoying himself. The IP's exhausted him, raised welts on his body, but he didn't get out of the pool. The IP's gave up on Ollie. They wouldn't attack a sailor who never got angry and never cursed.

He stayed indoors at night. Holes in the wood created a terrible draft. The wind shook the cottage roof. Furniture had the habit of sliding into Oliver. Mirrors rattled and developed splinters and cracks. The admirals moved out of Carver Cottage and slept in Georgia Hall. Oliver wore his underpants and three blankets to bed. He heard the field mice eating roots under the cottage floor. The noise of their skulls banging softly against the wood comforted him. He couldn't say why.

He had his breakfasts at Georgia Hall. They served hush puppies, little cornmeal cakes that the President had gotten him to try. Oliver grew addicted to them. He would gobble eight hush puppies at a sitting. Then he would jump into the pool with a swollen belly.

He climbed up the hill no more than twice a day. It might be a trim behind the Boss' ears for Madame

Shoumatoff, a note that had to be hand-delivered to an admiral or an aide, a dash with the Pup into the bushes. The Boss was preoccupied. He had Mrs. Rutherfurd, Shoumatoff, and affairs of state. He would drink an old-fashioned on the deck of his cottage without Oliver Beebe. He would go for rides with the tall, dark lady. His hands wouldn't stop trembling. He had trouble twisting Camels into his ivory holder, or picking up a prize Hong Kong stamp with his tweezers. He coughed a lot.

Oliver's existence at Warm Springs narrowed down to hush puppies and the swimming pool. He would swim, eat, swim, eat, swim, eat, and play with the dog. This ritual was broken one afternoon. Admirals and Secret Service men kept running up the hill. Marines skulked through the compound with readied bayonets. Women were sobbing in Georgia Hall. The IP's left their game of water polo. Oliver climbed out of the pool. He could feel a thick, ugly static on the clay road that led to Mr. Franklin's cottage. The front porch was crowded with Secret Service men, admirals, secretaries, and Roosevelt's Filipino houseboys. No one could get inside.

Oliver was still in his trunks, marking the porch with wet clay prints of his feet. He saw Shoumatoff and the dark lady rush from the guest house with their traveling bags. The dark lady had a shiver in her back. Someone was paging the child. "Mr. Beebe." The Secret Service ushered him over the porch and into the cottage. The admirals were chagrined. Oliver had more clout than any of them. But he was stuck in the vestibule. Doctors and Secret Service men flitted past the child as if he were some slight creature. A deep, horrible snore came through the wall. It frightened Oliver. What was a cow doing in the Boss' bedroom, a cow with a bad cold? The snoring wouldn't go away. It would stop and start again. Then Oliver heard a rattling sound, the labored breathing of a man. Then nothing at all.

An arm tugged at him. He was dragged into the bedroom by Kirkland Horn. The doctors went out of the room. The Boss was in his pajamas. His hands were folded. The fingernails had turned blue. The Boss' eyes were shut. His bottom lip seemed pulled out of shape. He had dark, crusty lines on both his temples. Horn dragged Ollie closer to the bed. What was Ollie meant to do? He kissed the Boss on his crusted temples. He didn't say goodbye.

Two Secret Service men came for the child. They walked him out of the cottage and gave him to the admirals. It had been a crazy hunch on Kirkland's part, to bring Oliver into the cottage and have him kiss a dead President. Beebe had a weird power over the Boss. But he couldn't kiss Roosevelt alive.

The Boss had a seizure around one o'clock. He'd been sitting with Shoumatoff and Mrs. Rutherfurd before lunch, when he complained of a headache and passed out in his chair. Doctors were summoned from Georgia Hall. The Secret Service carried Roosevelt into the bedroom. The doctors struggled to get him out of his clothes. Horn had to borrow the gardener's shears and cut away Roosevelt's trousers and shirt. They sponged the Boss and dressed him in pajamas. The doctors went at him with a blood-pressure cuff. Horn pulled bits of meaning out of their infernal jabber. Cerebral hemorrhage. Massive stroke. Blood roaring in the brain.

The old man had bitter chores to do. He got rid of Shoumatoff and the Rutherfurd woman. It wasn't the

unkind act of a Secret Service man. He would have liked
to keep Mrs. Rutherfurd near the Boss. But the press was
already hunkering around the cottage. He couldn't
afford to have some newshound from Atlanta swear to
bloody Jesus that Roosevelt had turned the Little White
House into a trysting place for himself and his dark-eyed
beauty, with Shoumatoff as Lucy's "nun." Horn had to
chase the two women out of Warm Springs. Then there
was Oliver Beebe.

The sailor was untouchable with Roosevelt alive.
He could drift in and out of Yalta, Pennsylvania Avenue,
and Hyde Park, sacred as the Pup. You didn't want to
mess with Mr. Franklin's child. Half a dozen agencies in
Washington kept a file on Oliver Beebe, including the
Secret Service. A dead Roosevelt couldn't hold Oliver
under his blue cape. There was enough jealousy distributed through Washington, D.C., to rip the white
pants off Oliver, and smear Roosevelt's name. Mr. Franklin's child had stepped out of the Navy with his scissors
and his combs, and the Navy would have to swallow him
up, like Jonah and the whale.

The admirals obliged Kirkland Horn. They drove
Beebe to Atlanta, where he was put on a bus bound for
the Navy Yard at Portsmouth. He didn't get off the bus
with shackles on his arms. No one laid a finger on the
child. He lived in a tiny room near the Portsmouth muni-
tions dump. That was the last of Oliver for a while.

Edgar and the Dogs

T he Boss was dead, buried in his mother's rose garden at Hyde Park, and Edgar had to deal with a new Commander-in-Chief. He didn't get along with Harry. He wasn't going to lie down with a haberdasher from Independence, Missouri. He wouldn't put Harry's picture on the Bureau walls. You saw nothing but "Roosevelts" at the FBI, with slender black ribbons tacked to the picture frames. Edgar would mourn FDR for as many years as he liked. He had his own little duchy near the White House. A President would have had lots of trouble digging him out of his corner at the Justice Department. Hoover was incorruptible. Also, you couldn't tell what he had in his files. He sat on information like a ferocious squirrel. He didn't have to bow to Harry S. Truman.

Edgar made his rounds. He couldn't run to Pimlico. The race tracks were shut on account of the war. But he could meet with Winchell in New York. He could share prime ribs with Mr. and Mrs. Babe Ruth. Eat raspberries dipped in white wine at the Stork Club. Or stay in Washington, D.C., and have his evening meal at Harvey's. He didn't have Oliver Beebe across the table from him. Edgar dined alone.

One night in April Edgar disappeared. It was only for an hour. The G-man hitched up the cuffs of his white pants and stepped into Nigger Lane. He visited Crawfish Alley and drank calvados with 'Dessa Brown. The girls in 'Dessa's crib giggled at him. They enjoyed their closeness to the FBI. Mrs. Brown wasn't on Edgar's roster. She wouldn't spy for the Bureau. But she might do Edgar a favor. The cops left you alone if Edgar Hoover was a friend of yours. Edgar hadn't come for any news. The calvados warmed his lips. Mrs. Brown didn't have to hide Jonathan Roosevelt from him. Edgar wouldn't arrest the man who had jumped on that Trotskyite at Lafayette Park and kicked him in the head. But Jonathan was obliged to hop between Mrs. Brown's different cellars. The Secret Service was looking for him.

He sat and had his calvados with Edgar and Mrs. Brown. "Where's Mr. Ollie?" he said, during a lull in the conversation.

"He's not with Harry Truman," the G-man said. "But I'll find him and let you know."

The G-man thanked Mrs. Brown and left her whore crib. But he didn't escape without notice. A pack of mongrel dogs watched him scuttle in the alleys. The dogs didn't snarl at Edgar, or bang into his high cuffs. They made little humming noises with their throats. Edgar figured they were hungry. He stood near the pack's inner belly, with the one-eyed dogs, and then moved on. That humming grew louder. The leaders didn't shy away from Edgar's pants. They blinked at him with yellow eyes, their scarred heads gliding past Edgar's crotch. The pack accompanied him to the end of Nigger Lane. The dogs wouldn't come out tonight on Vermont Avenue. Edgar called the Bureau from a pay telephone. A car arrived in three minutes and brought him home to Rock Creek Park.

Oliver Beebe

FORTY

I t was another tropical June, and a bog seemed to rise up from the Potomac as the city lay in its own deep swamp. Riders on the Pennsylvania Avenue trolley watched porches and roofs disappear from the White House in the Washington haze. The air stuck to your fingers and your clothes like some kind of crazy soup. You couldn't breathe in the alleys. The rooftop bars along the "white way" had to close. No one wanted to guzzle gin in a mud-green sky. At St. Elizabeth's, you couldn't live indoors. Doctors, nurses, and inmates crowded onto the porches to avoid that jelly in the air that could eat through a clapboard wall.

A young man was found on the lawn. He wasn't a drifter, or an escapee. He'd come to visit that retired first baseman of the Washington Senators, Otto Tutmiller. The young man had black hair, and eyes that looked as if they belonged at St. Elizabeth's. It was an abstracted gaze, common to half the population here. But the young man was no lunatic. It was only Oliver Beebe, dressed in civilian clothes.

St. Elizabeth's was his last connection with the District of Columbia. He couldn't walk into a White House run by Bess and Harry Truman. Without Fala, without

Mrs. Franklin, without FDR, it was a crumbling mansion with loose chandeliers and dirt under the carpets. He knew the Ox was nearly catatonic and wouldn't recognize him, but at least Oliver would have the comfort of a face *he* remembered and liked.

So he was squeezed onto a porch with doctors, nurses, and men in gray pajamas. The Ox had a buddy today. Vivian de Vries. Both of them had just endured an institutional haircut. They sat with cropped skulls. Vivian wouldn't say hello to Oliver Beebe. He thought Ollie still worked for FDR (the nurses hadn't told him Mr. Franklin was dead).

Ollie was on the porch for most of an hour. He looked familiar to the doctors, but who could recall the barber of an old President? Ollie left the porch and handed in his visitor's card. He didn't have to go searching for a bus. A limousine was waiting for him. Edgar's chauffeur invited Ollie into the car. You couldn't see Edgar himself behind the bulletproof glass. The G-man cherished his privacy.

The car drove off with Oliver Beebe. Edgar didn't have the magic to conjure up a forgotten sailor. One of his stoolpigeons had spotted Oliver Beebe at the Greyhound terminal. Edgar knew that the Navy had squirreled Beebe somewhere. But he couldn't get far enough into the Navy Department to come up with Ollie on his own. He had to depend on a ragged band of informants. The word had gone out. Mr. John Edgar Hoover was curious about the fate of Oliver Beebe.

He couldn't understand why Ollie had to sneak into D.C. without his sailor suit. It was difficult making conversation with the boy. "Kirkland died," he said. "A month ago. Horn . . . his kidneys failed."

Oliver didn't have any niceties for Horn. Nothing about pitying the old man. Edgar got out of the car. He had a long-distance call to make. The boy seemed more talkative when Edgar returned.

"Uncle, are we going to Harvey's for lunch?"

"No," the G-man said.

"Good, because I'm not in the mood for lobster."

They went out of the District in Edgar's car. Ollie didn't ask why they were riding in Pennsylvania and New Jersey. They stopped for ice cream cones. They had chocolate with lots of sprinkles and a little cherry on top. Edgar gave in to his weakness for news. "Oliver, where did the admirals put you?"

The boy said, "Portsmouth."

Edgar muttered to himself. They hid the boy under Edgar's nose, at a Navy base, and the Bureau couldn't unearth Oliver Beebe. The admirals were making idiots of the FBI. Margaret Truman sits at her piano, Harry takes his morning walks, and the Bureau had to scuttle in the dark. The sailor was talking again.

"Did he fish before he died?"

"Who?" Edgar growled.

"Old man Horn. He liked to fish."

Was Edgar supposed to know the fishing habits of every Secret Service man? "Yes," he said, to satisfy the boy. "Kirkland fished . . . Ollie, what did you do at Portsmouth for two and a half months?"

"I counted things."

Edgar stared at the boy. "What kind of things?"

"Shoelaces. Bowties. Peanut brittle. I was a clerk at the commissary."

"You sold peanut brittle to the sailors and their wives?"

"No. They wouldn't let me up front. I worked in the storeroom."

"And now?"

"Destroyer duty," Oliver said. "I'll be on the *Wendell Willkie*. It leaves for Guantanamo tomorrow morning."

"Did your captain give you a two-day pass?"

"Twenty-four hours."

"And they told you not to wear your uniform away from Portsmouth?"

The boy turned glum. But Edgar could tease out the mechanics of the U.S. Navy. Special travel orders for Seaman Oliver Beebe. Son-of-a-bitch! And they accuse the Bureau of having medieval ways. Edgar might drop a prodigal agent into some field office in Oklahoma, but he didn't bury sailors under a pile of peanut brittle. He hadn't kidnaped Oliver Beebe. The G-man was on an errand for the Boss' widow. Eleanor, the ugly witch. He'd heard from a spy of his in Poughkeepsie, New York, that Mrs. Franklin had been asking about Oliver. So he'd deliver Ollie to the witch for part of the afternoon, in memory of FDR. What was the Bureau worth, if it couldn't do a favor for Franklin Roosevelt, dead or alive? He'd dialed the witch at her cottage, and said he was bringing Oliver Beebe.

The sailor wasn't stupid. He could spell out the words on a road sign as quick as chauffeur Bill. They were going to Poughkeepsie. He recognized the old barns and fences of the Boss' estate. But they didn't stop at the big family house near the river. Edgar took a dirt road. Chauffeur Bill cursed the mean topography and the throw of the land. Branches and rocks dug under the fenders. Caterpillars died on the windows. They had to

wait until a bull crossed the road. Then the limousine
crept out of the woods. They were in a clearing now.
Didn't Oliver sleep at Hyde Park? This had to be Val-
Kill, Mrs. Franklin's place.

They arrived at a stone cottage and a swimming
pool. Mrs. Franklin climbed out of the pool wearing a cap
on her head. The skirts of her bathing suit were high
above her knees. Edgar, Ollie, and Bill got out of the car.
Mrs. Franklin waved to them. Even Edgar had to acknowledge that the witch owned an incredible smile. It
wasn't any pinko lure. Those big front teeth couldn't
have worked a hoax. She'd gotten grayer since the Boss
was dead. But there was nothing ghostly in her eyes.
They jumped out of that long, wrinkled face with a look
that was powerful and direct.

"Oliver dear. . . ."

She hugged the boy in front of Edgar and Bill, and
found bathing suits for everybody. The four of them
jumped into the pool. Bill was fond of swimming with a
cigar in his mouth. Edgar did the dog paddle from one
end of the pool to the other. Mrs. Franklin swam with her
elbows out. She blew holes in the water like a fabulous
seal. Oliver caught himself in the lilies that were growing
at the sides of the pool.

They had a snack on the cottage steps. Edgar was
grateful the witch didn't pry. Mrs. Franklin wasn't the
nosy sort. She never asked Ollie how come he'd disappeared. She teased the FBI a little. "Edgar, why can't you
get along with Harry?"

The G-man had already shed his bathing suit. He sat
on the hot stone in his white linen suit. The marsh flies
adored the pomade in his hair. They buzzed around
Edgar. But he wouldn't slap at them. He talked about

Harry Truman. "He started it, ma'am. He's been tattling to people that I have a stranglehold on the Justice Department. 'Edgar this, and Edgar that.' Let him junk me. I'll tinker on the piano, like that daughter of his. Give recitals in the park."

Mrs. Franklin laughed. And the G-man thought to himself: maybe she isn't such a pinko. He had her entire history on his index cards. The ugly girl who couldn't read or write at the age of six. Loses her father and mother before she's ten. Gets engaged to her cousin, the handsome young Franklin Delano Roosevelt. It's marriage, and kids, and life with Franklin's mother, old Sara, who rules the house. Franklin takes a mistress. The mistress runs away. She minds the children of a rich Jersey man, Mr. Rutherfurd. Then she becomes his wife. Only the thing with Frank aint dead. He's a President with polio. But he loves his ladies. Lucy's the one that persists. The Secret Service has to cover Franklin's tracks. But Edgar didn't raise a gang of simpletons at the Bureau. His men spied the President's car in Rock Creek Park. Edgar had to warn them. "That's Franklin Roosevelt in the car. Anybody who yaks about this will find himself a chicken farmer in Tennessee." And Franklin's widow? She survived thirty years of Lucy. Suppose Edgar got to like the wrinkles and the buckteeth? He whispered to the sailor. "What time do you have to be at Portsmouth?"

"Nine o'clock tonight."

Edgar peeked at his watch. "Holy mackerel. . . . Excuse me, Mrs. Roosevelt, but we have to leave."

Oliver and Bill dressed behind the cottage. The sailor didn't know how to say goodbye. Should he shake Mrs. Franklin's hand? He blubbered into her shoulder. Wanted to save the Boss' life. Kissed him, ma'am. But his lips stayed blue. And Kirkland snuck me out of Warm Springs.

Who could understand the sailor's blubbering? Mrs. Franklin touched his pompadour. "Ollie," she said. "You'll miss the Pup . . . Fala's in the woods, chasing squirrels."

Oliver had completely forgotten the dog. In his sailor's mind, he must have figured the Outlaw was buried with FDR. Mrs. Franklin strolled the cottage grounds, calling for the Pup. The dog didn't come. The limousine left Val-Kill. You could hear rocks grinding under the chassis. Bill cursed the road again. Country lanes could wreck a limousine. The constant smack of caterpillars against the glass was making the chauffeur blink. There was a skunk on the road, or a black possum. It skittered up to the car, with its swollen back.

"Lord," Bill said. "It's a crazy June when a skunk can turn into a traffic cop."

"That's no skunk," Oliver said. He opened the door. "Come on, you, we're in a hurry." Fala jumped into the car. The Pup had twigs in his coat that he dropped on Edgar's carpeting. He'd become a country dog. He was almost skinny without Mr. Franklin's toast. The Pup began to whimper as he nuzzled with Oliver Beebe. Did the sailor remind him of the White House, coffee, bacon, toast, and FDR? Ollie mumbled to the Pup, as if a President's dog could have picked up the intonations of Weehawken English. "Mr. Fala, I'm not a barber any more. They pushed me out of the attic."

Edgar wouldn't get the boy to Portsmouth if that conversation didn't cease. The Outlaw took advantage of an open door and jumped into the grass. Bill steered like the devil. He wasn't going to give that dog a second chance to creep back onto the road. He had his instructions. Portsmouth by nine. They drove through Dutchess County with the speedometer needle up to a hundred and five. You didn't have to fear God or man with Edgar in the limousine. State troopers caught up with them outside White Plains. The troopers burst into the car. Their temples pulsed under their stiff, pointed hats when they saw the white suit, the jowls, the pomaded hair. "Sorry, Mr. Hoover." You didn't fuck with the Bureau. Hoover might be running down a band of saboteurs out to blow up the water supply. "Can we help, sir?"

"Thank you, son, but we're fine the way we are."

The troopers got off Edgar's running board, and the limousine headed for New Jersey. The G-man had a touch of remorse. The FBI had mated Ollie and his sister, like a pair of laboratory birds. But Edgar didn't invent Vivian and Orlando Frayard. He had to seize what was out there. And he did confine Ollie to a box the Bureau had made for him. A President's barber could get into all kinds of trouble.

They arrived at the Navy yard three minutes to nine. Edgar hoped the admirals would take note of his car. Let them be aware that they couldn't swallow Oliver Beebe into their wonderful Navy. The boy thanked Edgar and Bill. He went through the gate with his hands in his pockets, a seaman at the end of a war.